ABOUT THE AUTHOR

PRINCESS JACQUELINE DE SOIGNÉE

has been living the enviable life of a princess ever since she was born.

She holds a bachelor of arts degree in classics from Vassar College; master of arts degrees in philology and art history from the University of Bologna and the Sorbonne, respectively; and certificates in fashion design* and floral design from Parsons School of Design.

After completing her education, she began working for the de Soignée Family Foundation, a worldwide not-for-profit organization with myriad philanthropic missions, most notably Jacqueline's literacy program. When she isn't toiling at the foundation, she graciously and joyfully engages in her favorite pursuits: shopping, rubbing elbows with the rich and famous, appearing in cameos in Jean-Paul Fameux films, shopping, charming and being charmed, writing, shopping and having fun with her friends. She is eager to share her princessly secrets with her readers.

A citizen of the world, she now divides her time between the de Soignée villa in Tuscany and ski château in Gstaad, her penthouse in Manhattan and salon in Paris. When not jetting hither and thither, she cruises the high seas in the family suite aboard the *QE II*.

(*lifetime-achievement honorary degree awarded by the dean of Parsons)

the Princess-in-Training Manual

Princess Jacqueline de Soignée

RED
DRESS
INK
™

First edition November 2003

THE PRINCESS-IN-TRAINING MANUAL

A Red Dress Ink novel

ISBN 0-373-25039-8

Visit Red Dress Ink at www.reddressink.com

Printed in U.S.A.

For my father

ACKNOWLEDGMENTS

A princess gives credit where credit is due, and always expresses her gratitude magnanimously.

Thanks to everyone at Red Dress Ink for their vision and enthusiasm for this project and for their dedication to making it a success—especially to my editior, Margaret Marbury, and her assistant, Zareen Jaffery; Laura Morris for all her creative marketing efforts; and the talented designers who created the fabulous cover and inside design, Margie Miller and Tara Kelly.

Special thanks to three of my most-cherished friends (who didn't want to be portrayed in this book): Eve, my first Princess-in-Training; Alexis, my guide in so many things, and my faithful cheerleader; and Erica, my mentor as a writer and my soul's twin sister.

To my literary agent and dear friend, Jay Poynor, my sincere gratitude for believing in this project from the beginning, and having such an excellent sense of humor, not to mention outstanding discernment.

Thanks also to Irwin, whose love for such regal necessities as genealogy and heraldry warm the heart of this princess who adores him.

Extra-special thanks to my father, for starting me off in such grand princessly style; and to my mother, for everything. I could not do what I do without their unwavering devotion and support.

Why I Had to Write This Book

Like many of my best ideas, the vision for this book came after a few saketinis too many at Nobu. I was celebrating my glamorous cameo in famed director Jean-Paul Fameux's latest action film. It would be a first for the royal de Soignées, but I was a princess on a mission. Royals have been getting such a bad rap in the past few decades. Between the political intrigue and the sex scandals, HRHs had really sullied the title of princess, and I was going to restore our good name.

I pull up in front of Nobu and the valet opens the door of my Lamborghini. I get out of the car, pivoting on the heel of one spike-heeled red-patent mule and flashing the expected dazzling smile.

"CUT!" yells Jean-Paul Fameux, the oh-so-fabulous film director, toast of every Cannes Film Festival, darling of Hollywood and my very good friend.

"Merveilleuse," Jean-Paul proclaims. "You are a natural!

A born star!" I love the way "star" sounds in his French accent. He lifts my hand to his lips.

"Oh, Jean-Paul, how you go on," I say. But secretly I'm excited. This is my first film appearance, and I can't believe how glamorous it is.

"Your presence will make my film a true masterpiece. I cannot thank you enough, Your Highness." Jean-Paul bows deeply.

He's not kidding with that Your Highness stuff, by the way. My full title is Princess Jacqueline de Soignée. The only members of our family to escape the French Revolution were my great-great-great-great-great-great-great-great-grandparents, Angélique and Louis-Luc de Soignée, who were saved from the guillotine by their loyal chamberlain, Jacques, disguised as a peasant. Jacques spirited them from France to Geneva, where they waited out the Reign of Terror, returning to France once royals were safe again.

More about all that later. After all, it's one thing to have been a royal princess all your life and quite another to become a film celebrity. So back to my moment in the spotlight of the cinema. How fabulous!!

As I make my way inside Nobu, a woman approaches me. She's dressed in all black. VERY film. Not any designer I recognize, but she pulls it off well. I notice she's sizing up my black leather Prada minidress and the mules. (Which, by the way, wouldn't have been my choice with the dress, but Jean-Paul insisted he wanted my shoes to match the Lamborghini, and who am I to argue with a cinematic genius?)

"Pardon the intrusion, Your Highness," says the woman. "I recognized you from the society pages."

I nod to encourage her; she seems so interested. Really, I'm just a regular girl. I don't go in for all that formal stuff. I'm much more excited about appearing in what will undoubtedly be THE hot movie of the year. I know it's only a walk-on—or a cameo, as Jean-Paul calls it—but still.

She continues. "I'm Trixie Loquor…a…um…friend of Jean-Paul's."

"Any friend of Jean-Paul's is a friend of mine," I assure her.

She smiles happily. Yay! Maybe now I'll have not one, but two friends in film.

I notice she's carrying a notebook, and, inclining my head toward it, ask, "Are you a screenwriter?"

"No…I am a writer, though. I work for *T.I.I.*"

"A writer. How impressive. I've never heard of *T.I.I.* Is it an entertainment-industry publication?"

"Well, you could say that. But enough about me. What brings you here? Just the film?"

I think she's being a bit forward, to be honest, but since she's a friend of Jean-Paul's, I let it go.

"That and dinner."

"With who?"

"Jean-Paul."

"Well, I'll make myself scarce then. Three's a crowd." She hurries off, calling over her shoulder, "Nice chatting with you, Your Highness!"

Before I can even respond, she's well out of earshot. Actually, I'm meeting Jean-Paul Corday, my chamberlain and dear friend, who is the descendant of the saintly Jacques who rescued my ancestors. His family has worked for mine ever since.

Jean-Paul Fameux will be popping in to the restaurant briefly, just to say goodbye. I didn't mean to give Trixie the impression that I'm dining with THE Jean-Paul, but what could I do? She left in far too much of a rush for me to elaborate. Besides, when she catches up with him, I'm sure he'll explain everything. It doesn't really matter, anyway. I mean, why would she care? She did seem awfully intrigued, though. Maybe she's a royal watcher or something. When Jean-Paul stops by, I'll ask him. Jean-Paul Fameux, I mean. Sometimes it's a bit confusing to have two good friends named Jean-Paul.

"Excuse me! Pardon me! Excuse me! Pardon me!" I say graciously, making my way through the usual crowd at Nobu as best I can. Most of the people are so absorbed in their mid-saketini conversations that they don't look up long enough to notice who they're moving aside for. Which is fine with me. I do notice a few discreetly point-ing in my direction and whispering to each other. I'm sure they recognize me. I just smile as they step aside to let me pass.

At last the hostess seats me at a relatively quiet back table for two, and a couple of minutes later my dear chamber-lain, Jean-Paul, arrives.

"Chérie," he says, taking a seat when I motion for him to. "How did it go?"

I give him all the details, finishing with Jean-Paul Fameux's pronouncement of my being a natural star.

"Fantastic!" he says, then orders saketinis for us.

"You still haven't told me what you wanted to talk about tonight," I remind him.

He's about to do just that, when Jean-Paul Fameux ap-proaches our table.

"I can only stay a second," Jean-Paul Fameux says. "You really were fabulous, *bébé*. I'll have a check sent to you."

"Send it to the de Soignée Charitable Foundation of-fice," I tell him. I'm donating my payment for the walk-on to the Foundation. It's so wonderful to actually have earned something to contribute to the work I do. Usually I just ask other people to donate money. A couple of years ago, I started a branch within the Foundation that spon-sors worldwide literacy. Working for it is how I spend most of my time. (When I'm not being a film celebrity, that is!)

"Right, you're turning the money over to your literacy thing," Jean-Paul Fameux says, remembering. "You know, I should introduce you to Oprah. Together, you could work miracles. Would you go on her show to talk about your project?"

"Absolutely."

"Done. My people will call her people, and I'll be in touch with the details."

He leans down for a kiss on the cheek and is about to dash off when I remember Trixie Loquor.

"Oh, before you go, I met your friend Trixie Loquor. Very sweet."

He stops in his tracks, wheeling around and slamming his hand on the table. "Trixie Loquor is NOT my friend. What did she say to you, Jacquie?"

"Just that she's your friend and a writer for *T.I.I.*"

"Did you tell her anything?"

"Only that I was meeting Jean-Paul here for dinner, but she hurried off before I could explain which Jean-Paul, so I'm sure she assumed I meant you—"

"Jacquie, Trixie Loquor is a rag-sheet reporter. *T.I.I.* is *The International Investigator.*"

By now my chamberlain has his hand over his forehead. "Tabloid," he says, knowing I don't read such things and would never have heard of it.

I sigh, embarrassed I'd never heard of *T.I.I.*, and furious with myself for thinking it sounded important just because Trixie Loquor had made it sound important. Groan. The bane of every princess: paparazzi, tabloids, scandals... It's enough to make a princess almost hate being a princess. I did say *almost*. I down a saketini to steady my nerves.

"Don't worry," I say brightly. "She probably hardly noticed what I said and scurried off to get some dirt on one of your film's stars, any of whom are far more interesting than I could ever be."

The Jean-Pauls exchange a glance, and Fameux says that he really must be off.

"Call me about *Oprah!*" I remind him, and he waves over his shoulder on his way out.

My chamberlain orders our sashimi and another round of saketinis, then turns back to me. "Let's see—you're appearing in a film and soon to be on *Oprah,* and now you've chatted with a tabloid reporter—"

I put up a hand to stop him. "I know, my father will not be pleased." (It's not always easy having a royal father.) "The film cameo and *Oprah* are for good causes—the tabloid thing will be a bit harder to explain… Perhaps my mother can intervene."

"We'll figure something out. Don't you fret," Jean-Paul soothes, patting my hand.

There are many perks to being a princess—not just the fabulous jewels, clothes and other accoutrements (all of which I adore, mind you!), but all the wonderful things I can do, not just for my friends and the people I care about, but also for the world at large. It's a blessing to be able to make a difference just by being me. All this wonderfulness outweighs the downside of paparazzi, tabloids and scandals.

By the time I'm into my second saketini, I've utterly forgotten Trixie Loquor and every tabloid on the planet. I'm just happy to be me: princess, philanthropist and film celebrity.

When the waitress brings our sashimi, Jean-Paul and I are deep into a discussion on what a bad rap princesses have been given. Granted, our line of thinking is somewhat saketini-induced, but there is a lot of truth to our opinion. Just think about it: "She's such a princess" is always said with such disdain, as if being a princess automatically means you're spoiled rotten or a simpleminded fairy-tale character, or a combination of the two.

And right then, I decide it's up to me to end the bad rap, to right the world's perception of the princess. Jean-Paul cheers me on. We're both inspired. Yes! I can do this. I will do this. (Perhaps I'll even bring up the idea on *Oprah*.) Hmm. But what to do? How to do it? (I mean, what if Oprah says no?)

"Well, *chérie,* that sort of brings up what I wanted to talk to you about," Jean-Paul begins. "I was going to suggest that you write a book."

Let me tell you, I am so flabbergasted by Jean-Paul's suggestion that I swallow a piece of sashimi whole. I am choking on sashimi, right in the middle of Nobu.

After I recover—thanks to some Evian and the ministrations of a very adorable waiter—Jean-Paul says, "I fully intended that all the proceeds from the book would go to the Foundation's literacy program."

I nod. "I should have guessed that. Forgive me," I say. "What kind of book? Please don't tell me you're suggesting a self-help book." Between you and me, I just don't understand self-help books. Ten steps to a magnificent you! *Blah, blah, blah.* Spare me. I simply don't get involved in things that I find distasteful.

Jean-Paul, in his ultracharming way, just smiles and says, "Of course not. I know how you feel about self-help books."

Sipping more Evian, I say, "Forgive me again. What *did* you mean?"

"*Show* other women how to be a princess—the best part of being a princess—by watching you. Teach by example," Jean-Paul tells me.

"Hmm. That could be fun," I muse aloud, my eyes wide. I am about to become not only a film celebrity, but a television personality and an acclaimed author as well. My saketini-enhanced mind races at the limitless possibilities.

The rest, as they say, is history. Following Jean-Paul's suggestion, I'm going to show you the real deal about being a princess. Not just the trappings—I mean, who would need a book to figure out how great those are?—but the way to learn how to really love yourself for who you are, just as you are, and to be loved once you do.

If I'm to be your mentor along the path to princessliness, you should know why I'm so eminently qualified, after all. The only difference between you and me is that I *am* a princess. That may seem like a huge difference to you, but that's only because you feel the huge difference between *being* a princess and *wishing you were* a princess. Being a princess is really about being happy with yourself. I know I've said that already, too. Some things bear repeating.

As for me, it just so happens that I recognized my princessliness early on, realized it was a good thing, and embraced and nurtured it throughout my life. By that I mean that I embraced my *Inner* Princess, in addition to happening to actually be a princess by birth. Being born a princess (or becoming a princess by means of marrying a prince) does not necessarily mean that you've embraced your Inner Princess; and embracing your Inner Princess definitely doesn't mean that you have to have a tiara insured with Lloyd's of London.

No matter who you are, if you want to be happy, you MUST call forth your Inner Princess and live your truth every day. And, yes, every woman has an Inner Princess, and we each have to discover, acknowledge, express, embrace and cherish our own Inner Princess, no matter who we are.

Learning to do that is the purpose of this book, and in it I'll show you how. Not by spouting a lot of do-this, do-that instructions, but by letting you watch me be me. Of course, I'll have to give you some tips and advice, too. What are friends for? I mean, I do want you to have the benefit of my experience as a princess. But first, some background on me.

To begin at the beginning, when I was born, my father promptly dispatched my mother's favorite lady-in-waiting to Harry Winston to procure my first diamond, and my grandmother sent maids-of-honor to commandeer the entire inventory of the Little Princess department of

Bergdorf Goodman. But these were just superficial trap-pings. We each make ourselves a princess by acknowl-edging that we already *are*. If you're feeling doubtful, don't worry: You're not alone, we're in this together, you and I. Just follow my lead. Before you know it, grace and savoir faire will just emanate from you continuously, making everything you do appear effortless and splendid.

From now on, you are a Princess-in-Training, and I promise to share with you everything I know about being a princess, and why it's so magnificent. We are going to have the most fun!

Being a princess is your destiny. See it. Believe it. Claim it. Dress for it.

On Sense of Self

A princess loves herself and loves being who she is.

1

As your princessly mentor, I realize that the best way to teach you how to be a princess is to let you see how a real princess lives. Like anyone else, a princess must work. Although I work for charity and not for subsistence, it amounts to the same thing. Contrary to popular belief, a princess is not meant to sit on her throne, arcing her scepter and looking beautiful all day. A princess must be productive, and use her skills and talents to the utmost. Luckily, my work at the Foundation allows me to do both—and that is where I'm headed right now.

Yesterday, I thought nothing could ever be more exciting than becoming a film celebrity, but writing a book is a marvelous experience.

By the way, in case you're wondering, yes, I touch-type. Being a princess doesn't mean thinking that any jobs are beneath you or that you're better than other people. My best friend, Clarice, who also happens to be my assistant at the Foundation, taught me how to type, and I taught her how to shop. Clarice taught me to type because I hated bugging her to do my typing all the time—it's not as if she doesn't have nine zillion other things to do every day—and I taught her how to shop because she asked me to. (Now she can spot a Prada at a hundred yards in deep fog. I'm so proud of her!)

Nine chances out of ten, you probably know how to type and maybe you're a Prada-spotter, too. Don't worry if you can't or if you're not, though. If it's important to you to learn how to type or how to spot labels, go for it. If neither one is important to you, that's fine, too. The point is to remember that you can do whatever you set your mind to, and once you really start loving yourself, you'll believe that. And then you *will* start to see yourself as a princess and carry yourself like a princess, and pretty soon everyone will treat you like a princess. You have to just trust me on this.

By the way, in case you're wondering, yes, my penthouse is fabulous. I live right off Central Park, and am close to *everything.* Not that it really matters; if it's that far, I just hop in the Lamborghini and off I go. (I have a chauffeur, James, but I like to be on my own, so he naps and watches ESPN more than he drives me. My father insists on my having a chauffeur, though. "Every princess has to have a chauffeur, Jacqueline," he says. It's usually *his* idea for me to show up at whatever affair we're going to in a tiara that gives me a headache. Sigh. As I mentioned already, royal dads can be…um…*challenging.*)

Truthfully, though, I like to walk whenever I can. I love being out and about, and getting to know people in my neighborhood. Just the other day, I was waiting to see a scarf at Hermès. The woman ahead of me, who happens to live in a building on my street and whom I've gotten to know because we both in-line skate in the park, offered to let the sales associate help me first.

"Please, Your Highness," she said. "I couldn't possibly let you wait."

"Absolutely not," I told her, insisting that she take her rightful turn. "And it's Jacquie, remember?" I reminded her. (Everyone calls me Jacqueline—Jacquie if we really get along well—so you can call me Jacquie, but remember, it's with a "qu" not a "k".) I know I'm a princess. All that fanfare isn't necessary, all that royal-court stuff. Yawn! Better than Sominex, believe me.

Anyway, my in-line skating friend gave me the hugest smile, as if I'd done something unbelievably wonderful.

I hadn't really done anything at all. It was her rightful turn. I never consider myself entitled to more than other people. I think that people find it a chore to be kind and gracious when they have a poor self-image. When you know how to honor and love yourself, honoring and loving everyone else just flows effortlessly. When you need other people to prove your worth to yourself, you will always feel lacking.

A true princess knows exactly who she is, and is proud of it.

A princess knows her regalness is an obvious fact requiring no overt behavior to prove it. It's important to recognize that sense of self is a permanent state, not a mood or emotion that changes with time or circumstance. You can have a bad day or have a dark mood or a cloud of negative emotions pass over you for a time without letting it impact your sense of self. Finding yourself in a dark mood is feeling irritable as a result of some situation or other, but not taking out your irritation on yourself.

Oh my God! Look at the time! I always try to be at the office by ten, and it's already past ten-thirty. Oh, well. Clarice will have everything under control. She always does. She is the absolute best. Come to think of it, yesterday she mentioned something that I was supposed to do this morning, but I was dashing out the door on my way to my dinner at Nobu. Needless to say, I wasn't paying rapt attention. Okay, I didn't hear a word she said. I'll explain when I get there, and she'll understand. After all, how often am I on my way to a film shoot?

Uh-oh. Clarice is standing in the doorway of my uptown office, looking none too happy. She's a true redhead, with very fair skin that is now quite flushed, and she's tapping her foot. Really nice Kate Spade pumps. I helped her pick them out.

"Hi," I chirp when I reach my doorway.

"Hi," she says, about as far from a chirp as she could get.

"Something wrong, sweetie?"

"Only that you're late for the board meeting."

"The board meeting is tomorrow at eleven," I say, remembering scanning my calendar for the rest of the week yesterday morning.

"No," Clarice says patiently. "It was scheduled for then, but when you were leaving yesterday, I told you I had to move the meeting to today at ten."

Oops. So *that* was what I was supposed to remember. Funny, compared to filming, the meeting seemed so inconsequential. But that's no excuse, and I detest being late for anything. It is most indubitably NON-princessly to behave as if your time is more valuable than other people's.

"Well…I…"

"You didn't hear a word I said when you were leaving yesterday, did you?"

I shake my head. "I'm truly sorry, Clar."

She shoots me an exasperated look. I realize now is not the moment to tell her how fabulous the filming actually was, or to let her know I'm soon to be a TV personality and acclaimed author as well. After the meeting.

I open the boardroom door and enter the room with a cheerful, "Good morning, everyone!" Breezing past the board members seated around the oval table to my seat at the head, I say, "I apologize for being late, but it was unavoidable. Let me briefly explain why, and I'm sure you'll not only understand, but be thrilled by the good news it portends for the literacy program."

They all perk up, smiling expectantly. All except Hortense Cranston, that is. Hortense is my least-favorite board member. The snob. I once heard Bill Wanamaker, another board member, say, "You'd think Hortense was the princess!" (That bad-rap stuff again. But don't you worry: Once my book hits the stores, there will be no more of that!)

"Last night I filmed a cameo spot at Nobu in my dear friend Jean-Paul Fameux's new film—"

"Is it subtitled?" asks Hortense, her mouth pursed as if she's sucking the world's sourest lemon.

"No, it's an American film. It's about an unorthodox street cop who exposes city corruption, thanks to his snitch—" I repeat verbatim the description Fameux gave me.

"I was assuming it was subtitled since you prefaced your little monologue by telling us how your endeavors will be so invaluable to the literacy program," Hortense says. "People have to *read* subtitles, Jacqueline." She smirks, and a few of the other board members cough in a thinly veiled attempt to cover their snickers. Snickers! I am horrified. How can they snicker at me? On the very morning that begins my new life as a film celebrity, TV personality and acclaimed author, no less. I am not about to stand for this. Especially not when Hortense Cranston is leading the charge.

"If you would have permitted me to finish—afforded me the same courtesy I afford everyone seated around this table all the time—the connection would have been apparent to everyone. Even you, Hortense," I finish with an icy smile. "Certainly you cannot assume that a Vassar graduate would not be aware that subtitles are *read*." It really bothers Hortense that I went to Vassar, because Vassar rejected her, so she had to go to Sarah Lawrence instead. She never got over it, even though she graduated from college before I was born. I notice even more board members are suppressing smiles and snickers now.

"Now then," I continue, smoothing the papers in front of me and taking a sip of water from the glass Clarice left at my seat, "my friend Jean-Paul is going to be getting me a spot on *Oprah* in the very near future, where I will discuss the literacy program with her." I pause again for effect and to gauge the board's excitement. They seem impressed, but in a quiet sort of way. "And I'm writing a self-esteem book, the proceeds of which will go to the literacy program."

"That all sounds grand, Jacqueline," says Bill Wanamaker, but in that tut-tut tone, as if I were a little girl excited about something that grown-ups would never consider important. Well, I guess I know what *he* really thinks of me.

"Oprah Winfrey is a bastion of the literacy campaign…" I begin, indignant, but keeping my cool.

"Oprah canceled her Book Club," snaps Hortense.

"I'm aware of that, Hortense. She is nevertheless one of the foremost advocates for literacy in this country. Let's just move along. I'll keep everyone apprised as things move forward," I say crisply.

I force myself not to focus on how disappointed I am by the board's underwhelmed reaction to my news about *Oprah*. I have no intention of letting anyone ruin my happiness about all my new adventures—my walk-on, *Oprah*, my book.

"Do let us know when the film will premiere."

I'm about to tell Hortense that I will, just so she won't show up in her vintage Chanel (it isn't cool retro vintage, it's just been hanging in her closet since the year zero, and she's worn it everywhere, every year since), but I think better of it. The Hortense Cranstons of the world don't deserve the attention the rest of us often pay them out of sheer frustration and irritation. A princess knows when to just let things go. I launch into the agenda, and the meeting proceeds smoothly and quickly.

When we adjourn, I thank all the board members for their time and participation, then head directly back to my office, closing the door behind me. Who cares that they all were so blasé! I'm not going to let anyone rain on my parade.

"Jacquie, can I come in?" Clarice's voice floats over the intercom.

"Please," I say.

She comes in, carrying a large mug that wafts the aroma of mocha java.

Before she can even ask, I spill the whole story.

"Who cares what they think? I think it's fantastic," Clarice says loyally.

"I do, too." I'm glad Clarice shares my enthusiasm.

This is the way a princess behaves: self-assured, strong, steady. I must be the princess that I am, inside and out. And so must you.

I smile at Clarice, and we both laugh.

"By the way, Clar, excellent response for a Princess-in-Training Graduate." (Once upon a time, darling, she was in training, just as you are now. I'm sure you'll do every bit as marvelously as she did.)

"Thanks," she calls over her shoulder on her way out of my office. I get the distinct impression that she might not think I have much practical advice to offer, but I tell myself I must be wrong. After all, Clarice loves me and is my stellar graduate, so how could she possibly think that?

Anyway, what's important is that, even though I was disappointed and upset, I recovered quickly, and am boundlessly psyched all over again. I'm sure Fameux will be calling any minute to tell me when I'm going to be on

Oprah. I should give it a day or two, though, because he did say that his people will have to call her people—and who knows just how long that might take, even though their cell phones are no doubt practically surgically attached to them. Sigh. But I'm not going to worry about any of it. I must get used to functioning at film-, TV- and book-pace.

You don't have to be perfect. You're a princess. Besides, even a diamond has flaws.

Now, as this morning's meeting proved, unexpected things do happen. What's important is that you not beat yourself up about them. Always try to do your best and to care about others. If you make a mistake, apologize, forgive yourself and move on. If people push your buttons, take a deep breath, center yourself and get through it as best you can. (Incidentally, I'm sounding a little like my friend Nirvana, with this "center yourself" stuff. She can be a little over-the-top with her guru and all, but some of it is really helpful. More about Nirvana later.)

I also want to say that since you are a beginner, don't despair if all this sounds a bit daunting. It's hard at first to get that loving yourself and being proud of what you do doesn't mean that you have to be perfect. I confess that even I, resplendent princess that I am, did not have a strong sense of self until I was six. (So what if you're starting a little bit later? Getting there is what counts, not how long it takes.) That's when I learned—finally, it seemed to me at the time—to arc my scepter with just the right mix of flourish and delicacy. Even now, I recall being in tears that I couldn't get it just right.

My mother, who'd been helping me practice for a costume ball I was going to, dressed as my idol, Princess Elizabeth (if you're thinking that this ball was my father's idea, you're right), sat me down on the tuffet next to her dressing table and told me that if I was to be a confident princess I needed to find my own way of holding and arcing the scepter, not imitate anyone else. She dried my tears and told me to try it again. Mindful of her words, I told myself, *I can do it. This is* my *scepter.* And, lo and behold, I made a perfect arc. You don't have a scepter—so what? The scepter doesn't matter. (Believe me, I do NOT go traipsing around the city with a scepter. Couldn't you just see me? *Puh-leeze!*) What matters is learning to be yourself and to trust yourself—that's the essence of a positive sense of self, of being a true princess. I didn't learn it because I was born a princess. I learned it because I made up my mind to be myself and trust myself. And you can learn it, too. I have faith in you.

And as you can see, even I need little refreshers every now and then. Having a strong sense of self doesn't mean that you never get angry or upset. Feeling your feelings is just human—you're learning to be a princess not a saint. I'll let you in on another secret (remember the first one was that we each have an Inner Princess): The scepter is a state of mind. By that I mean that we each have something that we can think about to make us remember that we are great just as we are. For me, it's that long-ago scepter practice. Call to mind whatever it is for you, and whenever you need a little refresher, just think of it. Sometimes you might not think of it in the moment when you feel the worst, and that's fine. We don't have to be perfect; we just have to do our best. Even more important, we have to be kind to ourselves.

Let me just go into my e-mail for a sec. Delete. Delete. That can wait. Delete. Nothing from the world of the silver screen… But my friend Mariana wants to have lunch today. After the board meeting debacle, I was planning to go for a reflexology massage during lunch, but Mariana so rarely eats lunch that I hate to say no. Mariana, who I met at Vassar, is a personal trainer, and Clarice and I think she has a serious eating disorder. However, she gives an incredible massage… I e-mail her that I'd love to have lunch, but wanted to go for a foot massage. She sends me an IM that she'll give me one, and then we'll go for lunch. Perfect.

Life is never simple, but it is as easy as you make it for yourself. Every princess knows that. So make life easy for yourself. The first step toward that is being true to yourself (i.e. your Inner Princess—so if that soft, sweet inner voice beckons, "bubble bath" in the midst of a chaotic day, find a bathtub and some bath beads). Right now, I'm indulging with some mocha java. Being true to yourself isn't a deep philosophical principle that requires years of contemplation in a lamasery (that reminds me of Nirvana, too), it's just knowing and accepting who you are and living the truth of that every day. The next step is laughing with your Inner Princess. A sense of humor, meeting life and your own shortcomings with smiles and laughter, is essential. It also leads to dignity, serenity and grace: three qualities no true princess ever lacks.

Maintain a sense of humor at all times. Especially about yourself. A princess knows how to chuckle at her own foibles.

In addition, having a sense of humor is infinitely empowering, as it helps you observe and remain in charge of your reactions. (Like just now when I knocked over the last few sips of my mocha java. Sigh. Maybe Nirvana is right, and caffeine really *does* make people jittery.) Most of the day-to-day situations that cause discomfort are things which we cannot control. I freely admit that even a princess cannot control *every*thing. No matter who you are, people and situations beyond your control will manifest, and that's just the way it is, as we saw in this morning's board meeting, which I really don't want to keep talking about. However, a princess can—and must—learn to control her reactions to what happens around her. Your reactions are always within your control, and just remaining mindful of this is extremely empowering. You saw how I handled myself in the meeting, and even though I wish I hadn't gotten as upset as I did, I still kept it together.

Maintaining this type of awareness with a sense of humor will help you even more. If you can laugh at the absurdity of a situation—and even more important, if you can laugh with yourself *through* the absurdity of it—you will inevitably persevere, prevail and triumph.

As I'm getting ready to head to the gym to meet Mariana, I tell Clarice where I'll be.

"Do you want to come, too?" I ask her.

She begs off. "A carrot curl and an alfalfa sprout are not my idea of 'lunch,' Jacquie," Clarice informs me.

Well, Mariana does have her moments. Clarice heads down to the lobby with me, walking me part of the way toward the gym on her way to run errands and pick up her lunch.

A piece of newspaper blows up onto the sidewalk in front of us as a cab speeds by, and Clarice stops dead in her tracks. "Jacquie, that's your Lamborghini!" She points to a photo on the front page of *The International Investigator* then stoops to pick it up.

"JACQUIE & JEAN-PAUL SIZZLE ON-SCREEN AND OFF!!" screams the headline. The larger photo is of me beside the Lamborghini in front of Nobu last night. Next to it are two smaller insets, one of Jean-Paul Fameux, the other a society-page head shot of me.

Clarice and I stare at the paper, speechless. "What a rag!" Clarice says. "Just because you did a walk-on. This is ridiculous. Tell Fameux to do something!"

"Don't worry about it, sweetie," I say. "It was a big misunderstanding." I fill Clarice in on my encounter with Trixie Loquor.

"Jacquie, you're going to be writing a memoir on how you survived depression after Trixie Loquor is done with you. Do you realize what all this means? Your father will—"

"Oh, Clar. Don't be such a worrywart. My father will understand, and so will Trixie when I explain it all to her. I didn't mislead her on purpose. Do you have any idea how confusing it can be to have two close friends named Jean-Paul? You've gotten their messages mixed up sometimes, yourself."

"No, I haven't. *You* have."

"What*ever*." Sometimes, she's SO nitpicky!! "The point is, it's confusing."

"*She* won't think so. You were in the movie. *Of course* she thought you meant Fameux."

"I'll call Jean-Paul when I get back from my foot-massage lunch with Mariana. Better yet, I'll call Trixie, too. We'll have a good laugh over it, I'm sure."

"Jacquie..."

"Don't worry." I kiss Clarice on the cheek and head toward the gym, happy and feeling fine except for the twinge in my instep from working the clutch in mules. Mariana's magic fingers will fix that in a jiffy. Mentally, I arc my scepter gracefully, as I imagine smoothing things over with Trixie Loquor, who will no doubt be so charmed that she'll never print an ugly thing about me or any of my friends ever again. Perhaps she'll even be inspired to give up tabloids altogether and go mainstream. I may be instrumental in the career of a future Pulitzer Prize winner! Honestly, the headline upset me only because it's not true and I hate being lied about. As for my father...I really need my mother to help smooth things over with him.

When I arrive at the gym, Mariana is waiting for me. I sit in her massage chair, and within seconds of her ministrations, the spasms in my foot have calmed.

"You're an angel," I tell her. "My foot is SO much better. Where to for lunch?"

"I'm going to beg off lunch," Mariana says. "*Look* at this." She shows me what she perceives to be a hunk of flab on her right hip. Mariana, sallow and dark-haired, defines "willowy."

"Look at what? You're a rail."

Mariana shakes her head.

"Would you have clients who trust you to make them skinny if you were fat?"

Mariana ponders this seemingly irrefutable argument. "They only think I'm skinny because they're so fat."

I realize that I am not up for this today. "You're slim and stunning, and I love you. I want to have lunch with you, but if you don't want to, we'll do it another time."

She nods.

"But you will eat something?"

"Of course, silly. After you go, I'll munch on my usual huge bowl of mung sprouts and blue-green algae shake."

No comment.

We hug, and I head back to the Foundation office, calling Clarice on my cell phone and asking her to order lunch for me.

Back to what I was saying about self-reliance before we got sidetracked by the tabloid headline and my meeting Mariana. Self-reliance means that you trust yourself, that you know you can handle whatever comes your way, and be stronger and more resilient as a result. (See, that's why I'm not a bit worried about this whole tabloid thing. I know I can explain everything, and it will all blow over in no time.) Trusting your own intuition is something you must learn for yourself. I hope that by observing my complete faith in my own intuitive powers, you will learn to trust yours. Let me tell you how I learned to trust my own intuition.

A while back, when I was a young princess—let's just say that I was old enough to have my own car, but young enough to not yet be on my own in Manhattan—I got to go to a very important party with my father, because my mother was away. It was one of those awful court affairs, and I had to wear a migraine-in-the-making tiara. And there was lots of bowing and curtsying and titles to remember, and I was really nervous. Let me tell you, I worried about this party day and night, obsessing over every little detail. Anyway, the fateful evening of the party arrived—finally!—and somehow, every aspect of the entire soiree was perfect. If I do say so myself, I was charming, gracious and adorable. My father was quite pleased with me, fortunately.

What a night that was! I can still remember Svetlana Yevgenyevna, the Russian princess I went to boarding school with near Lake Lucerne in Switzerland, dancing with Calvin Xavier St. Cyr, a Swiss banker, who was ancient even then. Every time they turned in a waltz, either his hearing aid or monocle would pop out, and he'd have to stop to pick it up. Then he'd forget where they were in the dance and clomp on poor Svetlana's foot. (Her instep has never been the same. Poor thing can't even think about wearing mules to this very day.) And then there was Lavinia Culpeper—born an English countess and married to a billionaire oil tycoon from Oklahoma—trying to marry off her triplets, the three "-icas"—Angelica, Veronica and Monica—to no avail. (Let me be kind and say that these girls had the personality of lint. Svetlana, who has since married their now-billionaire brother, Lance, assures me that they still do.)

But I digress. My point in bringing all this up is that I worried needlessly. At the time, of course, the worrying seemed completely justified—even necessary—to me. And you're right, I wasn't thinking of my mental-scepter image that time, either. Go ahead and laugh. Besides, I want you to see that I'm not above worrying or doing silly things, or any other human foibles. No one is. The key is to recognize your own foibles, laugh with yourself and move on. Life is too splendid and too precious to waste by worrying. A true princess learns that by acknowledging her foibles, she accepts them as a part of herself. You cannot carry yourself with poise until you accept every aspect of yourself.

You are becoming a true princess. Remember, your princessliness is more perception than reality: It's about how you feel about yourself, projecting that and waiting graciously for all around you to recognize the princess you already know you are.

Which brings up another important point about sense of self: choices. You do what feels right for you. Which doesn't mean you sit in judgment of other people, just that you know yourself and you're true to yourself, no matter what. Making a positive choice means you do what you do because it feels right to you and for you, not because you want to fit in. Fitting in is worthless if you have to become someone else to accomplish it.

So when Nirvana tells me I need to meditate more, or Mariana tells me I need to replace carbs with lean protein, I just smile and say, "Thanks. I'll think about it." Then I do what feels right to me. I love Nirvana and Mariana; I've been friends with each of them for years. (I met Nirvana at Vassar, too. She spent every school break with me, while her parents traveled all over India, Nepal and Tibet in the entourage of their guru *du jour,* a pursuit that Nirvana herself has also adopted. Sigh. She does worry me.) But I don't want to meditate and do yoga for more hours a day than I sleep, and I don't want to worry about every crumb I put in my mouth, either. I just want to be me, and to do what feels right for me—because that's what makes me feel happy. And that's why I hope you'll do it, too.

I choose what I know works for me, and I learn from what doesn't. Simple as that.

On Deserving—
and Expecting—the Best

Every princess deserves what she dreams of and deserves to have
her fondest dreams come true.

2

I spoke to Jean-Paul Fameux and Trixie Loquor. I reached
Fameux right away, but Trixie was quite hard to get ahold
of. Anyway, Fameux had fantastic news! Oprah is so excited about my wanting to be on her show, so I'm going
to Chicago to tape in two weeks. Isn't that just fabulous?!?! In two weeks' time I will have (1) filmed, and (2)
taped. For the segment, she and I will discuss the Foundation's literacy program, my book-in-progress and being
a hip princess in Manhattan.

As for Trixie, the news is not quite so fantastic. She
didn't want to listen to a word I had to say—was down-
right rude, to be honest—and accused me of setting her
up. Can you imagine?! And this, after I explained about
the two Jean-Pauls and everything. I still can't quite get
over it. But Clarice did call this one. (She feels just awful.)
On the bright side, one of the lawyers at the Foundation
called *The International Investigator* and got them to print
their version of a retraction: JACQUIE & JEAN-PAUL
JUST GOOD FRIENDS! So my father, who hears about

everything that happens in the world, somehow, has been appeased. My mother helped, of course. But I feel just terrible. Not because I mind being linked romantically with Jean-Paul—who is a hottie, but a confirmed bachelor (Clarice thinks he's gay, but I've never picked up on that)—but because I'm still wondering *how* Trixie Loquor could persist in thinking that I deliberately lied to her. Luckily, Clarice and both Jean-Pauls have reminded me to learn from the experience, then put it behind me. Truly, that is the princessly course of action. See? I have them to coach me, and you have *moi*. So tonight, I'm going to soak in a long, luxurious bubble bath while listening to my favorite Norah Jones album and indulging in Teuscher chocolates. Delish!

It is a relief that the whole tabloid thing has pretty much blown over. Jean-Paul is going to have a private premiere and bash at his place in St. Tropez. I am so *there!* Anyway, now I can focus on my ongoing film appearances (Jean-Paul is going to find more cameos for me because I'm such a natural), my upcoming show with Oprah, and of course, my book. I'll probably never hear from Trixie Loquor or *The International Investigator* again. And *never* will be too soon, believe me.

As I'm sure you can imagine, the whole tabloid thing was pretty stressing, mental-scepter image notwithstanding, so I've been doing what I can to destress. I find power walking to be one of the best things. I'm walking right now, in fact. It's early morning, so hardly anyone is out and about yet—unless they're still out from last night. Call me crazy, but this is my favorite time to power walk. I'm booking along Fifth Avenue, and one of my favorite places is coming into sight: Tiffany's. Sigh. I have to pause for a moment. I just ADORE Tiffany's! Clarice is always on my case about how much I love Tiff's and go on and on about it. Oh, well. Tiffany's *is* important. And there's also an important lesson to learn from Audrey Hepburn's character in the movie *Breakfast at Tiffany's*. She yearns for what's inside Tiffany's, what's beyond her reach. That's not what a princess does. A princess knows she deserves what she dreams of, and sets out to get it for herself. (That's what you need to start doing.)

Now, that doesn't mean a princess ever brags about how deserving she is, just that she is comfortable knowing what she deserves. People who go around bragging all the time may think they're proving their worth to others, but all they're really proving is how insecure they are. Having "the best" doesn't mean that you have to flaunt it.

Hold on a sec. Oh my God! There's an incredible chocolate-and-vanilla diamond pendant in the Fifty-seventh Street side window. That pendant is just what I'm looking for to wear with my new Donna Karan espresso charmeuse evening gown.

You may be thinking it's easy for me to expect the best, and that I've probably never had to make the best of anything. Not true. I understand why you're thinking it, though. That's exactly what Clarice thought when she first met me. I'll tell you the whole story so you can see what I mean.

When I first started running the Foundation's literacy program, Jean-Paul, my chamberlain, helped me with everything. After a while, poor Jean-Paul was just completely overworked, and even though he wouldn't admit it, I could see he was getting ragged around the edges. So I decided to hire an assistant to help me at the Foundation office. This midtown head-hunting agency sent a *ton* of people for me to interview, and each one of them was just *wrong*. After a few days, I was thoroughly discouraged. Then Clarice arrived for her interview. I thought she was fantastic—smart, composed, gracious—and I hired her on the spot. By noon of her first day, I realized that in addition to what I liked about her already, Clarice was also the most efficient person I had ever encountered. As her first week working for me was drawing to a close, she had the entire office completely organized and running as smoothly as my Lamborghini. I was amazed. Words could not describe my admiration or appreciation. I decided to run out and buy her a little something—a token to express my gratitude—and give it to her when she returned from lunch.

Off I dashed to Bergdorf's, happy as a clam. An hour or so later, I returned carrying a few Bergdorf's shopping bags. (Naturally, I bought a few things for myself while I was there. I mean, I was in Bergdorf's, my favorite department store.) The day before, I had worn a lovely Armani scarf that Clarice had admired, so I decided to get her one, but in a different color. I breezed past Clarice's desk on my way into my office, surprised to see her looking rather peeved, since her composure was one of the things I most liked about her.

After a minute or two, she came and stood in my doorway.

"Sorry to cut into your shopping time, Your Highness, but your two o'clock conference call with Reading Is Fundamental is on hold. Shall I have them hold or call back?"

"I'll take it right away. I'm sorry I lost track of the time. Thank you, Clarice."

She'd said it all with crisp efficiency, but I could tell she was really irritated. More than was warranted, in my opinion. Who doesn't lose track of time at Bergdorf's? I took the call, which only lasted a few minutes but accomplished a lot, then went out to Clarice's desk, holding the wrapped scarf behind my back. (I love giving unexpected little gifties! And Clarice was going to be SO surprised. Not to mention thrilled.)

Clarice, who has bionic hearing to go along with her bionic memory (seriously, the girl remembers everything), turned to face me as I approached.

"Your Highness, if you plan to go out shopping at lunchtime every day, please tell me. You seem to lose all track of time when you do, so I just won't schedule anything until after three."

"Clarice," I said gently, "it's Jacqueline, not Your Highness. I do lose track of time shopping, and I apologize if I caused you any concern. I went out to get you a little something to show you how much I appreciate all you've done in the past week." I handed her the gift.

"I can't accept it," she said gruffly, handing the wrapped gift back to me. "I'll just pack my things and go."

"Go? Where?" I sputtered, in utter shock.

"You're letting me go, aren't you?" Her eyes flashed at me, angry and hurt. "Every job I've ever had, this is what happens. It's like they want me to fix the mess they make of their offices but not hang around too long." She sank back into her chair, looking totally defeated. Truth to tell, she looked as if she might cry, but she didn't. "I've had enough of being Ms. Fix-It for people who don't appreciate it. I have too much to offer to let myself be treated this way. I mean no disrespect, Your Highness, but I won't tolerate it. I'm the most qualified person you'll ever get for this job, and—"

"Clarice, I have no intention of letting you go. I never did. Your former employers might have been crazy or stupid…I'm neither. This gift is just a token of my appreciation. I very much want you to stay if you're happy here."

Clarice looked up at me in complete surprise. "Do you really mean that, Your High—Jacqueline?"

"I never say things I don't mean."

"Please forgive my outburst. It's just that my career life has been like a revolving door and it's so frustrating for me. I need this job, and I felt so great because I thought I'd finally found the right place…"

"You have found the right place, Clarice, and I'm very lucky that you have. I understand why you've felt frustrated in the past. And I always want you to be honest and express your feelings. I can't depend on you if you don't."

Clarice nodded. "I've been so happy here that I almost started to think that we might be friends someday. I know that's ridiculous—you're a princess. I'd never dream you'd be friends with someone who worked for you. I can't believe I'm even saying all this to you."

"Don't be silly. I hope we will get to be friends." I put a tentative hand on her shoulder.

"You're just saying that to be nice," she said, regaining her composure. "I'm sorry if I made you feel uncomfortable."

"Clarice, I wouldn't have said it if I didn't mean it. I already told you that."

"I'm sure you have a million friends."

"Acquaintances, yes. True friends, only a few. I hope you'll be one of them someday."

She looked at me, mystified, as I handed her the gift again.

"I can't believe you got me a gift just to thank me."

I smiled at her, equally incredulous that she couldn't get over this fact. I did things like this for people all the time (and still do). Feeling that you deserve the best extends to others, too—to those you love and care about, and those who treat you with kindness and respect. I sensed that for all her gracious demeanor, Clarice did not expect the best for herself, did not honor and embrace her Inner Princess.

"No one's ever done that for me before."

"I'm sorry to hear that. But you'd better get used to it, because you deserve to be treated well, and I'm going to see to it that you are. And you'd better treat yourself well, too, because if I see that you aren't, you'll have me to deal with." (I can be pretty intimidating when I put my mind to it. All that regal-bearing stuff my mother taught me and had the ladies-in-waiting make me practice comes in handy. Hortense Cranston had best beware if I ever choose to let loose in the boardroom.)

Clarice merely arched an eyebrow in response.

"People should treat you the way they treat me, as if you, too, were a princess," I explained.

Clarice burst out laughing. "Jacqueline, it's easy for you to expect people to treat you like a princess. You *are* a princess. I'm just a working girl."

"Nonsense. You shouldn't accept people treating you badly for any reason, Clarice," I said firmly, then added more gently, "I know you think it's easy for me to say, Clarice, but it isn't. I expect the best—things, people, circumstances—because I know that's what I deserve, not because I was born a princess. What goes around, comes around. People treat me with the same respect and kindness with which I treat them."

We discussed my theory of the Inner Princess. She pondered this a minute, then realized I was right. "I think we are going to be great friends." Sometimes I think she still thinks that people are nicer to me because I'm a princess than they would be if I weren't. But I just don't believe that and I never will.

So that's the story. (By the way, she LOVED the scarf!) From that moment to this, we've been the very best of friends, and Clarice knows I love her for her, and it doesn't matter to me at all that I was born a princess and she wasn't. Who cares about things like that? What matters is that she loves me for me, and knows that things aren't easier for me than they are for other people. Well, okay, a lot of things are easier for me, but not the deep-down things. If you don't love and appreciate yourself, it doesn't matter what your station is, you'll always be miserable and nothing will ever satisfy or please you.

I know! Let's do what Clarice and I did: Explore examples of "the best," to expand your P.Q. (Princess Quotient), which is your innate connection to your Inner Princess and understanding of what she/you deserve. Before long, your P.Q. will be off the charts. Trust me. Simply put, "the best" comprises life's delights, while "less than the best" comprises everything else. Expecting the best means that you come to view these delights as your necessities. Your rights, even. If feelings of "At last! How wonderful!" come into your mind as you read this, splendid. If you still feel a bit daunted, not to worry. The "right of delight" will feel natural to you before long.

Just remember, at all times and no matter what, the premise of this lesson:

A princess never settles. For anything. You deserve the best and only the best. Expect it. Demand it. Enjoy it.

Before we begin the lesson in earnest, let me be clear about something. If you can't afford the goodies I describe, don't worry about it. Simply tell yourself, for example, "I deserve an Ilias Lalaounis platinum lariat studded with pink sapphires. Perhaps someday I'll be able to afford one. If I never own one, it's not because I'm not deserving of one." In the meantime, treat yourself to things you can afford, like sleeping late on Saturdays, meeting friends for coffee, taking bubble baths, lighting scented candles, nibbling chocolate truffles or doing whatever makes you feel treasured and pampered.

Now, let's explore some specific expectations, beginning with a true essential: precious metals. The precious metals, in descending order of value, are: platinum, gold and silver. (If anyone tries to convince you that copper is a precious metal, politely remind the person that pennies are worth a cent for a reason. Copper is lovely, particularly with a verdigris patina, but "precious" is a term reserved for the other three.) Among these three metals exists a further categorization, of which any true princess remains ever mindful:

As a rule (★ see below), silver belongs on the table. Gold and platinum belong on *you*.
Even if you can't afford gold and platinum, you can still *aspire* to having them. Above all, know that you *deserve* them. With the rules for precious metals understood, you are ready for gemstones. By that I mean you are ready to *expect* gems. How you wear jewels is a style issue. That you *have* jewels is an expectation of "the best."

Jewels, to me, are like my mental-scepter image: a symbolic reminder of my own princessliness. So, if nothing upon you sparkles, off you go to Tiffany's or Cartier or Bulgari—*immediately*. If you can't afford to shop in any of these, don't worry about it. The point is to know that you deserve jewels of that quality, and to feel like a princess wearing the jewelry that you *can* afford. Wear it *as if* it came from Tiffany's (or whatever design you wish it were), because what you deserve is to feel good about yourself, no matter what. The finer things can help you feel that way, while you're learning deeper ways of feeling good about yourself. But remember, they're only trappings, only things. If you don't feel good about yourself, all the baubles in the world won't cut it. Once you do feel good about yourself, a lump of tinfoil on a string tied around your neck will feel as good as a David Yurman (★ who, along with Lagos, is an exception to the rule about not wearing silver). But always remember: What really sparkles is you, not the stuff. Expecting gems and knowing you deserve them is an I-feel-good-about-me thing, not an I'm-nothing-without-them thing.

Diamonds may be a girl's best friend, but they're a princess's birthright.
If you're thinking that I'm focusing too much on jewelry, you are absolutely *wrong*. Forgive me for being blunt, but

you are. A princess is born to be bejeweled—bedizened, bedecked. Deep down, this is what you have always known, isn't it? Well, now you have the official word from me. You're learning so quickly and so well, and I am so very proud of you. Reward yourself. I recommend something radiant, iridescent or lustrous.

For the record, I must say that Clarice, who is a stellar Princess-in-Training Graduate, disagrees vehemently about the jewel thing. I think she's wrong, of course, but I'm sharing her opinion, in case you agree. Anyway, my whole point with the jewels is that wearing fabulous jewels makes me feel adorned and stunning. Not the same as feeling good about myself; I feel that way without them. But every woman deserves beauty, pleasure and celebration, and needs to treat herself to feeling all three. If I use the jewelry example and it doesn't do anything for you (GASP! Clarice still horrifies me with her lack of love for gems), come up with an example that makes you feel gorgeous and delighted and adored, and use it instead.

Just then Clarice pokes her head in my doorway. "Jacquie, you'll never guess who just called! My sister. She's engaged!"

We squeal our mutual delight.

"Tiffany's at lunch, Clar," I tell her. "We'll each get your sister something fab."

That's our lunchtime plan.

I am just so thrilled for Clarice. She's never shopped at Tiff's before. I can't tell if she's just playing it cool or really couldn't care less. I know she doesn't care about jewelry, but this is *Tiffany's* after all.

We head down in the elevator and enter the lobby, where the doorman holds the door for us, and the Lamborghini is waiting. (Clarice called to let him know we were on our way. I told you she's awesome.) The whole ride down to Tiff's, I can hardly contain my excitement.

Clarice assures me I'm more excited than she is. As if I hadn't figured that out on my own. Soon enough, we arrive at Tiffany's, and I park the car in the nearest garage.

Remembering the scene in *Breakfast at Tiffany's* where Audrey Hepburn actually goes shopping in the store and finds some inexpensive items, I encourage Clarice, "There are sterling-silver pens and key rings and all sorts of useful things that aren't that expensive."

"They may be lovely, but they aren't practical, Jacquie. You have to polish silver, and my sister won't want to bother."

So I steer Clarice toward the crystal vases instead. Every bride needs crystal vases for all the roses her new husband will constantly be bringing home. Okay, maybe he won't bring them home forever. When he doesn't, she can buy her own roses. Or whatever kind of flowers she likes. The point is, no woman can have too many vases. Clarice looks at a few of them.

"There are so many other things my sister will need. Practical, everyday things." She rattles off a whole list. The very thought of actually having to go obtain all these things is absolutely daunting. Thank God for Jean-Paul, my chamberlain. He takes care of everything. (At least, I don't think my penthouse came completely equipped with all the things Clarice just mentioned.)

Rolling her eyes, Clarice says, "You are so sheltered. I worry about you."

"Are you really going to leave Tiffany's without buying anything?" The very thought all but breaks my heart.

"Yes, but I'm sure you aren't, Jacquie *Ka-ching*," she laughs.

I laugh, too, even though Clarice is the only person I would let get away with saying something like that. A princess indulges herself in what she enjoys, lavishes what she adores upon herself and never apologizes for it—she relishes and savors every moment. I remind Clarice of this, and she agrees, but emphasizes that enjoyment and lavishing do not have to entail spending money. And I wholeheartedly agree.

I select a beautiful cut-crystal vase for Clarice's sister. I tell the sales associate to charge the vase to my account, and while Clarice is giving her the mailing address so they can ship it direct from the store to her sister, I motion to the store manager (who knows me, of course). He comes over and I tell him to charge and send the to-die-for vanilla-and-chocolate diamond pendant—the one I went berserk over this morning, and have been thinking about ever since—and a beautiful pair of earrings shaped like flowers, with pink-diamond centers and white pavé stones surrounding. And that's all I choose. Three things, and one of them a gift for someone else. (Now, I ask you, can you imagine Clarice worrying that I take shopping to an extreme? Ha!!)

"All set, Ms. *Ka-ching?*" asks Clarice with a grin.

"Quite." I grin back.

You have to just keep telling yourself that you are worthy of only the best. Even if you don't believe it at first, or feel silly saying it to yourself, you must. The more you tell it to yourself, the sooner you will believe it. Once you believe it, no one will ever again have power over your view of yourself—unless you give that power to the person. And why would you do that? A princess never lets others have power over her. This is actually advice I'm borrowing from a wise, inspiring and very great lady: Eleanor Roosevelt. What she actually said was, "No one can make you feel inferior unless you give them permission to." How true.

Now, let's review. A princess *claims* her own power, embracing and nurturing it so it nourishes and strengthens her. Then, the resultant light that radiates from her inner fortitude and serenity only amplifies the glow of her gems.

Real or symbolic, of course. If you agree with me as to the essentialness of gems, DON'T talk to Clarice about it. She'll be a very bad influence.

Always remember, nothing is too good for you.

On Poise and Charm

Every princess is charming* in her own unique way.

3

(*Note that this is why it's specified for Prince Charming. For a princess, it's just a given.)

I'm in the greenroom, waiting to go on *Oprah*. Isn't this too exciting? It's every bit as glamorous as you can imagine. I'm going to talk about the Foundation's literacy program, then about being a princess, writing my book and appearing in Fameux's new film for my "twelve." (Minutes, that is. In TV-speak, you leave off the word *minutes*. After being on *Oprah,* I'm going to know all these cool TV terms. It's such fun becoming a media darling—in film *and* on TV.)

Anyway, Oprah's producers decided the other twelve-spots will go to Jean-Paul Fameux himself. In one of them, he'll talk about how he got to know me, and in the other he'll talk about the new film, *The Stench*. (Yes, that's the one I'm in! The title refers to the corruption the hero exposes. *Très français, n'est-ce pas?*) The film's star, *the* Marco Trevini, couldn't make it. So his costar, Brandon Charmant, will be on instead. Neither of them was in the scene shot in front of Nobu, so I didn't get to meet them, but I will get to meet Brandon now. Isn't that too exciting? I'm going to meet a soon-to-be heartthrob. And Jean-Paul promises that I'll get to meet Marco Trevini in St. Tropez.

Jean-Paul is taping first, then I will join him. It's so fabulous being here in the greenroom. Speaking of which, wait a second. The associate producer's assistant's assistant is giving me some instructions. No biggie. She just wants to let me know that I'm on in ten, and have to go for a quick makeup check first. She leads me there, then tells me to wait. (Let me tell you there's a lot of waiting in film and TV! And princesses get a bad rap for making people wait. Ha!)

After a minute or two, I notice a man dressed in rags, with a dirt-smudged face, sitting on the floor diagonally across from me. I realize in a flash that he's a homeless person. I would never have guessed that homeless people would be allowed to stay inside the building (except for maybe in the lobby), but Oprah is such a compassionate person, I shouldn't be surprised. He looks up and smiles at me, a beautiful smile. His eyes are an incredibly clear blue. I can't tell you how moved I am. Despite his considerable troubles, this man is happy enough to smile at me for no reason.

"I think it's great that a princess is trying to get people to read. So many people don't care about anyone but themselves," he says to me from where he sits.

"Thank you," I say, returning his smile. I've never spoken to a homeless person before, but a princess is charming no matter who she's talking to. "I'm flattered you know about my work to foster literacy."

"Sure. I read the papers," he says, grinning.

I wonder if he was born homeless or fell on hard times.

Perhaps he was a victim of some of that awful corporate downsizing, and didn't have enough savings to tide him over while he looked for another job. Wouldn't that be too awful? The poor man probably hovers around newsstands trying to keep informed. Or worse, reads the pages of the paper he nestles beneath trying to stay warm on bitter-cold nights...nights when he's completely exposed to the elements, vulnerable to all sorts of horrible things. And this is Chicago, no less, so it's always windy, too. How could his lot in life be worse?

Before he has a chance to say anything else, I dash to his side. "Forgive me if I'm intruding, but I can't bear to think of you suffering as much as you must be. I wish you lived in New York, because then I could offer you a job..."

He chuckles. "That's great, Your Highness. Is it the makeup or did I really capture the essence of a homeless man?"

What is he talking about? He *is* a homeless man. Perhaps he's one of those poor unfortunate souls who was let out of a mental institution as a result of lack of funds. That's even worse than I thought originally! I must find a way to help this man.

Just then, the assistant comes back to tell me I'm on for the makeup check, grasping my elbow and leading me away. I glance over my shoulder for one last look at him, and he calls out brightly, "Don't worry, Your Highness. We'll catch up later."

I wonder what he could mean by that.

"Don't pay any attention to him," the assistant tells me. "All these nobodies thinking they're somebodies."

I think that's horribly uncharitable, but all I say is, "I'm sure he does the best he can. Neither of us knows what we would do in a comparable situation."

She gives me a rather odd look, then shrugs. I have my makeup check, then she leads me onto the set.

Oprah is as charming as I expected she would be. Gentleman that Jean-Paul is, when I arrive on-screen, he stands up, kisses my hand and says, "Princess Jacqueline is a natural. The camera loves her, as I'm sure you can see it would. I adore her, but as my very dear friend. Don't listen to rumors."

I smile at Jean-Paul, then the audience, turning to Oprah to tell her how thrilled I am to be on the show. Then Jean-Paul and I talk for a bit about how long we've known each other and what great friends we are. Oprah tells the audience that after a break, her third guest, up-and-coming film star Brandon Charmant, will be on. We break, and guess who walks onto the set? The homeless man I met outside the greenroom! A second or two later, he takes the seat next to Jean-Paul, who introduces us. Oh my God!! I mistook Brandon Charmant for a homeless man! Could this get any more embarrassing? Will I ever learn to not take everything and everyone at face value? Clarice is right: I have been hopelessly sheltered. I should have known when he said what he did about makeup that he was in costume. But wait, by virtue of what he said to me, he must have thought that I knew he was playing a role all along, right? Yes, of course he must have. (This is going to be our little secret, darling. Poise and charm at all times for every princess. Be charming and honest, but never reveal your secrets. This is a mistake no one ever need know about.)

We're on, and Oprah introduces Brandon Charmant to the audience, asking what the homeless getup is all about.

That adorable smile flashing and those incredibly blue eyes sparkling, he says, "I'm in costume for my role as the snitch in *The Stench*." (Duh, Jacquie!! Could this Brad Pitt look-alike really be a homeless man?!) Then he turns to me and says, "Thank you for helping me get into character earlier, Your Highness. How did you know I was a method actor?"

"Jean-Paul told me," I say without missing a beat. I shoot Jean-Paul a sideways glance.

Winking at me when no one else can see, Jean-Paul says, "That's right. I tell Her Highness about all my actors."

"I'm honored Your Highness would take such an interest." Brandon bows his head charmingly.

I just smile.

The rest of the taping goes smashingly. Oprah is very enthusiastic about my book-in-progress, and I'm going to come back on a regular basis to chat with her about the Foundation's literacy program. I tell her that we would be honored to have her become a member of our advisory board, and she says she would be delighted. Isn't that wonderful? Even though the board undoubtedly won't be as excited as they should be, I think it's fantastic.

As we're leaving the set, Jean-Paul leans in close to whisper in my ear, "Nice save, Jacquie. Don't let this one drink out of your Blahniks."

"Very funny, Jean-Paul," I shoot back, my whisper more like a hiss. "You might have told me, you know. And they weren't Blahniks, they were Louboutins." For a cutting-edge film director, he doesn't know much about designers.

"You pulled it off, *bébé*. No one even guessed." Jean-Paul steps away, giving me a kiss on each cheek. In a normal-pitched voice he says, "I'll call you to tell you when to come to St. Tropez for the private premiere."

"Bon voyage!"

I look around for Brandon Charmant, but he's disappeared. What a pity. I'll never forget that smile or those blue, blue eyes. I hope he'll be in St. Tropez, too....

Now, while I ride in the limo on my way to the airport and the flight home to New York, I'll tell you what

Jean-Paul meant when he said, "Don't let him drink out of your Blahniks." That was SO embarrassing. As I said, they were actually Louboutins, not Blahniks, but that isn't why the experience was embarrassing. Here's what happened:

A year or so ago, I jetted to Paris for a little R & R. (I jaunt over to Paris every now and then to rejuvenate myself, spending a week or two at my salon there. I do love having a Parisian pied-à-terre, and sometimes, I just get an irrepressible urge to pop in to Chanel a time or two, or to have a to-die-for crème brûlée at a sidewalk patisserie with a view of the Eiffel Tower. It goes without saying that a princess can be as spontaneous as she chooses to be. And her spontaneity is *toujours* graceful, dignified and chic...*bien sûr!*) Anyway, one night I went to a club near Montmartre, where I met this gorgeous Frenchman. We left the club and walked through Paris, stopping at the fountain at La Place de la Concorde, where he wanted to drink absinthe (*très français*) out of my shoe. Hmm. I freely admit that I was a tad intrigued by his request. Besides, I, too, find Christian Louboutins irresistible (especially this pair: mulberry *peau de soie d'orsay* pumps with fuchsia feathers across the vamp). However, I decided that drinking out of a shoe—even the sexiest Louboutin—is just a little weird. Okay, more than a little, and borderline gauche, to boot. What's a princess to do in such an awkward situation? I very graciously excused myself with an unbearable *mal de tête,* gripping my head in pain to lend authenticity to my excuse and offering a polite *merci* for a lovely evening, and headed back for my salon, making sure to keep my shoes securely on my feet, in case Pierre really couldn't control himself. (Thank God I wore the *d'orsays,* which are closed across my instep, and not mules!)

As if the whole experience in and of itself weren't awkward enough, it turned out Pierre was an actor, and the whole thing was just practice for a role. To make matters worse, he was quite bold in letting me know just how hilarious he thought my naiveté was, shouting his opinions after me, and whooping it up right there in La Place de la Concorde. I just kept walking and never looked back, but it was a humiliating scene nonetheless.

Anyway, I vowed never again to put myself in such a situation, which is why I decided to go with the flow on *Oprah* today, letting everyone think that I knew exactly what was going on. Every situation won't allow you to handle it this way, of course, but you can apply the idea behind it, which is that even if you are embarrassed—mortified, humiliated, devastated, whatever—you don't have to show it. This is not to say that you should deny your feelings. That's never a good thing, nor does it enable you to behave with poise. What I am saying is, you can acknowledge your feelings to yourself without revealing them to others, unless you completely trust the people. Keeping your cool, keeping your guard up, are essential to true poise and charm.

By the way, sweetie, you aren't thinking that it's a little excessive to jet across the Atlantic just to go to Chanel, are you? Because it isn't, but you're entitled to think it is, I suppose. (Hmm. Have you been talking to Clarice?) All I can say is, the importance of doing what you enjoy is never to be minimized (and if what you enjoy happens to be shopping, well, that's perfectly understandable). Every princess knows not just how to enjoy what she enjoys—and that it's fine to enjoy what she enjoys, even if no one else she knows does, so long as it doesn't hurt anyone else, of course—but also what is appropriate for every situation.

A princess doesn't wear evening clothes during the day, or sportswear to black-tie galas. Unique self-expression should be a positive reflection of how much you love yourself, not an opportunity to display that you need to defy convention just to prove something. When you know you have nothing to prove, people around you will get the message by observing how you carry yourself. A true princess is comfortable in her own skin, which lends her effortless poise. All who meet her find her charming. It would be kind of awkward—not to mention dull—to just say "no thanks" to an offer of absinthe drunk from your Louboutins (regardless of whether it's a "true" offer). I grant you, the headache thing wasn't the most original response, but the point is, remaining poised in the midst of an awkward, embarrassing or humiliating situation is something a princess must know how to do.

Contrary to popular belief, princessliness is not a walk in the park. It is a parade with fanfare, to be imagined by many but perfected only by the properly trained princess.
At this point, it's only natural if you find yourself reviewing your life up to now. Allow yourself this quiet time to reflect and envision your sparkling future as a true princess. If you are accustomed to the typical pace of today's society, this might appear indulgent to you. Remember that indulgence is quite essential, and before too long, you will recognize the importance of reflective time. Carve out this time for yourself, honor it and enjoy it. The important thing to keep in mind is that, as a princess, you set your own pace.

Accept that sycophants★★ will begin to follow you everywhere. This is an inevitable, albeit irritating, entailment of princessliness. Be kind: Remember, they only want to bask in your glory and glamour.
(★★Note that the sycophant is a distant relation of the paparazzo. Think of them as the gnats and mosquitoes of the princessly sphere.)

Simply stated, along with elegance and acceptance of the less-than-pleasant, you must learn certain other givens of princessly behavior in order to be truly poised and charming. Be prepared that some of this learning will require unlearning—to a negligible or substantial extent, depending upon your own P.Q. (Princess Quotient).

Let's begin with a learned behavior that I detest: self-deprecation. I have never encountered a more ridiculous manifestation of self-loathing than putting yourself down. If you are in the habit of doing so, cease and desist immediately. There are enough other people around who do and say things designed to make you feel bad without your doing it to yourself. I am very serious about this. If I catch you putting yourself down or beating up on yourself, I will seize your book and force you to listen to the Gloria Gaynor song, "I Am What I Am" 24-7. I agree that's a pretty extreme approach, but I'll do whatever I have to do to get you to accept and love yourself.

I had to subject Clarice to this, unfortunately. I only did it because I had no choice. Although she got off to a fabulous start in her princess training, she hit a rough spot midway, and needed me to step in. A drastic measure, true, but it worked like a charm. Now she thanks me and loves me for it. Mariana, on the other hand, is another story. She is my dear friend and I love her, but—alas!—I had no choice but to expel her from the Princess-in-Training program because she could not cease behaving in that deplorable manner. Nothing helped. The seemingly foolproof replaying of "I Am What I Am" had zero effect. (Not even when combined with "I Will Survive.") When all was said and done, Mariana could sing every syllable of both songs forward and backward, but *still* persisted in putting herself down. You witnessed her mung-sprouts-and-blue-green-algae moment, so you must see what I mean. Sad and painful as it is for me to accept, I must concede that no princessly techniques, no matter how extreme or creative, no matter how diligently and lovingly applied by me, seem to be able to bring her out of this tragic state. Mariana will have to find her own way, and the best and most I can do as her friend is to just love and support her as she is. And I do. (Needless to say, I usually don't eat dessert around her because her figuring out the sugar- , carb- and fat-grams on her calculator sort of sucks out all the pleasure of the indulgence, if you know what I mean.)

So whatever you do, DO NOT use Mariana as your role model. (You can hire her as a personal trainer if you want. She's the absolute best there is. She can StairMaster for hours on end and not even breathe any harder.) Self-deprecation is absolutely forbidden to a Princess-in-Training. You can't accept, believe in or love yourself at the same time as you're putting yourself down or being mean to yourself. You can't be happy if you hate any part of yourself.

With that horridness behind us, let's move forward to one of the loveliest aspects of poise and charm—and truest expressions of princessliness—the gracious acceptance of a compliment. Sigh. Receiving compliments is just sublime. So nourishing. So contenting. So *inevitable.*

A princess accepts compliments graciously because they are: (1) true; (2) deserved; (3) enjoyable.

Enough said.

On (Inner and Outer) Beauty

A true princess knows that she is beautiful from the inside out.

4

I'm back in New York, darling, and on my way to Elizabeth Arden for my monthly day of beauty. (I just LOVE that Red Door!) Mariana and Nirvana will be joining me, as usual. Clarice lets me treat her once a year on her birthday. (I do admire her for saving for what she wants, then getting it for herself—no princess expects others to fulfill her needs and desires—but it would be so much more fun if she would come more often and let me pick up the tab.) Mariana comes to Elizabeth Arden primarily for the cellulite treatments, even though her cellulite is microscopic. She also obsesses about being waxed from head (or should I say "eyebrows"—I completely understand and advocate the importance of good eyebrows, of course, but Mariana takes everything to the extreme) to toe. Nirvana, on the other hand, comes for the toxin-release wraps and the steam room.

I come for *everything*.

Today's agenda includes a European facial, mineral-salt

rub, seaweed wrap, steam room and massage. How heavenly does that lineup sound?

Meanwhile, I'm thoroughly enjoying the walk there. It's a beautiful day, and I'm loving every moment of blue sky and sunshine. Summer is definitely almost here: I just love June. Sunglasses come out (I've got my Guccis on), and so do sandals (Manolo Blahniks for me today). Not to mention the best part about summer: ice cream.

I stop at the corner, waiting to cross. Two girls arrive at the corner at the same time I do, and while we wait together, I can't help but notice the difference between them. One is tall and slender, quite pretty. She's wearing a very cute dress and sipping a Diet Coke. She's engrossed in whatever she's telling her friend, and she looks miserable. Her friend is average in size and looks, casual in jeans and a T-shirt. Her best feature is her smile, shown off by deep-red lipstick that's now smearing across her double-scoop chocolate ice-cream cone. (Judging from her happy expression, she shares my opinion of ice cream!)

Midconversation, the one with the cone stops eating to tug her friend's arm. "Forget him, sweetie. Let's just go back and get you a double-scoop, too."

"No way," says the skinny one, slurping the dregs of her Diet Coke. "I am not getting fat because of that jerk!"

"One ice-cream cone isn't going to make you fat!" exclaims her friend in a tone that reminds me of Clarice's and my attempts to convince Mariana of the same thing, always to no avail.

"Well…"

"Come on!"

"Okay."

They turn around as I cross, and I'm so glad the ice-cream eater prevailed. I hope the Diet Coke drinker will listen to her friend more. That ice-cream eater is a princess, if ever I saw one. She might not be the thinnest, prettiest or most fashionable girl you'll ever see, but she knows how to love herself just as she is and how to enjoy life.

I'm so glad that unexpected moment of everyday princessliness revealed itself. It's good for you to witness princessly behavior other than mine. Of course, since we're about to be spending the day with Mariana and Nirvana, you're going to be seeing plenty of *non*-princessly behavior. Sigh. They're my dear friends, and I love them, but I had no choice but to expel both of them from the Princess-in-Training program long ago. I already described Mariana's expulsion. Nirvana's was even worse, so let's just not go there.

Ah, here we are at Elizabeth Arden. Janie, the receptionist, rushes around to kiss me hello when I step inside.

"Mariana and Nirvana are already here. Nirvana is getting a toxin-release wrap, and Mariana's getting a wax. She said you would catch up. I hope that's okay."

"It's fine."

"In case you're interested, we're having a special today— top-to-toe with a Brazilian. For the wax, I mean."

I'm sure that these Brazilian aestheticians are terrific, but I've had my heart set on a mineral-salt rub, and shudder at the thought of one after a wax. Besides, Traci always does my wax, and I would never hurt her feelings, no matter how fabulous those Brazilians might be.

"Thanks, Janie, but I'm getting a salt rub, so no wax. And I'll stick with Traci, even though I'm sure your Brazilian aestheticians are fantastic."

"Jacquie, you are hilarious. Like you didn't know it's the technique that's Brazilian." She rolls her eyes, then laughs.

I smile at her. "Just a little waxing humor." Thank goodness for that quick save!

Janie continues, "Seriously, they are fabulous. So much better than just a bikini. It feels so sexy to have them wax off everything. ZIP!! *Nada*." She snaps her fingers and makes a whistling sound, then adds, "You gotta try one next time you're wearing a thong on a hot date."

Somehow, I don't think so. I'm no prude or a stranger to the waxing table, but that sounds horrid! I don't care how good it would make a thong look. If that's what it takes to be "The Girl from Ipanema," I'll definitely pass.

A princess allows her own unique beauty to emerge from her soul, without obsessing over every last inch of herself, just by feeling and enjoying her unique and ever-present radiance.
After my facial, salt rub and seaweed wrap, I sip water and nibble a plumcot while I wait for Mariana and Nirvana. We'll chat for a bit and have a snack before we hit the steam room. (Of course, Mariana's idea of a snack is water with lemon, and Nirvana will need to make sure no animals were harmed in the picking of the plumcots on the table. Sigh. Sometimes, those two really…) Oh, look! Here's Mariana now.

She walks up to me, and we hug. We sit down at a small round table and I offer Mariana a plumcot.

Mariana declines, horrified. "Too many carbs," she says. "What were you thinking, Jacquie?" Indignantly, she takes a long pull from her Dasani bottle.

I notice tiny pieces of lemon *and* lime floating in it. Hmm. Mariana is definitely living on the edge today. But how many carbs could there possibly be in one little plumcot? Mariana is obsessed, as I've already mentioned, and as you witnessed firsthand when I met her for the lunch-that-never-happened the other day. The girl is positively convinced that anything other than lean protein and low-glycemic veggies will deposit fat onto her body if she gets anywhere near them.

After she's recoiled sufficiently far away from the dangerous fruit, she tells me that she's planning extra time in the steam room because she's feeling "chunky."

"Mar, you're obsessing again," I say gently. Mariana weighs about a hundred and fifteen pounds soaking wet, and she's five-eight barefoot. When she stands sideways, you can only see her head; her body, in profile, becomes one-dimensional. Clarice and I wonder where she gets the stamina to do not just her own workouts, but to be a personal trainer, as well. Yet she's the best, and all her clients swear by her. No one can keep up with Mariana. Of course, her caffeine consumption helps a lot. I love my coffee, but Mariana has a java IV. (No cream and sugar, naturally—I drink it black, too, but only because I like it that way; whereas Mariana has nightmares about fat- and sugar-grams attacking her.)

Mariana moves her hands off the table and away from the carb-laden fruit. "It's bathing-suit season," she says softly, as if she's afraid there's a bikini or maillot lurking in the shadows, ready to jump out and demand that she try it on and be photographed for the *Sports Illustrated* swimsuit edition.

"So go to the beach in shorts and a T-shirt! It's just a piece of fruit, for goodness' sakes, not a hot-fudge sundae."

At the mention of such a decadent dessert, Mariana cringes, then squirms in her chair. "Here comes Nirvana," Mariana says, raising her arms in a wave that looks more like a distress signal than a greeting. I get the message. A princess knows when to back off. Mariana can live her life as she chooses to. All I can do is support her and love her just as she is. (I know I've already said that. I just get upset when I see my friend's self-deprecation. Ugh!)

Tiny Nirvana, her long light brown hair in a high ponytail, slips noiselessly into the third chair at our table. She presses one hand on Mariana's wrist and one on mine.

"Nirvana?" I say tentatively. You're never quite sure when Nirvana might be communing with a higher spiritual force, but with her eyes open and in the middle of a conversation.

After a resonant *"Om!"* and a hearty exhale, Nirvana beams at each of us. "I'm so cleansed!" she exults. "Multiple toxins have been released from my cells. I can *feel* the difference," Nirvana says, referring to the toxin-release wrap she's just had.

"That's good, sweetie," I tell her.

Nirvana sets on the table the large plastic bottle she takes with her everywhere. It's filled with what looks like swamp water. She uncaps it and takes a long swig.

I wince, grateful that I'm not close enough to get a whiff.

"You both should really try this."

"No thanks," I say.

"Does it help with weight loss?" Mariana brightens.

I shoot Nirvana a look.

"It helps with balance," Nirvana replies.

Mariana loses interest.

"It minimizes acidity by restoring alkalinity," Nirvana explains.

"I'm a woman, not a battery," I tell her. "Let's just go into the steam room."

I lead the way.

"When we get into the steam room, you have to tell me if you can still see cellulite. You have to be honest. Be brutal!" Mariana exhorts us, all but shrieking.

"Mariana, you have no cellulite. You are a twig." Turning to Nirvana, I say, "Would you please tell her she's being ridiculous?"

"Cellulite is an animal product. It's good to be rid of," Nirvana retorts, swigging more swamp water. Nirvana is a twig, too, but she doesn't have Mariana's willowy look because she's only four-eleven.

"Cellulite is not an animal product, it's a human product. Sometimes you're both impossible!" I take a deep breath, and follow the attendant into the steam room, feeling the serenity of my seaweed wrap evaporate as I grow more and more exasperated with my friends. (Upon whom I'm having no effect whatsoever, I might add. See? I told you I had no choice but to expel them from the Princess-in-Training program! I love them to pieces, but their obsessions get to be worrisome after a while. I'm sure you understand what I mean now that you've spent some time with them. I'm so glad Clarice is normal. And she thinks I'm obsessed with shopping! I'll have to have Clarice spend more time with Mariana and Nirvana, and then she'll appreciate the healthy, balanced way I approach shopping.)

A princess can charm her way out of any embarrassing situation, even if she loses her cool in the moment.

As we settle ourselves in the steam room, I notice no one else is there.

"Do you think the cellulite treatments are working?" Mariana asks, completely undeterred by what I said, pulling the flesh on her hips and thighs in a most unnatural, not to mention unflattering, way.

"I think you're gorgeous, sweetie," I tell her. "There isn't an ounce of flab or fat on you." I mean this most sincerely, even though I have to resist telling her she's hurting herself with this obsession. I need to let her find her own way. That's what every princess—and good friend—does.

Mariana breathes a sigh of relief, then smiles at me.

"You have the cleanest, purest flesh I've ever seen, Mariana," Nirvana tells her.

I shoot Nirvana a look. Mariana isn't cleansing herself for spiritual reasons, the way Nirvana does. Not that Nirvana isn't obsessed in her own way. A couple of years ago, Mariana and Nirvana went to a spa in Santa Fe, where they taught people to be "breatharians." That's right: to subsist on air. Of course, it's a spiritual-cleansing pursuit, and fine if you've decided to renounce the world and seclude yourself in an ashram. People who live in the everyday world, however, need to eat food! Nirvana, who managed to squirrel away some sunflower seeds and hazelnuts, was fine. But Mariana, embracing breatharianism 110 percent, wound up in the hospital with an electrolyte imbalance. She had to continue drinking Gatorade for three months after she was released and came back to New York. And she still hasn't learned.

Mariana and Nirvana are deep in conversation about how to completely eliminate sugars, carbohydrates and animal fats and proteins. I try to not pay attention, to just relax and enjoy the steam.

Nirvana asks me a question pertinent to what they're talking about. I completely tuned them out once the conversation veered toward finding a way to utilize the extractions of liposuction as a food source for children in third world countries. Even Nirvana and Mariana concede that growing children need some fats and protein, animal-based if need be. Apparently, they have concluded that such an enterprise should be undertaken by the Foundation. That's what she's asking me, I discover, once she repeats the question.

"Do the two of you really expect me to convince my board of directors to embrace such a harebrained idea? Do you think anyone other than the two of you would think this is remotely worthwhile? You're both obsessed! Do you hear me? OBSESSED!!!!!"

By the time I finish my tirade, I'm much redder than the steam could ever make me, and every shred of serenity is gone.

Two women have suddenly appeared on the other side of the steam room. (Hmm. I must have REALLY tuned out everything, not just Mariana and Nirvana's conversation.)

"We came here to relax and unwind, you know," one of the women says sharply, casting an irritated glare in my direction.

"Sorry," I say to her. (How embarrassing!) Of course, my outburst is understandable, but I certainly can't explain that years of frustration just happened to erupt in the middle of the steam room. "I'm rehearsing for a role in a new Jean-Paul Fameux film. I'm a method actress. My big scene is a steam-room brawl."

The women look impressed and smile in what I assume must be a mixture of awe and understanding. Another quick save! Thank God for my princessly self-possession.

My friends look at me but don't comment on my method-actress remark. "*Obsessed* is the word of the un-enlightened, Jacquie," Nirvana informs me.

"And the fat," Mariana puts in.

They resume their conversation, as if nothing else had happened.

In addition to being exasperating, sometimes they can actually be infuriating. I am not about to undo all the wonders of my spa day. Putting my wrap back on, I leave the spa room and head toward the massage area, where I wait for Ludmilla, my favorite masseuse. She's from Ukraine, and a childhood spent pulling beets and pota-toes gave this woman hands that are absolutely magical when it comes to kneading muscles. At this moment, I need kneading. Thank God for Ludmilla!

Anyway, while Mariana and Nirvana remain in the steam room (apparently, fat cells and toxins lurk every-where), I surrender to Ludmilla's artistry. As I relax again, I reflect on my friends. Really, Mariana and Nirvana are not so different from a lot of women—counting calories and fat- and carb-grams, jumping on the bandwagon for every new diet and lifestyle trend—albeit somewhat more obsessed. Suffice it to say that this is one of my biggest pet peeves—as if you couldn't tell from my outburst. No woman is born to look like a stick, or to worry about every crumb she puts in her mouth, or to feel that she isn't worthwhile unless she espouses the pop-psychology/spirituality *du jour*.

There are hairdos and hairdon'ts.
A true princess knows the difference.

Well, I've had my full-body massage and I'm just feeling wonderful. So relaxed. Not a sign of stress in sight. Ludmilla is leading me toward the hair salon now. I love getting a massage, but the effect on the hair is *not* pretty. I'm the first person to emphatically say that looks are the least important thing about a person, however, I don't want to go around scaring every child in Manhattan—which I would do if I walked out of Elizabeth Arden looking like this!

Self-acceptance and poise are the cornerstones of beauty. Nothing is more beautiful than a self-possessed woman.

Now that I've been recoiffed, I'm ready to go. I don't go in for the whole makeup bit. If I have a big gala to attend—or an evening with a potential Prince Charming— (no, I still haven't met him)—I'll pop in to have my makeup done. Otherwise, I prefer the natural look. Which is not to say that I'm against makeup. If you like wearing it, go for it. I just hate the feel of it on my face all day long. It's a personal choice for each of us. What's important to remember is that you are gorgeous with or without the matte-finish foundation, with or without the mascara, with or without the highlighter, with or without all of it. You are gorgeous and wonderful just as you are. Every princess knows that. (But don't forget a good moisturizer).

Are you thinking that Elizabeth Arden is not that far from Tiffany's or Bergdorf's? So was I! (Great minds think alike, darling.) However, I'm not going shopping today. I'm going straight home. Here's James coming down Fifth now to pick me up. He comes around to open my door, settles me in and drives off. (I do hope he isn't missing anything terribly important on ESPN this afternoon.)

Now, there's another important thing that I must share. It's sort of private, but I know I can trust you. I have a mole on my right cheek. It's absolutely adorable, if I may say so. But at one point, one of my father's ministers suggested it be removed, as it would be unseemly in photographs. (Needless to say, he's no longer a minister. The nerve of him!) I was about twelve at the time, and you know what a sensitive age that is. I was inconsolable for days, imagining the paparazzi just lying in wait to find the angle that would make The Mole look enormous. I couldn't look in the mirror without bursting into tears. Finally, I decided that I was being ridiculous. I realized that mole was as much a part of me as any other feature. Things like that just don't matter. If you love yourself just as you are, then you have to love every aspect of you just as it is—including moles. What might seem like an imperfection is really just an example of how unique your beauty is—how unique *you* are. Remember:

A princess does not shy away from natural defects. She readily frequents *gioiellerie* and *joailleries* in pursuit of pearls—of every size and hue—which, after all, are never perfect.

Here we are at home. I'm going to relax on the chaise for an hour or so before I have to get ready for dinner. I'm meeting some people from the National Endowment for the Arts at Lespinasse in the St. Regis Hotel. (I have a gorgeous Roberto Cavalli to wear for the occasion, and fabulous opalescent D & G's to go with it. We're discussing some grants that the Foundation is offering to young artists.)

But I want to leave you with one final, essential thought,

regardless of whether you decide to go to a spa or not, or to have a makeover or not, or to change your hairstyle and/or color or not:

You are as beautiful as you believe yourself to be. Don't expect anyone else to see—let alone value—what you yourself don't.

On Style, Fashion and Shopping

A princess always looks fabulous because she knows that she does.

5

Bonjour, chérie! Today, we are going on a shopping excursion. An all-day shopping excursion, to be precise. Won't that be too much fun? I couldn't be more thrilled! It's a quarter to ten on a glorious Saturday morning, and as soon as Clarice arrives, we'll be on our way.

Ah, the concierge just called to say that Clarice is on her way up, so I'll just swallow the last of my mocha java, and we'll be off when she gets here. (Unless, of course, she wants coffee, too.)

To a true princess, style is everything. *Her* style, that is.

A princess embraces her own sense of style, in addition to knowing all there is to know about prevailing fashion trends. Individualism is far more important than designer labels, but a big part of effectively embracing your own style—not to mention displaying it with aplomb and flourish—is being proficient in the *au courant* styles. Let's just do some shopping, and you'll see what I mean. First stop: Manolo Blahnik. (Note that it's always best to shop for shoes as early on in the excursion as you can, so you're feet aren't swollen from a whole day of walking and standing.)

"Ooh! Those are so you, Clar! You have to try them on," I tell her as soon as we get inside Blahnik's, nudging her toward a fabulous pair of stilettos. A strappy affair with ties around the ankle that I spied through the window as we approached the store.

"Manolos are not a working-girl shoe, Jacquie."

"That depends on where the girl works, sweetie." We both laugh. I can tell she's just dying to try them, though. She never wants to admit how into designers she is.

"Clar, you can't go through life without *ever* having Manolos on your feet. At least once." I pick up the shoes and hand them to her.

Clarice takes them reluctantly and asks a nearby sales associate if she can see them in her size. They look fantastic on her, and she is in her element in these spike heels, let me tell you. She only staggers a bit when she looks at the price tag as she slips off the shoes, but I can tell that she just loves them.

"Maybe they'll still be around during the annual sale," I suggest hopefully.

"Even at fifty percent off, I'd be in hock," Clarice says, placing the shoes back in the box gently.

"I could just—"

"Absolutely not! I will not have you buying things for me. I buy what I can afford, end of story, Ms. *Ka-ching.*"

"Whatever you say, sweetie."

I turn to check out the rest of the lineup. What have we here? A new *d'orsay* pump since my last visit. My, oh my. I confess I have a weakness for *d'orsay* pumps, and these are black satin, with an overlay of black chantilly lace. Fabulous!

"Wouldn't these be just the thing with my black satin Vera Wang?" I ask Clarice.

She nods yes.

Just a sec. I *have* to try these on, and then we'll go. There's one woman ahead of me, I think. I can't figure out *what* she's actually doing. She looks a bit overwhelmed, to be honest. Hmm.

A sales associate approaches. "Are you being helped?" she asks the confused-looking woman.

"I don't see any heels that look like cotton."

Clarice and I exchange a puzzled glance.

"Cotton?" repeats the sales associate.

"The boutique where I bought the dress for my son's wedding told me to look for a cotton heel," insists the woman, her voice approaching shrill. (Shoe shopping can be daunting to the uninitiated. I *must* step in and help.)

"Pardon my intrusion," I say, much to the relief of both the woman and the sales associate. "I think you mean *kitten* heel."

Her cheeks bright pink with horror and righteous indignation, the woman exclaims, "Oh, no! I'm an animal rights activist. I couldn't possibly—"

"Not to worry," I interject. "No real kittens are involved."

Clarice rolls her eyes at me. She hates it when I'm "the informer of the uninformed," as she calls it. But what I do is true noblesse oblige, in addition to the fact that I just can't abide anyone struggling this way when I can help. Especially with something so simple. Imagine the poor thing scouring Manhattan in search of the elusive—and nonexistent—"cotton" heel. I remind Clarice that it would have been most non-princessly not to help in such a situation. She agrees, if a bit reluctantly.

The sales associate accompanies the woman in pursuit of kitten heels, just as my regular associate emerges from the back and grins as she sees the *d'orsays* I'm holding. "They came in last night. I was just leaving you a message," she gushes, then whispers conspiratorially when she reaches me, "I held aside your size. Be right back." (She always does that for me. I'm a 5½, and they only get one in my size per store. She's such a sweetie. And don't listen to Clarice: My annual spending at Blahnik is NOT higher than the budget of most third world countries.)

The *d'orsays* fit like a glove and feel heavenly on my feet, so I charge the pair to my account. I remind my sales associate to call me the second the new Mary Janes come in, and she promises she will. Manolo Mary Janes are just too fabulous for words.

And we're off again.

A princess carries herself as if she thinks she looks stunning no matter what she's wearing.
I do want to remind you that, although we'll be going around to designer shops and departments today, that doesn't mean you have to shop there on your own if you don't want to. Getting yourself into debt is not a princessly course of action. A princess always has a Plan B: finding a way to make what is affordable *fine enough* to be worthy of you. By looking at designer collections (or magazines, etc.) to see how they combine pieces, you can use your creativity to *look* designer, head to toe, even if you can't shop that way. More important, if you believe that you look fabulous, you will. All that matters is how *you* think you look, not what anyone else thinks. Your style is your own; use it to your best advantage. Every princess has her own brand of glamour.

And now, my list of must-stops (we'll pop in to as many as we can today):

Giorgio Armani
Bergdorf Goodman
Prada
Manolo Blahnik
Burberry
Dolce & Gabbana (D & G)
Pucci

This list wasn't one of my better ideas. I've only just started. My full list would take up the entire book. Never mind. Just remember, it's easy and fun to be a fashion plate—or just look like one. Never sell your sense of style and individuality short. Your "look" might become THE new look.)

Here we are at Pucci. Clarice and I love to come here because all the swirly colors are such fun and make us feel happy, no matter what. (How could a place with a hot-pink door and matching staircase NOT be the most fun?) Clarice is ogling the same scarf she does every time we come in here. Little does she know, I ordered it for her for Christmas. *Shh!* I want it to be a surprise.

A princess never wears anything that doesn't fit her *perfectly*.

Another customer is worried that the dress she's trying on doesn't fit properly. She's right. The sales associate is trying to talk her into buying it, though. I hate when they do that. Never allow anyone to talk you into something that doesn't feel right—whether clothes or anything else. A princess knows herself and trusts herself without needing validation from other people. That's why God invented three-way mirrors for fitting rooms.

Sigh. The poor thing. She really needs help. I must restrain myself, however, as Clarice is giving me "The Look" again.

"Come on, Clar. The woman needs major help. She keeps asking where the loafers are, for goodness' sakes. Obviously, she doesn't know if she's in Pucci or Gucci. It's so sad."

Clarice is not being at all charitable toward the fashion challenged. "What can we do? If she doesn't know the difference between Pucci and Gucci, she's beyond even your help, Jacquie," she says, taking a halter in swirls of coral, peach and garnet red off the reduced rack and showing it to me.

"Wrong with your red hair," I tell her, indicating the halter. Then I add quietly, "No one is beyond my help." As I've told you, Clarice was nowhere close to being a fashionista until she met me. (Though I must say, the girl was born with the ability to find almost anything at a reduced price. She is the only person I know who has ever found a marked-down Roberto Cavalli.)

Clarice laughs, chiding me about being the informer of the uninformed, then adds, "What was I thinking? Of course you can help her, and she obviously needs you." She shows me another halter, this one in swirls of lime green, lavender and indigo, and I give her the thumbs-up. While she goes to try it on, the is-this-Pucci-or-Gucci shopper approaches me.

"Excuse me," she says hesitantly, a look of true desperation in her eyes. Believe it or not, she looks even more lost and confused than the woman at Manolo Blahnik. "Do you work here?" she asks, more like a prayer than a question.

"No. I'm just shopping. However, if I can help, I'd be happy to."

"Can you tell me where the loafers are?"

Very gently, I say, "There are no loafers here. You're at *Pucci,* not Gucci."

The woman's eyes widen as she gasps, "How embarrassing!"

Her speech pattern tells me right away that she isn't a New Yorker. "Visiting?" I ask.

She nods. I tell her how to get to Gucci, and she's on her way. See what little trouble that was? And it made her so happy. Pucci and Gucci are both fabulous, but neither one replaces the other.

I turn on my heel and head back toward the fitting rooms in search of Clarice. The halter looks as fantastic on her as I knew it would. This only depresses her, because now she can't decide which to save up for: the scarf or the halter. I tell her if I had to choose between the two, I'd pick the scarf, which is big enough to tie into a halter if you want to. She agrees that's the most practical choice. (She's going to LOVE her gift!!) We leave Pucci, and head for Bergdorf's.

Now, you remember what I said about how to look like you're wearing designer clothes even if you can't afford them. It's true, of course, that you best accomplish that by the way you carry yourself. A princess can wear a burlap sack and look elegant, because she knows she IS elegant. When you're in training, though, this can be daunting, even with an off-the-charts P.Q. The key to true princessly elegance is accessorizing with flair. Here are some tips for exuding the elegance *par excellence* that you are destined to achieve:

Always wear gloves with after-five wear. They lend you elegance, sophistication, drama and mystique; a certain *je ne sais quoi* that is required of the true princess.

The true princess always has signature items that she wears with her own unique panache. A silk scarf, a wide-brimmed hat, a night-light–sized solitaire...*

A princess always wears enormous dark sunglasses. Regardless of prevailing eyewear styles, this is a must. Paparazzi lurk everywhere. No principessa in Roma or Firenze is ever without her oversize *occhiali*, lest she find herself suddenly in the midst of a paparazzi onslaught.**

(* Note that C.Z. is perfectly acceptable.)
(**I've had my share of unfortunate paparazzi episodes over time, and had I not been safely concealed behind

enormous Christian Dior, Gucci or D & G shades, I don't know WHAT I would have done.)

As I've said, depending upon your individual P.Q., you may or may not be a true fashionista in your own right. If you are, wonderful! If you aren't, not to worry. Clarice learned with lightning speed, and can now spot any designer in seconds—and at a markdown, no less! With the proper training and dedicated practice, so can you. Perhaps you don't consider fashion and style to be that important. That's okay, so long as it's because it just doesn't interest you. However, if it's because you feel intimidated, that's a no-no. A princess is not intimidated by anything. You can be a front-row fashionista with the best of them if you choose to. It's entirely up to you. And remember, what you're thinking of as your I-feel-like-such-a-slob-today wear could just be the grunge or heroin chic of tomorrow. You're a princess: Anything is possible!! Do not underestimate how much your particular style can influence the fashion world.

A true princess possesses a limitless knowledge of all things fashionable, instantly discerning Manolos from D & G's or Louboutins from Jimmy Choos, even at a mile away in a dimly lit club, and regardless of whether she can presently afford to buy them.

Clarice and I are back outside now, famished and searching for a place for lunch. We duck into a small café. We ask for a table for four so we'll have enough room for my bags, and the hostess seats us, leaving us to look at the menu. While scanning the salads and trying to decide between niçoise and Caesar, I notice that the man seated diagonally behind Clarice has a python coiled around his neck. What to do? Clarice is terrified of snakes. Will telling her help or harm? I can't decide. Fortunately, he's paying and leaving. But Clarice sees the python as the man walks past us, and she turns white as a sheet, gripping my arm for dear life.

"It's all right. He's gone."

"Did you see that thing? It was huge." She takes a deep breath and gulps some water from the glass in front of her.

"I thought it was fascinating," I tell her truthfully.

"Please don't go into the snake thing, Jacquie."

The "snake thing" is this (and I'm sorry if I'm offending any snake lovers): Snakes are reptiles. Reptiles eat bugs. I, true princess that I am, hate bugs. Over and above their usefulness as natural exterminators, snakes are transformed into the most stunning accessory items. I took one look at that python and thought only of all the icky bugs it could rid the world of, not to mention what a magnificent pair of knee-high boots it could become at the end of its productive life. Sigh. One woman's fear is another's accessory fantasy.

One final thought I want to leave you with:

A princess knows that toting two evenly balanced, filled-to-capacity-with-"necessities," large shopping bags is the best form of strength training and aerobic activity a princess can find.

On Dealing with Difficult People

A princess uses her poise and charm to her advantage at all times—especially the most trying times.

6

Forgive me if I sound a bit pressed for time, darling, but I have a hot date tonight. Guess with who. Give up? Okay, I'll just tell you. Marco Trevini. Isn't that too fabulous?! *The* Marco Trevini, Milanese hottie and heartthrob *du monde,* and I are off to TriBeCa for what will undoubtedly be an unforgettable night. (Perfect for an evening with an international superstar and sex symbol is head-to-toe D & G, strapless pleather with matching go-go boots. But enough about what I'm going to wear. I'll bet you never thought you would hear me say that!)

Let me tell you how it all happened. Jean-Paul Fameux called me at the office yesterday to say that Marco Trevini had been hounding him for my number, and would it be all right if he gave it to him. Would it be all right? No, it wouldn't be *all right.* It would be unbelievably fantastic. I mean, we're talking about Marco Trevini!! However, all I said was, "Of course. Getting to know him would be such fun!" Last night Marco called and asked me out to dinner for tonight.

Marco said that he's been my secret admirer for a long time, but never thought I would be interested in dating an actor. Could you imagine? Only a woman in a coma would turn down Marco Trevini. When Fameux told him about my walk-on, he decided he was going to make his move. "I told myself, 'Marco, it's now or never,'" he said to me in that Italian accent that turns my knees into jelly. He said he actually came to Nobu that night, but lost his nerve and left. Then he decided he was just going to tell Fameux how he felt, and hope he would help. As if Marco needs anyone's help! Knowing that he was nervous makes him even more adorable.

Of course, a princess must expect the men she dates to appreciate her, to feel lucky to be in her charming and lovely presence. Again, in a self-loving way, not an arrogant one. I'm just so thrilled to be going out with a movie star! (It's my first time, you know.) And he just seems so sweet and lovable, in addition to being such a sex god. I couldn't be happier. Besides, let's just say that dating hasn't been my most successful pursuit of late. My last date was an Oklahoma oil tycoon, who my friend Svetlana introduced me to. He was as stiff and boring as the III after his name. After that I swore off tycoons. Then, after several months of diplomats, artists, photojournalists, political dissidents and a count from a little European principality that isn't even on the map, I decided to just swear off dating, period. (That's also when I began to avoid the word *date* as if it were the plague. I was approaching depressed, to tell you the truth. So was Clarice. We commiserated often, frequently in the company of truffles from Teuscher, or over pastries, *tartufo* or *gelato* at Ferrara's in Little Italy.)

Marco arrives, hot as ever in his black Zegna, with his flashing black eyes and full lips. We kiss, and it's not just a thank-you for the dozen red roses he brought me.

"I knew you'd be as good as you looked," he half purrs, half growls in my ear. "We better get going before I eat you."

As if I'd mind *that*.

After some more "lip appetizers," we speed downtown in his Aston Martin, top down, so it's all but impossible to talk. But that's fine. We have a whole magnificent evening stretching ahead of us. Mmm! Marco valets the car, and when he comes around the front of it, reaches for my hand. (Talk about fireworks! I've never felt sparks like this in my entire life, and all we've done is kiss and hold hands.)

We're seated at a cozy little table at Chanterelle (*très intime* and chic), and Marco is telling me all about how hard it was for him as a struggling actor in Milan. He did a lot of modeling to pay the bills, but acting was all he ever wanted to do. Jean-Paul Fameux spotted him at a Hugo Boss show. The rest, as they say, is history. (Of course, I knew how Jean-Paul discovered Marco. At the time, I could have killed myself for not having gone along, even though I never go to the men's runway shows. Perhaps it's time to rectify that.)

Stroking my hand in the most endearing way, Marco asks if our family ever fell on hard times. Rather an odd question, but I'm sure he's just a bit daunted by the whole royal thing. I'll charm him out of that in no time. I tell him the story about multiple-great-*grandmère* and -*grand-père* Angélique and Louis-Luc, and assure him that the de Soignées have been happy and healthy ever since.

"And prosperous?" he asks a bit too eagerly.

I nod and smile, but his focus on the family fortune seems to be intensifying, and I'm not exactly pleased about it. A princess is to be loved for her magnificent self alone; her *complete* self, that is, not for her money, looks or any other single thing. I tell myself that Marco must just be more nervous than I had thought. After all, even though he's a huge star, he's a new star, and must be a bit in awe of all the glamour. My princessly patience and charm are no doubt exactly what he needs, along with the tender loving care I intend to shower upon him. And deliciously receive in return.

Happily, Marco stops asking about the de Soignée financial history and holdings, and goes back to his heavenly way of caressing my hand. He kisses the inside of my wrist. And I…well…let's just say that he obviously knows what he's doing. Hand-holding has never been this pleasurable. I'm utterly swept away, until I notice he gasps upon seeing my emerald bracelet. More like a pant, really. What is going on? You would think that an actor could do a better job of covering up his true intentions. This date is definitely *not* going the way I had hoped it would, fabulous hand-caressing notwithstanding.

Our cocktails arrive (vodka martini for me, classic martini for Marco), and I resist the urge to drown my sorrows. Instead, I try to make conversation, but Marco seems hypnotized by my Tahitian pearls. His behavior has completely *ruined* my fantasy of our soon-to-be-legendary love affair. (I confess I'm a *hopeless* romantic.) I don't want to believe it of Marco, but the only men I've ever known to find gems this fascinating worked at Tiffany's or Winston's…or in clubs in the Village. He doesn't fit either of those categories, so I have no choice but to accept the worst: He's a bimbus (male version of bimbo, that is) and a gold digger.

Then, as if what had already happened wasn't bad enough, the worst thing that could happen, happens. Above the rim of my martini glass, who do I see walk into Chanterelle and head straight toward where Marco and I are sitting? None other than Trixie Loquor herself. *Groan.* Now I'm going to have to be all gushy about being out on the town with gorgeous Marco Trevini, when I suspect he's only here because he's interested in my money and position. Though I'm sure I don't know why. He's a star, after all, even if a newly rising one. All the sweet things he said on the phone meant nothing. Oh, well. It's just one night of my life, and it's his loss, not mine. I'll just make the best of it. I could do a lot worse than a night out with *the* hot film star of the universe.

By the time Trixie reaches our table, I have mustered an appropriately dazzling smile.

"Well, well, well. I guess you and Jean-Paul really are just friends, after all," Trixie says, her tone so greasy it drips oil.

"I never lie," I say sweetly.

"More than I can say for your date." Before either of us can respond, Trixie turns and calls, "Come on, Adrienne. We've got him this time!"

Charging behind her is a woman from out of 1987: hair teased out and up, and dyed a shade of red I'm quite certain I've seen on some vintage sedans; skintight leopard-print minidress and matching mules. "You!!" she screams at Marco, her lavender-eye-shadowed lids opening wide. In the next instant, she lunges at me, but Trixie pulls her back, hissing, "I told you who she is when we walked in. Control yourself. You don't want to go to jail. Or worse. Let him take the heat, not you."

"Ms. Loquor, now would be the time to start explaining yourself," I say icily as Marco sits silently across from me, his face the color of Elmer's glue.

"Why don't you let Mr. Trevini do that, Your Highness."

All three of us look at Marco.

Out spills the story, Marco's voice the tone of lead, but peppered by Trixie's evil laughter and Adrienne's shrill epithet-hurling. Remember, if something (or someone) seems too good to be true, it (or he) usually is. Marco—real name, Mark—Trevini is really from Hoboken, not Milan; his accent is courtesy of Berlitz, his background the invention of his agent. The only thing he didn't lie about was his last name. The redhead is his ex-wife from Hoboken, who he walked out on when he went to Milan to model. (His agent's idea. By now, I'm beginning to wonder if making a play for me was, too. Is *anything* about him real?! I wonder. Of course, as tight as those Zegna pants are, I don't have to wonder about *everything*, but that doesn't matter anymore.)

Trixie finishes the story by telling me that Marco—I mean Mark—decided I would be his ticket out. Adrienne sued him for more alimony when he made it big, threatening to expose him with Trixie's help. (No doubt a tell-all of the hottest new hottie would make her so-called career, so she agreed to trail him to get the "whole story.") Long story short, Marco/Mark needed cash—preferably an endless supply. I realize that's why Trixie was at Nobu in the first place, and he ran because he saw her, not because he was tongue-tied at the prospect of meeting me in the flesh.

Well. What more can I say?

As the maître d' is approaching to see what the ruckus is about, I glare at all three of them, stand up and say, "This is the end of my involvement in this matter. It had better stay that way." I level my eyes at each of them, then turn on my heel and sail past the table. The maître d' asks if I'm all right, and I assure him that I am, but that he'd best see about the rest of the party, who are undoubtedly not the types Chanterelle wants to have around.

I leave and start walking uptown. I don't want to stick around as long as it would take for James to drive down to pick me up if I called from my cell. The walk makes me feel a little better, but pleather go-go's are *not* made for walking, so after a few blocks I hail a cab. Settling into the back seat, I feel calmer but still outraged at being lied to, not to mention hounded *again* by Trixie. And underneath it all, I'm sad to have met yet another Prince Not-So-Charming.

I am determined to relegate this unfortunate episode to the past. The *remote* past, to be precise. Nevertheless, I'm still upset. Understandably so, of course. A princess never denies her true feelings, but uses the following mantra of self-expression: feel, express, let go, move on. (I learned to use mantras from Nirvana, and even though a lot of the things she does are definitely stratosphere material, the mantra thing really works. This particular one is mine, not hers. Hers are all Sanskrit chants.)

Sorry, darling, I know I'm not bouncing back in true and admirable princessly fashion. But it's just so…disappointing! So infuriating! Not to mention awful that there's no one around to go for a *tartufo*. (Clarice is on a date, hopefully having a wonderful time; Nirvana will be deep into her evening *bikram* yoga, and wouldn't eat ice cream, product of an innocent cow, anyway; Mariana would spend so much time calculating the fat and sugar content that the poor *tartufo* would melt before she decided if she could eat it, or calculated how many StairMaster sessions she'd have to do to work it off. Sigh.)

Well, I must do something. I simply will *not* allow anyone or anything to make me feel miserable for long. Despite the fact that my romantic evening with a movie star was a complete disaster, and despite the fact that I unwittingly fell into the clutches of Trixie Loquor yet again (God only knows what she'll write this time!), I am going to enjoy the rest of my evening. Somehow. But first, I must call to warn Jean-Paul Fameux, even if all I can do is leave a damage-control message. He'll need to know about this before the film comes out. Poor Jean-Paul!

This is a good lesson for you, and although I am distinctly not happy that it happened, I am glad that you got to see it, nonetheless. Now you understand that even I must encounter and deal with difficult people.

Every princess must. Unfortunately, there is no inoculation against irritation or aggravation. A princess today is not a princess of yore who can just ask her prince or knight in shining armor to do away with the peevish person in question. She must, instead, learn how to rely on herself to defuse the irritation/aggravation, and determine the outcome she'd like for the situation. That outcome does not always necessarily manifest itself, but your expectation of it and attitude toward it always must. Determine for yourself what you want to have happen, then do everything in your power to create the atmosphere that will allow it to. If what you'd hoped for isn't what transpires, do your best to accept it and move on, provided that you know in your heart you did the best you could.

Remember, part of the defusing process is knowing who you're dealing with. There's nothing wrong with being tough when you need to be; however, a princess knows how to temper necessary toughness with charm, poise and dignity.

A princess gets what she wants *most* of the time, but she walks away with her self-respect all the time.

Each time you handle a difficult person or situation, you automatically do it better, because you're wiser each time. The important thing to remember is that difficult situations and people are just that: difficult. Don't beat yourself up when they are. Just do the best you can and have faith in yourself. If it's a bit easier each time, then you're making great progress, but don't expect it to ever be truly easy. It just never is, not even for a princess.

Some people just need to be smacked, but a princess smacks wearing a velvet glove.

I think it's fair to say that the behavior of both Marco and Trixie definitely qualified each of them for a well-deserved smack. (The obviously brokenhearted Adrienne I truly feel sorry for, even though the memory of her bad dye job and red-lacquer-clawed would-be pounce is one I surely won't forget as soon as I'd like. Her behavior might have been ill-bred, but it's understandable given the circumstances.) Marco really more so than Trixie. Tabloids are just a given, unfortunately, and even though Trixie's presence in my life is annoying, she is only doing her job. No matter how much I might not like it, that is the truth, and a princess accepts the truth and makes her peace with it. As for Marco—Mark, what*ever!*—it's not that cut-and-dried. Lying and manipulating for your own gain at the expense of someone else who can't possibly know what you're about is inexcusable.

So having established that both of them are undeniably smack candidates, let's examine the other part: how to smack with a velvet glove. The art of the velvet-gloved smack is something every true princess must cultivate and perfect. There's no room for a doormat princess except in fairy tales. A princess has to learn how to take care of herself, and the velvet-gloved smack is one of the most reliable and useful tools she has.

Think about the way I handled Marco, Trixie and Adrienne. I could have ranted and carried on, even slapped Marco (since he surely had it coming), or demanded that Adrienne and Trixie be removed from Chanterelle. Satisfying as any or all of that might have been in the moment, it only would have served to bring me down to their level. A princess is never brought down to anyone's level. A princess sets her own standard and expects others to rise to meet it. If they don't, they simply aren't worth her time, effort or attention. The velvet-gloved smack is simply you standing up for yourself without making a scene;

it's letting the offender know that you aren't going to tolerate being mistreated. Period. End of story.

Of course, there are offenses that truly warrant an actual physical slap, *sans* glove. Had Marco merely been a date from hell whom I caught in such an outrageous lie far away from the clutches of a tabloid stringer, I might very well have given him the *sans*-glove treatment. Not to mention a well-timed slosh of my martini into his face. But a headline like "SLAP-HAPPY JACQUIE LETS LOOSE IN TRIBECA," would have accomplished nothing and probably would have made me feel even worse, and my father apoplectic. So I suppose it's just as well. Things have a way of working out the way they're meant to. When they don't, reread your favorite chapter, break into a box of chocolates, take a lavender bath, go for drinks or coffee with your girlfriends, or go shopping. (Speaking of chocolate, where did my chamberlain put this week's box of Teuschers? If ever there was a moment requiring a champagne truffle, this is it!)

Rely on yourself. No matter what. This is what a true princess does.

Self-reliance isn't about remembering to do everything perfectly in the moment, it's about knowing and trusting that all you need to do will reveal itself to you. Self-reliance means that you just trust yourself and whatever higher intelligence you believe in, having faith that everything will turn out fine. Then, you do the best you can. And that's that. (My mental scepter is firmly in place once again.)

On Wining and Dining

A princess understands all the connotations of "good taste."

7

Hello, darling! I'm oh-so-much better than when we last met, after the dreadful Marco-Trixie-Adrienne debacle. (Which I'm now referring to simply as The Debacle.) Let's not even go there.

Now I'm waiting for Nirvana to arrive with her newest guru, whose name I cannot possibly pronounce but will try to spell: Mahanirijawarlaldhjiswami. (I think I got it right.) I've met several of Nirvana's saffron-robed pundits, but she's only been this one's devotee for a few weeks. It should be interesting. In deference to the vegan status of Nirvana and her guru, I suggested we meet for an afternoon pick-me-up at the Soy Luck Club. (My first choice was to go for high tea, but Nirvana informed me—a bit haughtily, I might add—that Sri Maha would never eat a scone, the animal fat–laden butter of which would incur more karmic consequences than I could ever imagine. The Soy Luck Club immediately came to mind then, as I freely confess to being a frosted soy smoothie addict.)

I love Nirvana to pieces, but the vegan stuff can cause strife. Once, she invited me over for dinner and served portobello mushrooms in lieu of steak. Hmm. Don't get me wrong, I adore portobello mushrooms, but eating a mushroom is not the same as eating a steak. Clarice suggested that perhaps Nirvana's hours upon hours of yoga and meditation each day have transported her to a parallel universe, where she has come to truly taste the mushrooms as steak. Hmm, again. I think it's nothing more complicated than self-deception. Nirvana wants to believe that the mushrooms are a replacement for steak, so she's convinced herself that they taste the same.

Let's remember that, although Nirvana is a good friend and I love her, I did have to expel her from the Princess-in-Training Program. I accept her trying to convince herself that a mushroom is a steak. I even accept her being a vegan refusing to eat fruits and veggies that have to be dug up or picked, and consuming only those that fall from the tree or vine when ready—which often means rotten. Sigh. Nirvana follows these rules religiously, and that's why I worry about her obsessiveness. The last time she came back from Katmandu, she nearly got herself arrested for accosting a woman in a Mongolian lamb coat. Nirvana, who really got far more into the Adopt-a-Yak program when she was in Nepal than she should have, mistook the Mongolian lamb fur for that of her new favorite animal. Not that she ever does all that well with accepting anyone wearing fur, but a coat that looked to her like her adoptee yak, Siddhartha, really pushed her over the edge. It turned out all right in the end, but it wasn't pleasant, to say the least.

Anyway, far be it from me to tell Nirvana, Mariana or anyone else how to eat, but eating is supposed to be an enjoyable experience. Yes, I'm all for eating healthfully most of the time, but a decadent treat now and then isn't going to harm anyone, either (serious health conditions and food allergies excepted, of course). If eating becomes a burden, something is wrong. Nirvana's obsession with vegan rules and Mariana's compulsive calculating of fat- and carb-grams are not examples of healthy eating; they're examples of making yourself miserable. Rules of healthy eating should guide and support, not imprison and terrorize.

Hold on a sec, my cell is ringing. Nirvana. Turns out her guru won't come to Soy Luck Club, either. Something about having to know *exactly* how the soy products were cultivated before he would ingest them. *Quelle surprise!* I order a frosted soy smoothie to go. Since I'm downtown, I decide to head over to Prada. (I just adore the fitting rooms there. You can actually adjust the lighting and mirrors yourself. Isn't that too fun? This isn't going to be a real shopping trip, but I can't resist the beckoning I know so well: "Pra-da, Pra-da, Pra-da." It almost makes me understand what "Om" does for Nirvana, to be honest. Almost.)

As it happens, this smoothie is out of this world. But I freely admit that if it tasted horrible, I wouldn't drink it just because it was healthy. That's why vitamin and mineral supplements come in tablets and capsules that you can swallow with water without tasting them. I mean, that is a simple concept, isn't it? Sometimes I think Nirvana enjoys making these things complicated because she's convinced that if simple things require effort, it's because she's more spiritually evolved than other people. In truth, simple things are supposed to be simple, and complicated things are supposed to complicated. Period.

Last night I was out with friends at La Grenouille, and definitely overindulged in the amazing chocolate soufflé. (Be aware that the only *grenouilles* I see socially—dates from hell, liars and manipulators notwithstanding—are in

French restaurants. The only princessly response to a frog's croaking is: *Jamais!*)

It's girls' night out tonight. Clarice, Mariana, Nirvana and I all are going to Le Cirque 2000. Actually, I think the girls are just doing it to cheer me up post-Debacle (I'm cheering myself up by wearing my new marabou-trimmed sweater from Prada), and I think it's just too sweet of them. Nirvana will brave the world of carnivores, and Mariana will square off against myriad fat- and carb-grams, just because they love me. That means a lot to me, it really does. I treasure my friends, as every princess should.

Le Cirque, of course, will be *formidable*. (In case you're wondering, yes, French cuisine is my favorite. And yes, I plan to indulge in something out of this world again tonight, so an extra-long power walk or in-line skating set is on for tomorrow.) Let me emphasize that, while I do watch what I eat and compensate for indulgences by exercising more, I don't obsess the way Nirvana and Mariana do. Neither does Clarice. No princess would ever do that to herself. A princess just enjoys herself, takes care of herself, and knows that balance and moderation in all things is the way to eat—and to live.

A princess enjoys herself on her own terms, deciding for herself how to have a good time.

Clarice and I are headed for Le Cirque. Mariana and Nirvana are meeting us at the restaurant. Mariana, of course, is walking to and from the restaurant, to burn more calories. Nirvana may be a bit late depending upon her *bikram* yoga routine. Some days she needs a longer cool-down than others. As we discuss this, Clarice rolls her eyes, reminding me that she's checking Mariana's purse for the calculator.

Inside the restaurant, Clarice, noting from the size of Mariana's purse that the likelihood of a calculator's presence is slim to none, takes Mariana's arm. She informs her *sotto voce,* "If the calculator appears, sweetie, it's toast."

Mariana, after a flash of a deer-in-the-headlights stare, chuckles good-naturedly. I wonder how small a calculator she's managed to conceal in that purse. My guess is that she's planning to check the grams consumed every time she goes to the ladies' room.

As we're being escorted to our table, I see my friend Svetlana, her husband, Lance, and his triplet sisters, Angelica, Veronica and Monica. We stop to say hello to Svetlana, who Clarice and Mariana know. I say hello to the others, and Svetlana introduces Clarice and Mariana to her husband and sisters-in-law. When I ask how they're enjoying New York, Svetlana gushes about how she can't believe how long it's been since she was last in the city. We make plans to meet for lunch and a visit to the MoMA the following day.

"Well, I for one can't wait to get back to Tulsa," says Veronica, and her sisters echo the sentiment. I roll my eyes at Svetlana, when they and Lance can't see. I see for myself that the three "-icas" are the same as ever, just as Svetlana told me. Poor Svetlana, all alone with just them and the oil wells. Lance does seem like a sweetie, though. He's been in nonstop meetings since they got here, but he says he loves New York and can't wait to see *The Producers* two nights from now. The three "-icas" are positively underwhelmed.

We say our goodbyes and continue to our table. Sometimes it's nice when things don't change. In the case of the three "-icas," however, a change of personality would be nice. Or should I say an *addition* of personality. They don't seem to have *one* even to share amongst the three of them. Oh, that was a bit mean, I suppose. I'm sorry. Just for that, I won't say a word about their wardrobes.

Soon after we're seated a waiter takes our drink orders: Pellegrino for me, a cosmopolitan for Clarice, Evians for

Mariana and Nirvana. For the most part, I'm a Pellegrino drinker; usually, I never have more than one martini at parties or on dates, and a glass of wine with dinner. I wish drinking made me get all giggly like Clarice does (she is just so adorable and such fun when she gets all giggly), but after drink number two, all I want to do is curl up in a ball and go to sleep. Not too much fun, huh? So you can understand why I'm not much of a drinker. As opposed to Mariana, who never drinks because of the calories. Or Nirvana, who, of course, never drinks because she prefers her inhibitions to be released transcendentally. I'm not passing judgment. If you want to drink, drink; if you don't, don't. But Mariana and Nirvana don't for obsessive reasons, and that's never a good thing, as every princess knows. A true princess does, at all times, what feels best and right for her. (Of course, if doing so will intentionally hurt another person, she needs to factor that in to the equation, and modify her choices accordingly.) She doesn't do things to conform to anyone else's judgments or preconceptions. (Just a little tip, though: Less is more. A princess knows how to enjoy herself without jeopardizing her self-respect. By all means, indulge in evenings filled with martinis and cosmos, but don't drink so many that you don't remember the evening the following day. That would be most definitely nonprincessly, indeed.)

A princess knows it's no coincidence that "wine" and "dine" rhyme with "fine."

Clarice raises her glass in a toast. "To our wonderful friend, Jacquie. May our favorite princess find her Prince Charming soon."

"May we all!" I say as we clink glasses all around. I give Clarice's forearm a squeeze, and she winks at me. "No talking about The Debacle, girls," I remind them. "This is going to be a happy night."

"Let's order," Mariana says. "I'm starved."

"I would think so. From what you've told me, you haven't really eaten since 1996," Clarice replies.

I shoot Clarice a look. I mean, I agree with her (actually, I think it was more like 1994), but this is supposed to be a fun evening.

Much to my surprise, Mariana just smiles and says, "Sometimes it feels that way to me, too. I just can't stand the thought of being fat."

"But you're not fat. You're skinny!" Clarice and I say in stereo.

"They're right, Mar. You are thin," says Nirvana, who usually supports Mariana's excessive eating habits by telling her that eating less is clean, pure and more spiritually evolved. "Tonight, let's all just eat and enjoy."

Clarice and I exchange a glance. Maybe the guru *du jour* isn't so bad, after all. Even Mariana, who usually goes along with Nirvana's stuff in the hope that she'll get a few juice fasts or further instruction in breatharianism in exchange for her show of solidarity, seems surprised.

In any case, everything we order is absolutely delectable. Supreme. *Nonpareil.* Even Mariana and Nirvana are eating happily. Mariana doesn't even hesitate when she orders beef bordelaise for her main course. Of course, Nirvana sticks to cheeses, salad and bread, but doesn't grill the waiter about how any of them were prepared. Both of them are truly throwing all caution to the wind. I couldn't be more pleased. That's what nights out with your girlfriends are for: celebrating, indulging, reveling…in whatever ways you choose. I don't want Mariana, Nirvana or Clarice to be what they're not—I love each of them just as they are—but I do love seeing them enjoy themselves. And tonight, all we girls are having a wonderful time. Almost like a birthday. (I love birthdays, by the way. I celebrate mine for a week. Clarice says that's only because I was born a princess, but actually it's because I was born an Aries.)

Clarice orders veal and I have the bordelaise, same as Mariana, which will be perfect with the merlot we order for the table. The sommelier decants, I sniff the bouquet, then sip some. *Ahh!* Gloriously smooth. I nod to the sommelier, who decants for Clarice.

Clarice sips her wine, turning toward me after the sommelier departs, and pronouncing, "Sm-o-o-o-o-o-th!" Then she practically collapses into a fit of giggles. (Didn't I tell you she's absolutely the cutest thing? I never feel happier than when I'm out with Clarice in a giggle-fest.)

The four of us chat and laugh for a bit, then the waiter brings our cheese course (which is Nirvana's entrée). The cheeses are outstanding, and Clarice and I are delighted to see Mariana and Nirvana both helping themselves to Brie with joyous abandon. After we've finished the cheese, I order demitasse for each of us, and Clarice and I ask the waiter to bring us *glacés* for dessert.

"I'll have the same," pipes up Mariana. At first she seems to shock herself with the request for ice cream, but then she just beams at us.

"Me, too," echoes Nirvana.

"I adore ice cream," Mariana tells us after the waiter leaves.

"Me, too," Nirvana says again.

If Mariana is calculating what it will take to burn off calories and work off fat, and if Nirvana is assessing the damage done to her delicate acid-alkaline balance, neither of them lets on. All four of us are ear-to-ear grins.

"Everyone adores ice cream," Clarice tells them. "But that doesn't matter, what matters is that you do. It's our night on the town, girls. Splurge!!"

Everyone needs to indulge themselves—frequently, in my opinion, but especially on girls-only nights like this.

Of course, indulgence is one thing; addiction, another. (Let's not get into that ridiculous idea Clarice has about my being addicted to shopping. Ever since I said that I would consider that I *might* have, shall we say, "shopping issues," she's been relentless. I mean, it isn't as if I can't get through a day without shopping! I just don't like to think about it, and I'm not going to spoil this fun evening by thinking about it for another second.)

A princess is sure to have her daily dose of vitamin I: as in, "indulgence."

The *glacés* have arrived: *noisette, framboise, pêche, chocolat, vanille.* They divided them in the kitchen, so we each can have a taste of all five flavors. *Formidable!* Each flavor is more delectable than the other. (Just so you know, *noisette* is my all-time fave. Simply *magnifique!*) True, I'll be sticking to salads and plain fish for a while after last night's and tonight's feasts, but it's worth it. Life is about enjoying yourself to the fullest. Every princess knows that. If you go along every day just waiting for that day to end, you're existing, not living. That's a shame and a pity. You must make room for pleasure and joy in your life, no matter how sad, disappointed or frustrated you might feel in the moment—even if the moment is ongoing or feels eternal. Plus, indulgences give you something wonderful to look forward to.

Sometimes you just have to choose to be happy if happiness doesn't come to you naturally. Treating yourself to the things you love—indulging yourself in something wonderful every day—is a good way to begin this process. For lots of people, a delicious dessert or a fine meal is just the indulgence needed. I don't advocate food replacing other things in your life, but if chocolate truffles beckon on a trying day, I say, "Heed the call." (Of course, it goes without saying that shopping is another form of indulgence that is *toujours* effective, with far less risk of addiction than truffles.)

But back to indulgence. Indulgence is a "daily require-ment" of life as a princess. If truffles and shopping don't appeal to you, that's fine. Pick whatever you like to indulge in—bubble baths, writing in a journal, sleeping an extra fifteen minutes, lighting an aromatherapy candle, whatever it is that makes *you* feel indulged.

We leave the restaurant, and I'm certainly feeling in-dulged now. Mariana and Nirvana each say they're ready to call it a night. If they're going home to work it all off, that's their choice, and I support them. I hope someday they each will learn how to truly enjoy without punish-ing themselves afterward. We each get to take baby steps with whatever is hardest for us. And indulgence means something different to everyone.

The four of us exchange hugs. Clarice and I wait for the Lamborghini to be brought around, while Mariana and Nirvana start walking downtown.

"Come over for dinner tomorrow?" Clarice offers. "Poached salmon and arugula-and-endive salad."

"Sounds wonderful. What should I bring?"

Clarice shrugs.

"How about fruit salad for dessert?"

"With watermelon and plumcots?"

"Of course!" I assure her. Those are our two favorite fruits.

"Sounds perfect." She grins at me. "You don't know the sugar content offhand, do you?" she teases.

"Sure I do. It's just right."

On Rubbing Elbows

A true princess makes hobnobbing an art form.

8

Darling! It's so good to be back! Oh, I forgot, you didn't know I was away. Okay, I'll have to make a very long story very short, because Contessina Sfilato-di Moda's New York runway show is going to start in a few minutes (I've already been to Prada, Armani, D & G—all of them—and this is the last one.) For the past couple of weeks I've been at the runway shows in Milan and Paris. (Fashion Week in every city is always a blur. A bright, beautiful, joyous blur, *bien sûr,* but a blur nonetheless). Contessina, whom I regret having to admit I never truly appreciated before the Milan show, is a true style genius, and hers have been the best everywhere. Don't believe all those rumors that she's a complete psychotic. People are so jealous of obvious talent that they will stop at nothing short of ruining the person. Truth to tell, it's all a bunch of vicious lies, thought up and promulgated by the likes of Trixie Loquor.

That reminds me! I haven't told you what happened after The Debacle. After I called to give Jean-Paul Fameux a heads-up about Marco/Mark Trevini (which

I did prior to Trixie's horrid headline, "PRINCESS SLUMMING IN HOBOKEN! MARCO SAYS, 'AR-RIVEDERCI, MILANO!'," hitting the stands, thank God!), Jean-Paul went ballistic. "I will not work with that scum after what he did to you, *bébé*," were his exact words to me. Then Jean-Paul and his producers held a press conference, where they announced that *The Stench* will be released somewhat later than planned, and with a to-be-announced leading man. The big secret is, Jean-Paul is going to cut all Marco's scenes and reshoot them with himself in the lead role. Very Truffaut, *n'est-ce pas?* The producers are a little skittish about Jean-Paul's box-office draw as a star, so I'm going to be his primary financial backer, which means I get screen credit as executive producer. Could I be more excited?! I think not. And the adorable Brandon Charmant will be replacing Marco as the lead in the new movie Jean-Paul is going to start filming in a couple of months. Anyway, as a result of it all, Marco Trevini is completely washed up, so if he was hoping that a scandal would increase his box-office draw, too bad, so sad! Hopefully, Brandon Charmant will become a huge star. It would be wonderful if something good came of Marco's awful deception. And I couldn't be happier that Jean-Paul's reputation remained unscathed.

As for mine, the Foundation attorneys insisted upon an *International Investigator*–style retraction, and I gave interviews in the *New York Times,* and *Time* and *People* magazines to set the record straight. Trixie Loquor is still on the loose, of course, but I have no concern of ever hearing from her again. (Remember that scandals and tabloids are the ever-present nemesis of every princess, but I am not about to dwell on either one.) As you can see, I got so caught up in all of that, and then I had to be off for the runway shows…and the time just slipped away from me completely.

In any case, I'm back! Clarice is here beside me. This is her first runway show. Every season I invite her to come with me, and she finally agreed. Of course, she said she was only coming so I would stop bugging her, but I can tell she is beyond excited. I always get invited to the shows, front-row seating, of course. (Another one of those born-a-princess perks, darling. One of my favorites, I must say!)

Every fashionista on the planet is here. Contessina is just the hottest thing. After I bought her entire *collezione* in Milan, everyone else followed suit. How I *adore* being a trendsetter! Wait a second. Someone is making her way across the row to talk to me. As she comes closer, I see that it's Claudine Chinobert, editor in chief of *De Rigueur* magazine. I almost didn't recognize her with her cherry highlights. Her hair used to be a hundred percent jet black.

"Jacquie!" she croons, air-kissing me on both cheeks.

"Chi-Chi." Everyone calls Claudine "Chi-Chi." I introduce her to Clarice, who holds her own, even though I can tell she's a bit overwhelmed in the presence of the "fashionistas' fashionista." Chi-Chi has that effect.

"You bad girl!" Chi-Chi scolds. "You've gone over to Sfilato-di Moda, and every spread I have lined up is on Prada. You might have let someone know!" Chi-Chi's voice is approaching the shrill decibel of meltdown.

"Chi-Chi," I soothe, "I couldn't let anyone know when I didn't know myself! Was I supposed to turn my back on utter genius?"

"All I'm saying is, to go from Prada to an unknown—"

"Contessina Sfilato-di Moda isn't an unknown anymore."

"Thanks to you."

"And you, Chi-Chi. Who else would I grant an exclusive feature story to on my new favorite designer?"

With that, Chi-Chi goes from shrill to thrill. "Fabulous!" she purrs. With two more air kisses and an over-the-shoulder "I'll call you," she's off as suddenly as she arrived. Dinner with Chi-Chi at Alain Ducasse, and I'll ensure Contessina's American fame.

"This is why I've resisted these things up to now," Clarice hisses in my ear.

"Come on, Clar. This is all part of the fun."

"Puh-leeze, Jacquie! Look at the other people in the front row. It's a Who's Who of Beautiful People. Not to mention that the silicone, Botox and collagen would have to be measured by the ton."

I wink at her, suppressing a laugh. "It's part of the show, sweetie. Just enjoy yourself. Contessina is fantastic. You're going to love her stuff."

"This row is a show in and of itself," persists Clarice, nodding toward a supermodel-turned-actress a few people away. The woman hasn't taken her eyes off her reflection in her compact mirror since she arrived.

"Not everyone can be a princess," I remind her gently. "Remember the training required. And not everyone has your enviable innate P.Q., Clar. Dedicated students less fortunate than you will have a far more arduous training."

Clarice nods with a sigh of newfound compassion for the self-absorbed, emaciated (yet noticeably inflated in all the expected places) celebrity who has just tucked her compact inside her Gucci and picked up her head sharply with a deeply snorted sniffle and discreet wipe of her finger across the bottom of a conspicuously red nose. Clarice and I exchange a knowing look. Obviously, that mirror has more uses than one. Sigh. (Perils abound in the glam life. Of course, a true princess needs no high besides life itself, and her joy in being who she is.)

The music and dry-ice smoke start, signaling that the show is about to begin. Raising my voice a bit so she can hear me above the thrum of the bass guitar, I tell Clarice, "Take a few deep breaths."

Clarice raises an eyebrow but obeys.

And a good thing, too. She can laugh all she wants, but the air at a runway show is heady, indeed, with this many slaves to fashion in one place. I thrive on it, though. Clarice will, too, but it does take a bit of adjusting. It's sort of like adjusting to the air in Gstaad on a ski trip, or to the taste of Belgian chocolate if you're used to any other: You know it's rich and wonderful right away, but you have to take small doses of it to make sure it will agree with you. Until you're used to it, of course.

Clarice beams from ear to ear. She's adjusting even more quickly than I expected. Goody! It's fine to shop for what you want at deep discounts, but every princess needs to go to a runway show at least once.

Here comes the first model! No matter how many runway shows I attend, the first pair of stilettoed legs striding down the runway is always a thrill. I love the anticipation, the glamour, the showmanship. (I also love the list of goodies to check off with those cute little pencils! I am the ultimate fashionista, after all, and must ensure that Contessina didn't sneak in any new items for the New York show.)

Be back when the show is over, darling! *Ciao* for now.

A princess always refers to high-powered fashion designers by their first names.

The show was *favoloso!* Even better than Paris and Milan. It must be New York. I only have a few check marks on my list. That Contessina! She snuck in a deep charcoal suede miniskirt with matching bolero. How could I say no? (Clarice remarks upon my only checking two items, saying I must have really cleaned her out in Milan. I just wink at her. Of course I cleaned her out in Milan! Have I not been saying what a genius Contessina is?)

I turn to Clarice, who is a bit overwhelmed in spite of herself. "Oh, Clar," I say. "Isn't Contessina fabulous? She understands the importance of black. Even her non–black and almost-black styles look black!" What could be better?

"Uh-huh," Clarice says, her voice a bit higher-pitched than usual.

"Breathe!" I instruct, *sotto voce.*

Well, we've turned in our lists, and the front-row attendees have gone to mingle. Clarice isn't all that comfortable hobnobbing, even at Foundation functions when she has to, so I take her under my wing, as always. I want this day to be perfect for her, the most fun she's ever had. I want her to remember it and smile about it forever.

"Let's go chat with Contessina," I suggest.

Clarice blinks, then stares at me.

"You are so adorable," I tell her, taking her arm and squeezing it.

Contessina is not too far away, flanked by models and positively radiant in the glow of her first successful New York show. She turns and sees me.

"Jacquie!" Disengaging herself from the models, she comes toward me, arms extended.

"Cara!" I say, returning her two kisses on the cheek. *"Bravissima!"*

I gush for a moment or two about how fabulous the show was, then introduce Clarice, who is taking deep breaths, but on the verge of hyperventilating from sheer excitement and awe, nevertheless. (Contessina may not be *the* hot designer yet, but the whole atmosphere is a bit overwhelming for the uninitiated.)

Contessina is an angel, kissing both of Clarice's cheeks, too, and telling her how thrilled she is that she enjoyed the show. Any friend of mine is a friend of hers, she says. How sweet is that? I told you she was an angel. I adore the woman. And not just because she understands the importance of black—that makes her the genius I tout her as being, not an angel.

I whisper to Contessina about my conversation with

Chi-Chi, promising I'll let her know what happens after we've had our meeting. But I instruct her to prepare herself for soon-to-be fame as fashion designer *par excellence.* The radiant smile and thank-you hug she gives me must mean that she's rid her mind of all those horrid tabloid lies. Thank goodness!!

"I have a gift for you, *carissima,*" Contessina promises.

"How thoughtful. You needn't have." But I can't wait to see what it is. After the Milan show, she gave me a silk camisole encrusted with the tiniest iridescent bugle beads. The most exquisite thing I've ever seen. Not wanting to monopolize her time, I kiss her twice on the cheek again, tell her to mingle with the rest of her guests and invite her to brunch at the Plaza on Sunday. She unhesitatingly accepts, kisses Clarice and me goodbye and moves into the crowd.

The glamour is beginning to fade for Clarice. She's back on the inequities of front-row seating. "People deserve respect, regardless of who they are. Regardless of how much money, power or aristocratic lineage they have. Am I right? After all, you yourself always say that, Jacquie."

"Well, sweetie, of course you're right. But front-row seats aren't about respect. They're about how much you're known to buy at a runway show."

"*Ka-ching* seats," Clarice says a bit dejectedly.

"Life isn't fair, even for a princess."

Clarice's eyes widen and her cheeks turn deep pink. "Oh my God! Oh, Jacquie, I didn't mean *you* with that money, power, aristocratic stuff—"

"I know you didn't, sweetie." To make her feel better, I invite her to join Contessina and me for brunch at the Plaza.

Born-a-princess perks are fabulous, to be sure, but never more important than a friend's feelings. Besides, I do know what she meant. She's talking about the sense of entitlement that we've already discussed. Truth to tell, the people who feel the most entitled usually have the least cause. Every princess knows that. (I gently remind Clarice of all this, and she hugs me and says she has to get back to the office. I gave her the day off, but there's no reasoning with her. She is the most conscientious person I know.)

After Clarice leaves, I scan the crowd to see who I might want to chat with. In the next instant I find myself looking up into the bluest eyes I've ever seen. Guess who? Brandon Charmant. How perfect is that? And I must say that cleaned up (i.e. not in homeless garb), he is…well… one of the most gorgeous men on the planet.

"Your Highness," he says in a baritone voice, which alone could make him a star, and gives me the most charming little bow.

"Brandon! It's so good to see you. Please…no need to bow. We're friends. And you must call me Jacquie."

"All right, Jacquie."

"What brings you to Contessina's show?"

"Jean-Paul made me promise not to tell you."

"You mean it's a secret?" I adore secrets, except when I don't know what they are.

He nods in mock solemnity. "Someday, I'll be able to tell you. For now, I really must run. I hope I'll see you again very soon."

"I hope so."

He gives me a huge smile, then lifts my hand and kisses the back of it.

Then he's off as quickly as he arrived. I'm going to have to call Jean-Paul Fameux to get the scoop on this. Secret, indeed!

Oh my! Between the show and Brandon's unexpected arrival, I completely lost track of time. Next week, the Metropolitan Museum of Art is opening a costume exhibit—Queens throughout History: A Sartorial Overview—and I'm on the advisory board. We have a meeting in half an hour. *Ciao* for now, darling.

★ ★ ★

Since Contessina's runway show, all my time has just been *consumed* by the exhibit at the Metropolitan. I agreed to be on the advisory board, not to be the curator, for goodness' sakes! But the chief costume curator had a personal emergency, so I was pressed into commission by the rest of the board, being the member most knowledgeable about all forms of fashion. (Ha! I should tell Clarice that all my fashion knowledge and shopping expertise have served to prepare me for public service.)

There's a big fete tonight in honor of the exhibit's opening to the public tomorrow. I'm wearing my fabulous new Sfilato-di Moda tonight. Oh! I never even told you what Contessina's gift was, did I? Remember the beaded camisole I went on and on about that she gave me in Milan? Well, she knew how much I loved it, so she made me a black satin gown, bias-cut and to-the-floor, with diagonal swaths of jet beads. Floor-length iridescent black! Anyway, that's what I'm wearing, along with black satin Louboutin mules and a black Judith Leiber *minaudieré* with an Art Deco clasp. And my D & G full-length black evening gloves, of course—my trademark.

For a princess, elegance is effortless, and she doesn't need a costume of any period to achieve it.

The fete is a huge success. Everyone who's anyone is here. They all remark on how wonderful the exhibit is. How dazzling. How comprehensive. I discuss the cultural effects of the change from farthingales to panniers with a history professor from Columbia. Ugh! I can't imagine wearing either one of those torturous-looking contraptions. The professor then asks what I think of corsets. Hmm. *Not much,* I think. But I respond by saying that I'm greatly relieved that men have gained enough enlightenment to recognize that a woman's body should not be compressed, contorted, constricted or in any way harmed just to appear more attractive to them. He nods politely and beats a hasty retreat. Well done! What did he expect me—or any woman—to say? "Please let us wear corsets again, so our spines and rib cages can be knocked out of alignment, and we can go around fainting at the drop of a hat." I don't think so.

Besides, elegance and beauty never arise from hurting yourself. They come from within and are reflected outward. This can only happen when you feel comfortable and good about yourself. The costumes on display may look magnificent, but must have felt like torture chambers. *Quel dommage* that the women who wore them had to suffer so much for the sake of fashion.

An older lady in a St. John evening suit approaches me. I recognize her from the society pages, but can't remember her name.

"Good evening, Your Highness." She extends her hand, and I take it. "Millicent Bickford."

Bickford. Oh, yes, it's coming back to me now. Her husband's a surgeon at NYU Medical Center. Very prominent. They do a lot of fund-raising for medical charities.

"Of course." I smile. "You and your husband do such good work."

"I've been admiring you all evening. You look absolutely stunning. I haven't been able to take my eyes off that choker."

(I'm wearing a French Art Deco diamond-and-emerald choker, borrowed from my mother. My dress is backless, and the neckline hits just below my collarbone, so only a choker would do. This one is exquisite, if I do say so myself. Vintage Cartier.)

I thank her, admire her St. John and black pearls, and ask how she's enjoying the exhibit.

"It's outstanding," she pronounces.

"I'm so glad you think so. Which was your favorite piece?"

"Come and I'll show you."

She leads me to the *pièce de résistance* of the exhibit, a frothy court gown originally owned by Marie Antoinette. Standing before it, I stroke the back of my neck. (Not because of the choker. It's a reflex whenever I think of Louis XVI's doomed queen, and my own forebears' narrowest of escapes. If not for Jacques Corday…besides, but for two hundred or so years, Marie Antoinette might have been me. Royalty does entail certain risks, after all.)

"How were they ever able to assemble all these items? I didn't even know any of Cleopatra's personal effects still *existed*," exults Millicent. A special display included some of Cleopatra's combs and hairpins, courtesy of my great-aunt, Camille de Soignée, the widow of my great-uncle Philippe, and a renowned Egyptologist, long since retired, who didn't want credit given in the exhibit.

"The curator asked me to…assist her," I say softly. I abide by Auntie's request, but Millicent is savvy enough to connect the dots.

"Well, that explains it!" she says. "We're so lucky to have a person of your fine taste, standing and philanthropic inclination in our midst, Your Highness."

"Thank you, Millicent. Please call me Jacqueline." I smile, then add, "We're lucky to have people as concerned with championing medical research as you and your husband."

We say goodbye, as Millicent's husband motions to her to come meet the couple he's talking to, and one of the museum directors asks me to join him for a photo-op.

**Never underestimate the scope of your influence.
You are a *princesse du monde!***

The evening is a huge success, and the museum directors can't stop thanking me. I keep assuring them that I'm glad I was able to help. It isn't as if sorting through costumes is exactly a hardship for me—they are, after all, the fashions of their day. (One cloth-of-gold coronation gown is absolutely gorgeous, I tell you plainly, and I happen to have a pair of Manolos that would be perfect with it. Sigh.) If I can help others, I'm always too happy to do so. And it is truly wonderful to feel the appreciation and gratitude of the curator's staff, whom I worked with to mount the show. Next week, I'm taking the assistant curator, Jeannine, and an adorable little intern, Pam, for lunch at Compass, and they're taking me clubbing in the Village, to a hot spot called Sweet Rhythm, which I've heard good things about.

The point of my telling you all this is that you never know who you'll meet or whose life you'll touch. A princess is ever mindful of this. The larger your sphere of influence, the more important it is to be yourself, and to be the best possible you. That's the only real way to be a positive influence on anyone. That's what makes people want to rub elbows with *you,* not the other way around. Contessina doesn't give me gifts *just* because I'm a devoted patron who happened to jump-start her American career (by the way, the meeting with Chi-Chi was smashing, and the feature is going to put Contessina's name on the lips of every fashionista from coast to coast), she does it because she enjoys being around me. Millicent may have approached me because she found my choker dazzling (she isn't exactly bauble-deprived herself, you know, thanks to her husband's renown as a surgeon), but she extended our conversation because she enjoyed my company. So even if you don't have all the rubbing-elbows trappings, you are still a princess, still the woman every person in the room with taste and discernment flocks to and wants to be around.

Enjoy your influence, your glamour, your everything. I'm so proud of how well you're doing. Your P.Q. is already through the roof, no doubt (if it wasn't naturally when we began).

On Entertainment

A princess makes life a ball.

9

It's girls' night out again, darling! Downtown, this time.
Clarice, Mariana and I are meeting the girls I know from
the Metropolitan, Jeannine and Pam, at Sweet Rhythm in
the Village.

I'm head-to-toe Prada for the club scene: black leather
miniskirt, black mohair sweater, black knee-high boots.
Very Village. Even though I'm really an uptown girl, I
love a good downtown adventure. And I love making
new friends. Jeannine and Pam seem great, and were
thrilled to include Clarice and Mariana. Which is terrific
because I am never happier than when all my friends are
having a good time. (Of course, Nirvana won't be joining us. She's in the process of a ritual cleansing prior to
a midnight meditation with her guru. Something about
Venus lining up with—Pluto? Neptune? Uranus? I can't
remember which planet—for the first time in however
many gazillion years. It's this huge cosmic opportunity to
meditate with her guru at this time, she said. When she's
done she'll have erased aeons of karmic debt. If Nirvana

were really happy, I'd be happy for her, but she never looks happy. Anyway, she's trying to talk Clarice, Mariana and I into going on retreat with her to a spa in Sedona in a few weeks…and we'll probably go just to see what it's all about. But I digress.)

Clarice and I arrive at about ten-thirty, and the place is already packed and hopping. The bouncer gives us a bit of a hard time (I think he was just trying to hit on Clarice), so I ask to see the manager. When he arrives, I'm shocked to see it's Pierre from La Place de la Concorde, who wanted to drink absinthe from my Louboutins. (You remember. Ostensibly he was a method actor getting in character, but I think he just had a foot fetish and probably still does.) Pierre, infuriatingly enough, has a rather skewed recollection of our meeting in Paris. In his memory, *I* wanted him to drink out of my Louboutins. Right.

"Well, Pierre," I purr, "regardless of how you remember that evening in Paris, you will let my friend and me into the club. Kindly tell your bouncer to step aside."

"Your Highness, my apologies," says Pierre with a sweep of his arm, falling all over himself in the process, and nearly getting tangled in the velvet ropes he undoes to usher us into the club. "Your friends are already here. Please follow me."

I graciously refrain from reminding him that I should not be confronted by a bouncer even if my friends weren't already here. (You know I don't like to pull rank, darling, but some things are simply unacceptable. By the way, in case you're wondering how Jeannine and Pam got a table when there's such a crowd outside that *I* was stopped by the bouncer, Pam's brother is the band's bassist.)

Pierre steers us to the table where Jeannine and Pam are sitting. He seats us, then turns and smiles broadly at me. His foot fetish betraying him (I *knew* it!), he glances surreptitiously at my boots, then thinks better of it. I mean, a knee-high boot would probably take an entire bottle, maybe even two.

"Thank you, Pierre," I say. "Another friend, Mariana, will be joining us. Please see to it that she's allowed in without a hassle."

"My brother left all the names with you," Pam puts in.

Pierre gives me a short bow, moving so stiffly his beret flies off his head. "I will see to seating her personally, Your Highness. And the first round is on the house."

I nod my thanks.

"Mar could slip through the ropes without anyone seeing her, Jacquie, so don't worry," Clarice chuckles.

A few minutes later, a flushed Pierre brings Mariana to our table.

A true princess helps those around her feel as comfortable doing what feels right for them as she does doing what feels right for her.

We settle into our seats, prepared to have an amazing time.

"We waited to order till you got here," Pam tells us, motioning to one of the waitresses. "And it worked out great. Free round and all."

The waitress comes over and reminds us, "This is your free round, girls." She starts with Pam, who's closest to her.

"Boilermaker," says Pam.

"Dirty martini," says Jeannine.

"French cosmopolitan," says Clarice, squeezing my forearm. She's been dying to try one ever since she saw it in a Grey Goose ad.

"Vodka martini," I say.

"Same," says Mariana.

I cast a sidelong glance at her, hoping she isn't ordering a drink just because we're out with people we don't know.

Clarice doesn't miss it, either. "I've never seen you order one of those before," she says pointedly.

Mariana shrugs it off. "Time for a change," she says briskly. Clarice and I exchange a glance. Maybe those *glacés* had a more profound effect than I even guessed.

We chat for a bit, but are soon drowned out by the band, which returns after the break they were on when Clarice and I arrived. Speaking loudly and slowly to be sure we understand, Pam tells us not to make a big display trying to get her brother's attention. It's very uncool from the musicians' perspective. He'll have drinks with us at the end of this set.

Our drinks arrive, and Mariana takes a good-size swig.

"Sweetie, that's not Evian," I tell her as Jeannine and Pam turn their chairs so they're facing the band.

Mariana spurts, then coughs. "I can tell," she finally manages, coughing again. Mariana has never had a drink in her life. She was so terrified of gaining the freshman ten in college that she put herself on a radical diet in high school. When she discovered the calorie content in alcohol, she vowed never to touch a drop, and never did until tonight. "I guess I shouldn't have ordered something that looks like water and has no smell, huh?"

"Next time, get a Manhattan," I suggest. "They're too sweet to gulp."

Mariana cringes at the word *sweet,* no doubt feeling the carb-grams looming, and says, "How about just scotch on the rocks?"

Patting her shoulder, I say, "Mar, just get your usual club drink. It's what you like." Mariana doesn't like to just order water at clubs, so she gets club soda for fizz factor. I know I'm always talking about Mariana needing to set aside her calculator and just enjoy herself, but she gets to do that in her own time and her own way, not because someone else is pressuring her or making her feel awkward or uncomfortable.

Mariana smiles at me, brightening at the suggestion of club soda and nudging the martini glass away with two fingers.

We spend the rest of the evening enjoying our drinks and the music. (Mariana keeps her martini to the side and happily orders a large quantity of club sodas, pleased that Jeannine and Pam don't even notice.)

"So Clar, how's that French cosmo?" I want to know.

Winking at me, she purrs, *"Ooh-la-la!"*

"I was going to say the same thing about Pam's brother," Jeannine confides.

The rest of us can see why.

"Go for it, girl!" Clarice tells Jeannine. "Ben Affleck with a bass."

Sweet Rhythm is definitely a keeper. And it looks like Jeannine and the bassist will be sharing some rhythms before too long…but in a more private setting.

Yawn!! Oh, excuse me, darling. We practically closed the club last night, and I'm EXHAUSTED this morning. The only word I can focus on right now is "coffee," which I will hopefully find brewed in the kitchen. Hmm, let's see. *Yes!!* God bless Jean-Paul. There's a whole pot of mocha java just waiting for me. I couldn't be more grateful. Okay, let me just pop in an ice cube so I can take a few substantial swallows and I'll be good to go.

Now, aside from clubbing, you're probably wondering what else I do for entertainment. There are *oodles* of things I enjoy doing, but of course, many of my evenings are occupied by charity fetes, galas and things of that sort, which I have to attend either because of the Foundation, or as the official de Soignée representative (read: my father insists, and I must obey—a born-a-princess duty of which I am distinctly NOT fond.) Still, obligations notwithstanding, I go to film premieres, and to restaurant, gallery and show openings.

Hollywood premieres aren't my favorite. (Unless it's a Jean-Paul Fameux or Pedro Almódovar film, in which case, I am so *there!*) Anyway, what can I say? I'm just not a Hollywood/L.A. person, and never have been. You would think that, with my love of Evian, avocados and tofu, I'd fit right in, I know, but I can't get into it, even after a full day on Rodeo Drive, so I usually just hop the next first-class flight out of LAX to LaGuardia. At heart, I'm just a Manhattan girl. I do love film retrospectives, though. I flew out to L.A. for an Audrey Hepburn retrospective, followed by a costume party where every guest had to come dressed in an outfit from their favorite Audrey flick. My *Breakfast at Tiffany's* costume won first prize. (Deservedly so, if I do say so myself—with a brunette wig, gloves and authentic Tiff's goodies, how could I lose?)

Aside from that, though, I'm really more of a Broadway fan. Broadway openings are just the best. When *Hairspray* opened, I was there in a Pucci sheath, D & G go-go boots and BIG hair (mine, just teased). When *Mamma Mia!* opened, I wore the most fabulous pair of multicolor floral-print Thierry Mugler bell-bottoms and a lavender satin djellaba cut to fall a few inches above the knee. The paparazzi were practically falling over one another fighting for the best shot. Ha! Oh, and when *Contact* opened a few years ago, I was there in my yellow dress—a Sonia Rykiel original, I might add, with Charles Jourdan lemon *peau de soie* pumps. (Incidentally, I was dating one of the producers, who told me all about the Girl in the Yellow Dress before everyone else knew all about her, and before he proved himself to be a *very* green frog.) And it goes without saying that I use all these appearances to get to meet important people who will support the work of the Foundation.

Of course, restaurant openings are a blast, too. When

Alain Ducasse opened, naturally, I was there. You know how I adore French food. Just for fun, I wore a Jean-Paul Gaultier Apache-dancer outfit—tight black slit skirt, fishnets, a black-and-white-striped tee, T-strap spike heels, black neckerchief and bloodred beret. Alain was ecstatic. He sent me home with a year's supply of pastries. (I am not exaggerating. Clarice had to beg me to stop bringing her éclairs every morning.)

Now, just because I enjoy these openings and participate in the festivities with my little costumes doesn't mean that I view myself as the entertainment committee. Nothing could be further from the truth. I enjoy wearing costumes, so I wear them. One film producer who attended the party following the Audrey retro found that out the hard way. He sauntered over to me in that "hey, baby" smarmy way and gave me his card, telling me to put it in a safe spot in my Rolodex.

"I don't have a Rolodex," I told him, sipping my martini.

"That's cool, baby. PalmPilot, then. And gimme your card," he ordered, patting the cigar in his jacket pocket. "I want you to come for a screen test on Monday."

A screen test?! *Excuse you,* I wanted to say, but restrained myself. Instead, I demanded, "Do you know who I am?" (A fabulous princess-by-birth perk, pulling rank on the sleazy and smarmy. Nothing can compare to a true princessly put-down in the satisfaction department.)

"I know you're supposed to be the girl from *Breakfast at Tiffany's,*" he said, annoyed. "And you look pretty good."

A woman standing not far behind him leaned over and whispered in his ear as I watched his face turn white, then gray, then pea green.

As a waiter passed, I deposited my martini glass and Mr. Smarmy's card on his tray, turned on my heel and walked away, hearing him sputter, "How was I supposed to know? She looked just like Hepburn in that movie! I figured she was a kid from the Valley." Alas for him, he hasn't made too many successful films since then. *Tsk, tsk*.

A princess does not entertain. A princess *is* entertained.

I don't mean this in a demanding or stuck-up way, of course. A princess loves to regale, amuse and charm those she cares about. As you are well aware by now, no one is more charming than a true princess. But a princess does not feel *compelled* to be a source of amusement. That's the difference. And she certainly expects those she associates with to be charming, witty and a joy to be around, just as she herself is. Not that she expects her friends to *perform* for her—of course she doesn't. (She's a princess, not a producer. Although, being an executive producer is just fabu!) But she does not waste her time with people whose company she doesn't find delightful. Period. And if she wants people to perform for her, she gets the best seats in the house. Which is exactly what I have for tonight. (*The Lion King* for the twelfth time, in case you're wondering.)

Sometimes, of course, I'm not in the mood to go out. I just don't feel like getting dressed up and all. (A stretch to imagine, I know, and it doesn't happen often.) In that case, I pop in a DVD to watch alone, or invite Clarice over—with munchies, of course! There's nothing like curling up on the sofa with a laugh-out-loud, then cry-your-eyes-out chick flick. Or something that's just cute and fun. Aside from *Gone with the Wind* and just about every movie Audrey Hepburn ever made and all the wonderful Hollywood classics (and every Fameux film, of course) some newer movies I just love are *Legally Blonde, Divine Secrets of the Ya-Ya Sisterhood, Kate & Leopold*... I could go on and on. I really love movies, it's the Hollywood premiere scene that I can't stand because of the paparazzi. (Next newspaper photo of a New York premiere that you see, look closely for me. I'll probably be at the edge of the photo with a gloved hand held up in warning at the paparazzi. For goodness' sakes, can't a girl just go to the movies?)

Off to Broadway! *Ciao* for now, darling. Hugs and kisses!

On Vacationing

A princess knows when it's time to just get away from it all.

10

Bonjour, chérie! I'm in St. Tropez with Jean-Paul Fameux. *The Stench* (version two) is in the can, and since I'm executive producer, Jean-Paul insisted that I come for a private screening before the big "private" premiere. I went to see the rushes, too, hoping Brandon Charmant would be there, but at the last minute, he didn't show up. *Quel dommage!* Jean-Paul promises that Brandon will come to St. Tropez. Anyway, St. Tropez is *formidable* as always, and we watched the film last night. Definitely Cannes material. (My walk-on is *magnifique,* if I may say so.)

Right now, Jean-Paul is trying to convince me to go topless. "You are in St. Tropez, *bébé.* You behave so like an American, no one would believe you are of French heritage."

"But Jean-Paul, I was born in America. Of course I behave like an American!" It's true that usually I follow the when-in-St. Tropez guidelines and wear my bikini *sans* top, but ever since Trixie Loquor, I'm more concerned about paparazzi than ever. I explain this to Jean-Paul.

"You are in St. Tropez!" he repeats. "What's wrong with you?"

"Jean-Paul, I'm not arguing with you about this. It's out of the question."

"I'm sorry. I didn't mean to upset you, *bébé*." And as he reaches out to hug me, his wristwatch catches the closure on my top and it comes undone.

FLASH! CLICK! SNAP!

Oh my God! I cannot *believe* what just happened. (I can, of course, given the way things have been going lately, but it's no less upsetting.) Apparently, a paparazzo hiding in the next cabana was just waiting to descend upon us. Ugh! In a flash, Jean-Paul throws a towel over me and lunges for the camera. Thanks to his stunt training for his role as the cop in *The Stench,* he tackles the paparazzo and gets the camera, which he opens to expose the film.

"Just friends, still?" The unmistakable rasp of Trixie Loquor falls on my ear with all the melody of scraping sandpaper. (Seriously, the woman must chain-smoke three packs a day.) She is so furious, the steam curls out of her ears.

"I protect my friends," hisses Jean-Paul, shoving the man. He turns to reclaim the camera, but Jean-Paul gives him a don't-even-think-about-it glare, and he heads off with an I'm-outta-here toss of his head at Trixie, who he's obviously in cahoots with.

"I'll finish both of you off this time!" she vows, turning on her heel and following her photographer off the beach, the sand she kicks up sticking to her head-to-toe black in splotches.

Jean-Paul heard that Trixie was furious when he ruined her coup by announcing that he was pulling Marco Trevini from *The Stench*. All the retractions the Foundation lawyers have been demanding have put a decided crimp in her style. She came to St. Tropez gunning for the both of us. Too bad she's going to be so disappointed. *Never* cross a princess!

"Pay her no mind, *bébé,*" Jean-Paul tells me.

I smile at him, but the charm of the beach is gone for both of us, so we gather our things and head back to Jean-Paul's house. After we change, we decide to go out for a late-afternoon coffee, settling on a bistro near one of the hotels. I need to use the ladies' room, but the bistro's is out of order, so I walk to the hotel to use theirs. It's an old-world rest room with true water closets, not stalls. The first door is locked, so I go into the second one, where I'm most distressed to hear moans and a thump against the dividing wall. Rest room etiquette is always a sticky situation, even for a princess. After I wash my hands, I tap gently on the door, deciding the person could truly be ill. I barely have time to jump out of the way before the door bursts open, revealing the source of moaning and thumping: Trixie Loquor, her arms and legs locked around Archibald Cranston, Hortense's husband. In the same position, they tumble to the floor, as the busted door crashes.

"Well, if it isn't Trixie Loquor, the illustrious journalist of our time! Going for the Pulitzer with this one?" I keep my voice pleasant and my eyes sharp. "Archibald, Hortense never mentioned that your media empire extended to a vote for that prize."

"There's a lot about Archie that Hortense doesn't know," Trixie informs me.

"Obviously," I say. In that instant I realize that in addition to the highbrow magazines that haughtily bear the Cranston Publishing banner, as well as his vast real-estate holdings, Archibald owns tabloids, too. I also know for a certainty that prim-and-proper Hortense knows nothing about these tabloids or about her husband's cheating. Hortense would never stand for either one. Even my flush of glory at having trapped Trixie Loquor in a far more compromising position than she's ever trapped me (or ever will), I feel a pang of remorse for Hortense. I don't like the woman, but even she deserves better than this. I keep my face inscrutable as the lovebirds disentangle themselves.

"All I want is Archie. Who cares about the damn Pulitzer?" Trixie spits, standing up and adjusting her too-short, too-tight skirt, now quite twisted from her activities. Archibald is so stunned, he hasn't even managed to zip up. (I try not to stare, but get enough of a glimpse to be able to tell you I'm beginning to understand why Hortense is so chronically, shall we say, dissatisfied. Trixie is obviously doing this for career advancement.)

"Only the people who are good enough to win them," I reply sweetly, satisfied to see that I hit a nerve, in addition to exposing her. Then I realize that I won't have any proof of anything. It will only be my word against theirs.

With that, from the other side of the main door to the ladies' room, I hear Jean-Paul's voice. He took the photographer's camera with him when we left the house and put in a new roll of film, saying he'd always wanted to snap paparazzi shots. I pray he didn't leave it on the bistro table.

"Don't worry about it, babe," Archibald tells Trixie as he staggers to his feet. "You've got enough on her." He starts groping her again, as if I'm not even standing there. Trixie goes along. What is wrong with them? (If I find out they're method actors, too, I'm going to absolutely scream, then check myself into that spa on the Dead Sea for a month.)

"Three's a crowd!" I say breezily, slipping outside and motioning frantically to Jean-Paul, where he stands at the concierge's desk a few feet away.

"There you are! Are you all right?"

"No time to explain. I'll open the door. You just start snapping that camera and don't stop!"

"Jacquie—"

"Now!" I order, in my most imperious tone, flinging the door open.

Jean-Paul does as he's told, seeing who we've cornered in the same second he starts snapping. I whisper in his ear that the man is Hortense Cranston's husband, and I'll explain the rest of what I've figured out later.

Trixie does her best to lunge out of Archibald's embrace to seize the camera, but they're standing with her back against the wall, so all she manages to do is topple them both. (Few among us have Mariana's agility, after all.)

"Kudos on finishing us off," I call over my shoulder as Jean-Paul shuts the door and we hurry out of the hotel.

After getting the film developed and FedEx'ing it to the Foundation the following day, I call Hortense, wanting her to hear the news directly from me.

"You will have my resignation when you return. A tabloid owner should not sit on the board of a literacy foundation."

"Archibald doesn't sit on my board, Hortense."

"But I do."

"And obviously you knew of none of this. I will not accept your resignation unless you no longer wish to serve."

"Why are you doing this when we've fought so in the past?"

"One thing has nothing to do with the other."

"I'm going to be humiliated, you know," she interjects.

"Not by the Foundation or by me."

"Thank you. I won't forget your kindness."

I'll say she won't! Not that I'm worried about it. Somehow, all this has transformed Hortense, or maybe I'm seeing her in a new light. The ability to forgive is an important princessly attribute. Bear in mind, however: A princess forgives but never forgets.

Hortense and I say our goodbyes and hang up.

After all this, I'm really not up for Jean-Paul's big premiere. Since I've had my private screening, I beg off until the New York premiere. I just need to go off by myself for a bit, and even the prospect of seeing Brandon Charmant isn't enough of an incentive to stay. Thankfully, Jean-Paul understands.

A princess knows when it's time to just get away from the getaway, too.
(Some vacations require another vacation.)

Buon giorno, carissima! I'm at my villa in Tuscany. Ah, *la dolce vita!* I simply adore the villa. It's just south of Siena, and not far from Florence. It really isn't even all that far from Rome, by train or car. (In the Maserati that I drive here, I can get to Rome in no time.) Right now, I'm just enjoying my cappuccino out on the veranda. Sandro, the gardener, keeps the jasmine and lemon trees just beautifully, and the scent is the most heavenly you could imagine. Sandro's wife, Simonetta, who is the most adorable woman, dries the flowers and makes potpourri and sachets out of them, which she sells in Siena, but always sends a lovely batch of each to my mother and me. Isn't that so thoughtful? This is the perfect place to recharge my battery after The Debacle and all that went on in St. Tropez.

Now, you may be thinking that my vacation from the vacation could have been the upcoming retreat in Sedona with the girls. Somehow I'm not thinking that's going to be much of a vacation. More like a few days in a row at Elizabeth Arden, but with a lot of bizarre-sounding prayers and my feet falling asleep in the lotus position. (I'll probably need another vacation after Sedona, too. So will Clarice. Maybe I can finally talk her into taking a cruise with me. There's a permanent de Soignée suite on the Q. E. II. Talk about relaxing! If we hadn't promised Nirvana, I would just bag Sedona altogether. But I'll tell you all about Sedona when we get there, darling. Meanwhile, back to Tuscany.)

I'm off for a spin in the Maserati now. Destination:

Florence. The *gioiellerie* along the Ponte Vecchio beckon, darling, and I must heed the call.

Bella Firenze! No wonder they call it that. It's absolutely gorgeous here. Aside from the quaint charm of the city, there's a slew of magnificent buildings, and I can't tell you how many fabulous works of art in the Uffizi and the Accademia. (It's worth a trip to Florence just to see Michelangelo's *David* live—whoever modeled for that was one hottie, let me tell you...talk about perfection. "Mercy," as Clarice would say.) It's impossible to take it all in in one trip. In fact, there's SO much culture here, I'm not even going to attempt to absorb any today. Today, I am here strictly for the Ponte Vecchio, strictly for *gioielli*.

I decide to pop in to Bottega Veneta and Ferragamo before heading for the Ponte Vecchio. There is a bag in Bottega that is just too adorable. Garnet-red calfskin trimmed in espresso brown. Sublime. While the salesgirl (they still call them that in Italy) is wrapping it up, I see a pair of boots out of the corner of my eye and turn to get a full view.

Gasp! They're over-the-knee, aubergine woven leather with suede ribbons that cross around the ankles and tie like espadrille laces. And they're fully lined in aubergine suede so the woven leather won't scratch, and also so you can cuff the top and have a triangle of suede tuck down just below the knee in front, if you don't want to wear them over the knee. I have never seen such a beautiful pair of boots in my entire life. Not even at D & G. (Don't say that I said so. I feel so disloyal. But I can't lie.) Sigh. There is no way I'm leaving without these boots. I ask to see them in a 5½, and of course they fit like a glove. I have them wrapped up to be sent to the villa along with the bag, then head straight for the Ponte Vecchio, bypassing Ferragamo because my taste for suede and leather has been sated for today.

I can smell the Arno wafting on the breeze as I approach my favorite jeweler in all of Florence: S. Vaggi. These are master craftsmen who've been setting jewelry for centuries. Every piece of theirs that I have is hand-set, and I've never seen any other pieces that even look remotely like them. They're truly one-of-a-kind. That's always fun, to have things that are unique and not like anything that anyone else has. And you don't have to spend a lot of money to achieve that. Just go to thrift shops, yard sales, vintage shops, and you'll find plenty of unique and interesting things. As you already know, it's all about creating your own style, not spending a ton of money you can't afford.

Today at Vaggi, I select a woven white-gold bracelet that looks like a bangle but actually is a regular bracelet with a flat clasp. It looks hard but flexes to the touch. Each piece of the weave is hand-set. A work of art, and exquisite, too. Hmm, what's that platinum Byzantine-style chain? *Ooh!* That's gorgeous, too. And that small but intensely colored Burmese ruby enhancer over there would look just *favoloso* hanging from it. My mother's birthday is coming up, and she would just love that (then, of course, I can borrow it!). I wait for the bracelet and the necklace and enhancer to be wrapped in those adorable little suede pouches Italian jewelers pack jewelry in.

I can't wait to see my mother's face when she opens her gift! She'll be so excited. If you think your mother is hard to buy for, try having a royal mother. But she'll love this. When she and my father went to Thailand and Myanmar, she was all psyched to get a Burmese ruby, but they had to cut the trip short, so she never did get to pick one out. And now she'll have one. I love finding the perfect gift, especially when I'm on vacation, and everything I shop for becomes a souvenir.

After some serious Ponte Vecchio "therapy," I feel all the stress of both The Debacle and St. Tropez melt away. And I must say, I've lost all track of time. Annamaria, the cook at the villa, gets very upset if I'm late for meals. (It only happened once, believe me. Italian is a beautiful language, but not when spoken between sobs.) I hop in the Maserati and head back to the villa. The sun setting on the Tuscan hills is truly a spectacular sight, and I arrive at the villa just in time. What a relief! I can't stand to see Annamaria cry. On my way from the Ponte Vecchio to the car, I picked up some candied lavender and violets—her favorites—so she becomes quickly contented when I greet her with a cheerful *"Buona sera,"* and present her with her adored *confetti*.

Whew! I dash upstairs to change for dinner: risotto with black truffles and cannellini beans, and arugula and pecorino salad. My mouth is already watering. Annamaria is the best cook in Tuscany.

When traveling, a princess strives to stay in palaces, châteaux, villas and five-star hotels/resorts. Any other accommodation is really "roughing it," as far as a princess is concerned, but she makes the best of things.

Back in my suite, I breathe in the heavenly scent of the jasmine and lemon trees. Francesca, the housekeeper at the villa, keeps all the linens stored away with the sachets that Simonetta makes, and she fills all the drawers and closets with the sachets, too. The entire villa is a haven of constant aromatherapy. Just divine. Much as I love my penthouse, nothing compares to the way I get pampered here at the villa. True, day after day, week after week, year in and year out, it would probably start to get on my nerves. But a week or two is easy to enjoy. *Very easy.*

Francesca even sees to it that there's a small but exquisite piece of handmade bittersweet Italian chocolate on my pillow every night, right in the center of that sublime four-hundred-count cotton pillowcase. (The cotton is so soft and smooth, it feels like silk. Even the cotton towels in the bathroom feel silky. I use Frette linens at home, and they're wonderful, but these Italian ones are simply beyond compare. Why have I never thought to have some sent to New York? I scribble a hasty note to remind myself to talk to Francesca about this.)

I change into silk pants and a silk knit twinset. (It's Armani—I only wear Italian in Italy, and my new cache of Contessina Sfilato-di Moda has not yet arrived, aside from the gifts she gave me. She was so surprised by the groundswell of popularity that she was woefully understocked and is working like a demon to fill up for a trunk show at Bergdorf's, which I'm presiding over.) Slipping on a pair of Gucci backless loafers, I head for the dining room.

After another few days, I've had my fill of serenity. Delicious as the food is, glorious as the surroundings are, luxuriant as the pampering by the villa household staff is, I am all but overwhelmed by a hankering for Manhattan. I feel oh-so-rested and completely recovered from both The Debacle and St. Tropez, but truthfully, I miss my friends (especially Clarice) and I miss my New York life. I can never stay away from Manhattan for too long. Tomorrow, I'll call the pilot and tell him I'm ready to head back home.

Vacations are wonderful and necessary. But just as a princess knows when to get away, she also knows when it's time to go home.

On Relaxation

A princess knows that relaxing is one of the three R's.*

11

(* The other two are "rejuvenating" and "replenishing.")

Hello, darling. I'm just refreshing an arrangement of hydrangeas and lilacs that I put together yesterday. Flower arranging is one of my hobbies—very calming and lots of fun, too. I enrolled in a floral-design program at Parsons a few years ago, and when I finished the course, I was awarded not only a certificate in floral design, but also one in fashion design. The dean told me to think of the latter as a "lifetime-achievement honorary degree." Wasn't that sweet? I don't take it seriously, of course. True, I have a natural flair for fashion and style, as every princess must, but that doesn't make me a designer.

There. That looks so much better. The hydrangeas looked fine, but the lilacs were getting a little weepy. This is my favorite assortment: The cream, purple and blue in the flowers pick up the Aubusson carpet in the room perfectly. Besides, I just adore being surrounded by flowers. My chamberlain is such a dear. Jean-Paul dashes off daily to bring me fresh flowers. In fact, the pink torch ginger I had in my breakfast nook died yesterday, but I told Jean-Paul not to replace it until I'm heading back from Sedona. What a lovely welcome that will be!

The time has just flown by since I got back from Tuscany, darling. The girls and I are off to Sedona tomorrow. I know I was hesitant at first, but then I thought, *What could be bad about a week at a spa?* And now I can't wait. Clarice has managed to convince me to try flying coach, after all. I was horrified at the prospect at first, but decided to make the princessly best of it, and now I'm looking forward to it as a grand adventure, and have been practicing elbow positions while sitting in armchairs during the past several days. (I can't even bear the thought of being considered an armrest hog, whether by one of my friends or by a stranger and fellow traveler. I think I've got elbow etiquette down, though. Thank goodness.)

Clarice and I were looking through the spa brochure the other day, and there are all sorts of wonderful features and amenities: facials, steam therapy, mud baths, reflexology, hot-stones massage, seaweed wraps, mineral-salt rubs—you name it. Just like Elizabeth Arden, but when you turn on the massage table and get to peek out the window, you see red rocks and mesas instead of standard New York sights. (It's been ages since I've had a mud bath, and I'm so looking forward to it.) Oh, and there was something about rosemary aromatherapy massages for energizing in the morning and lavender aromatherapy massages for relaxing before bedtime. Doesn't that just sound heavenly? The rosemary regimen in the morning is supposed to be in lieu of caffeine. Gasp! Clarice and I have decided to just not think about the implication there. I mean, how relaxing could caffeine withdrawal possibly be? I'm sure they mean it as an option not a requirement. Clarice isn't so sure. I've told her not to worry. (There's bound to be a Starbucks not too far away if we get desperate.)

Wait a sec, Nirvana is on the phone for me. She's trying to "sell" me on the meditation and yoga for the gazillionth time. Sigh. I keep telling her that she should just enjoy what she wants to do while we're there and let the rest of us do the same. Truth to tell, I'm just not a good meditator. I really don't get it. When I focus on cosmic good intention and turn my closed eyes up toward my "third eye," I don't attain illumination. I do get a cluster headache, though, and the muscle running from my jaw to my neck sort of clamps up. (Which is why Clarice says that TMJ really stands for "the meditation joke.") All in all, not what I consider to be relaxing. As far as yoga goes, they only do *bikram* at this retreat, and I do not consider exercising in front of space heaters relaxing, rejuvenating or replenishing. Ridiculous is the only R that applies to such an undertaking.

"How can exercising in front of a space heater possibly be healthy?" I ask Nirvana.

"The heat makes your muscles more supple and also releases toxins," she tells me, speaking slowly and patiently. I'm not sure whether this tone is meant to calm me or show me that she thinks I'm a nonilluminated type needing to be enlightened. Hmm.

"Nirvana," I say gently, "I was over once when you were in the middle of one of those—er—sessions. You could have fried an egg in the room, that's how hot it was."

She draws in her breath, and I realize I might have offended her with the animal-product reference. "Sorry," I add quickly. "You could have—um—fried tofu. Or seitan."

Nirvana relaxes a bit and pronounces, "You're exaggerating, Jacquie."

I am not exaggerating in the slightest. I had a plumcot in my bag for an afternoon snack, and after I left Nirvana's it was a *prune*cot.

"Look, Nirvana, as I keep telling you, you'll do what

you want to do while we're in Sedona, and let the rest of us do the same," I suggest for the umpteenth time.

"But I want all of you to experience these processes. Especially *bikram*. It's a cosmic—"

Although I usually don't interrupt, I must here. "Nirvana, I'm going to Sedona to feel comfortable not combustible. Gotta run, sweetie. See you tomorrow."

I hang up and shake my head. When I'm exercising, the only things that get cranked are the tunes and the A/C. Space heaters? I don't think so.

I really must run, because I'm meeting Clarice for coffee and cheesecake. We figure we'd better have our last sugar, fat and caffeine fix before we head off to the wilderness.

"Treat" and "retreat" have far greater differences than just that little "re."★★

(★★ Which is why "retreat" is not one of the three R's of the princess!)

Sedona is magnificent. What a majestic landscape! What clean, dry air! What an absence of boutiques and chic bistros! Hmm. I'm sure the weeklong respite will be as relaxing, rejuvenating and replenishing as I expect it to be, but I could *never* live here. Nirvana said it was "raw nature." Perhaps she's right. A princess is *not* a creature of nature. A princess is civilized at the very least. And pampered at the very best. Not to worry, though. I will make the best of it, as every princess always should.

We've been shown to our rooms and advised that dinner will be served in an hour, after which we'll have our before-bedtime lavender massages. Thank God! The coach flight was bearable and really wouldn't have been too bad if I wasn't accustomed to flying first-class (and no errant elbows, I'm proud and happy to report!), but we're all a bit stiff and all in, not to mention famished. (Flying coach is something I don't plan to do again in the near future. Sigh. A true princess will do anything to make her friends feel comfortable.) I take a shower and change, then mark all the spa amenities I want to try during the coming week.

No sooner have I finished making notes on my brochure when a gong begins sounding, reverberating throughout the building—not to mention every eardrum therein. Perhaps this is the Sedonan version of the dinner bell. I rise, open the door to my room and step into the hallway, only to find myself plastered against the wall by the gong's next reverberation. Or was it an earthquake? Clarice comes out of her room, too. We brace ourselves against the wall in preparation for gong number three, but it seems the second will be the last. Mariana and Nirvana come out of their rooms, too, and Nirvana leads the way to the dining room. Clarice and I bite our lips to keep from bursting out laughing.

Once we've been seated and served, there's no cause for amusement. We each receive a plate with a medallion of seitan, seven mung sprouts and five shreds of Chinese cabbage. Even Mariana gapes at the small portion.

"What a lovely appetizer," I say, feigning optimism that an entrée—any additional food—will be forthcoming before morning.

Nirvana rolls her eyes at me. "This is more than ample for anyone pursuing advanced spiritual evolution and enlightenment."

"Thanks for telling us this was a fasting vacation," Clarice puts in. Hunger makes her a little cranky. "If we're very good, can we each get a carrot?"

"Of course not!" Nirvana is horrified. "Carrots have to be *dug up,* Clarice." Nirvana lowers her voice at "carrots," lest any other attendees be as offended as she herself is.

Clarice kicks me under the table.

"This isn't a normal portion for adults, Nirvana, and some of us came here for a week at a spa not a lamasery."

After a deep cleansing breath, Nirvana advises, "Better eat up. We only have ten minutes."

"What do they do for a power lunch?" Clarice says under her breath.

Right about now, I'm ready to retreat to New York on the next flight—even if it's the red-eye, coach class. (I wonder if Elizabeth Arden will do a weeklong thing. I'll have to check on that.)

After what I'll loosely refer to as "dinner," we have our lavender aromatherapy massages, as promised, but they are far from sublime. The lavender smells heavenly, of course, but their idea of a massage is my idea of a pummeling. Maybe it's just because I'm irritated about "dinner." In any case, I'm back in my room now, and so exhausted that I'm sure I'll fall away, despite the rumbling and growling of my very empty tummy. I climb into bed and snuggle down for a good night's sleep. In the morning I'll feel better, and just spend the entire day at the spa. (Hopefully they give yummy fruit snacks like at Elizabeth Arden Red Door.)

BONG! BONG! BONG! BONG! BONG! BONG! BONG! BONG!

I'm jolted out of bed by an infernal noise and reverberation. *What?!* As my head clears, I remember the gong from the night before. Do they herald midnight here? It's pitch-black outside. I glance at the nightstand clock: five o'clock. Can this be the morning wake-up call? Those dawn meditations Nirvana's been going on and on about can't possibly be mandatory. Let me go out into the hallway to see what I can find out....

Well, just when I thought that this retreat was absolutely *devoid* of any treats whatsoever, it only gets worse: At five o'clock every morning, we will be awakened, taken for our ten-minute rosemary pummelings—massages—then marched in for meditation until nine. After that, breakfast (who knows? three nuts or a thimbleful of oats would be my guess), then a hike, followed by *bikram,* and another meditation. Then we have an hour for spa amenities, followed by dinner and lavender massages. I'm ready to bag Red Rocks, and head back to Red Door and real food, but Clarice convinces me to at least see what the meditation is like, so off we go.

The mantra of a princess needs to be pronounceable.

Post-rosemary, we're each given a garment that looks sort of like a caftan (but with a bulkier fit and a flap of material that goes over one shoulder, and made of rough fabric in that hideous shade of yellow-orange that Nirvana calls saffron, "the color of enlightenment"), and told to sit on the floor in the lotus position. Sigh. I knew it. By the time we leave this place, my ankles will be shot. I'll need a week of reflexology in New York before I can walk in Manolos.

Nirvana's guru, who is leading the meditation, arrives, bows and greets us with *"Namaste."*

We bow and return the greeting.

He walks over to a large frosted-glass bowl, picks up what looks like a drumstick with a foam ball at the end of it, taps a few spots inside the bowl, then rubs the outside rim several times, unleashing an otherworldly low hum. (Might be an interesting sound at a club after a day's worth of caffeine and a martini, but at fifteen minutes past ungodly, it's unbearable. And in very poor taste, if you ask me. Some people have sensitive hearing. Some people like to sleep beyond when the moon goes down. Some people like to eat. Conclusion: This is a very rude and inconsiderate establishment. Indubitably NON-princessly.)

"Release samsara," intones the guru.

Clarice and I exchange a sidelong glance. Those more advanced, Nirvana included, mumble back what sounds like, "Dhourywardjaklapi." The only Samsara I've ever heard of is the perfume.

"Release maya," he intones.

I have no intention of babbling incoherently, wearing a scratchy (not to mention HIGHLY unfashionable) garment and sitting with my feet falling asleep and my spine in what feels like a soon-to-be permanent cramp. Nor do I have any intention of starving myself for a week or staying at a spa where I can only avail myself of the amenities for an hour a day. And I certainly have no intention of exercising in the equivalent of a kiln.

A princess knows when she's had enough.

I rise noiselessly and pad to the back of the room, then wait for Clarice and Mariana to notice and follow. Just as carefully, I open the door behind me, and no sooner have I done so, when the guru does the bowl thing again, asking in heavily accented English what we're doing.

"This isn't what we expected, sir, so we're leaving," I tell him graciously.

"Not allowed to leave. Not till I say so."

Nirvana gapes at me with a look of fury and mortification, as the guru rushes to the back of the room.

"With all due respect, sir, when I recognize that I've had enough, or something is wrong for me, I don't continue with whatever it is."

"Approved for program, must stay."

Suddenly, it dawns on me that Nirvana did not tell us the whole truth about this "retreat." I cast her a warning look. "Not staying," I tell him firmly.

"Stay!" he commands, exhaling so vigorously he blows his own beard out at a ninety-degree angle.

Noticing that Mariana is staring intently at the guru's face, I nudge her and she gives me a look.

"You have entered parallel consciousness and cannot leave until I say you are ready."

"Then we can go back to where we came from?" asks Mariana. "Like Jackson Heights?"

Huh? Clarice and I exchange a glance. Mariana was born and raised in Queens, but would hardly refer to it as where she was going back to.

The guru, however, is noticeably squirming.

"You're no more a guru than any of us are! You're Arvind Patel from Jackson Heights. I remember you from high school!"

The guru shakes his head vehemently, mumbling some sort of mantra, but by this time all the devotees are looking at him askance, even Nirvana.

"Well?" I say sharply, tapping my foot (half with impatience, half to get the blood circulating because it fell asleep midlotus).

"Never heard Jackson Heights," he says post-mantra.

"No? Perhaps you've just forgotten. Remember Officer Mott? He busted you for taking money for 'reading' a Magic 8 Ball, insisting that yours was 'sacred.' 'Blessed by Shiva and Lakshmi,' was your claim, as I recall." Mariana stares him down, her eyes gleaming in triumph and satisfaction. (I wonder what ersatz Magic 8 Ball "reading" caused her so much heartache or humiliation that she hasn't forgotten it in all this time, but it would be rude and non-princessly to pry.)

The guru peers at Mariana, then seems to realize who she is. In his shock, the Bengali accent vanishes, and he says, "Mariana Ortiz?"

Mariana nods.

"You're so thin!"

"That's the first lie you haven't told since we got here," I remark.

"You'd better start telling us what's going on," Clarice demands.

Clarice and I each put an arm around Mariana, and Mariana speaks softly so only we can hear. "His Magic 8 Ball said that if I didn't give up chocolate malteds—which I had every day in high school, when I wasn't exactly slim—I would weigh three hundred pounds by the time I was twenty."

"Magic 8 Ball only had standard answers, sweetie. Why did you believe him?" Clarice asks.

"He told us his family was psychic and persecuted by Nehru, so they fled to the U.S., where they could practice their gift and help others in peace. Of course we all believed him!"

"We've all done things we look back on as foolish, sweetie," I tell her as Clarice rolls her eyes at me.

Mariana gives me a sideways squeeze.

Meanwhile, Nirvana is leading the charge to expose the guru. "Do you think this is some kind of joke? People look to their guru to guide and inspire. How could you do this?!"

"Blind trust is always misguided. You'll all receive full refunds. *Namaste.*"

As he pushes through the crowd to exit, Nirvana grabs my arm. "Jacquie! Do something! Tell him he can't get away with this."

"He's not, sweetie. He's refunding our money. We can't ask for more than that."

We're waiting in the airport for our flight now. Each of us has already polished off two muffins and a venti latte at the airport Starbucks. Yes, Mariana and Nirvana, too. I've never been so ravenous in my life. This is the first relaxing moment I've had since we arrived in Arizona, despite the jolt from the caffeine and sugar. The rest of the girls agree, even though the caffeine is making Nirvana twitch.

The only good that came of the experience is that Mariana realizes she doesn't have to starve herself, and Nirvana understands that she can't go around believing every word a person says just because he's wearing a saffron robe. Mariana will still watch what she eats and strength-train, but she won't be obsessed. Nirvana will still meditate, do yoga and be a vegan, but she won't be obsessed, either. (She does look a bit queasy, but I'm not sure if it's a result of her clay-footed guru or the muffin-latte spree.) All I've ever tried to do was help them see that obsession is unhealthy and un-self-loving. Now they see it for themselves.

"We never got to think up our mantras, though," Clarice teases.

"Speak for yourself. I've always had one," I tell her. "Pra-da. Pra-da. Pra-da." (I hope you don't mind my sharing our private joke with the girls.)

Clarice cracks up. "What are mine and Mariana's?"

"Cos-mo, for you. No-carbs, for Mariana."

Clarice laughs even harder, and Mariana joins in, then tells us she wants to make hers "low-carbs" instead. Baby steps, but definite progress. Clarice and I applaud her.

Nirvana says she's sticking to *"om-shanti,"* but she's not finding a new guru anytime soon. I hope she means it. I would hate to see her get hurt again. "Thank God Mariana spoke up!" she adds.

We all applaud this time, then collapse into a fit of uncontrollable laughter. Nothing like a good laugh with your friends to ease all tension. And tomorrow, I'm going to spend the entire day at Elizabeth Arden. I've already called Jean-Paul, who'll make the arrangements, and also have pink torch ginger waiting for me—and delivered to each of the girls' places, too. After the Sedona ordeal, we each need a pick-me-up.

They're boarding our flight, darling, so I must dash. Always remember that relaxing pursuits make you feel refreshed and serene, not stressed and irritated. And it doesn't matter who tells you what should make you feel relaxed or enlightened. Only you know, deep down where it counts. Do what works for you and ignore anyone who gives you a hard time about it.

I knew I never should have trusted someone who wouldn't drink a yummy frosted soy smoothie!

On Romance

*A princess doesn't play hard to get, a princess IS hard to get,
and she doesn't stay with any man who doesn't deserve the treasure she is.*

12

Everything has just been copacetic since returning home from Sedona. Mariana is eating without her calculator (even though she still is positively the Energizer Bunny on the StairMaster for an hour a day, seven days a week), and Nirvana has switched from *bikram* yoga to Tae Bo (she still meditates for almost as many hours a day as the rest of us sleep), which she's taking in a class with Mariana. (Princess-in-Training is looking good for both their futures.) As for Clarice and me, we're our same princessly selves—although I am much wiser as a result of The Debacle, my St. Tropez experience and all that preceded them both. A true princess knows that life is an adventure, with more to learn from it every day, so she keeps her mind and heart open.

Speaking of hearts, mine is still pining for Brandon Charmant. I suppose it's really not fair to say it's my *heart* that's pining, since I barely know him. But…well…you know what I mean, darling. I do so want to see him again! I surely thought I would have heard from him by now. Every time I ask Jean-Paul Fameux what he's heard from

Brandon, all he says is. "Be patient, *bébé*. Brandon will call you. He's just busy rehearsing for his next role. Don't worry." Most annoying. (Mind you, Jean-Paul offers no clue as to what this role is, even though it's the lead in *his* film that Brandon is preparing for. If he thinks I'm going to be executive producer when he won't even tell me the plot, he's got another think coming!) The last guy I fell for was a bimbus and a lying gold digger. (I know that term is reserved for women who hunt for rich men, and I hate that. Marco/Mark Trevini is a gold digger if ever there was one.) So why would I worry about Brandon Charmant, who only turns up every now and then, always when I least expect it, then disappears just as suddenly, leaving me to wonder whether he really is as interested in me as I am in him, or just gets a rush off the chase.

Still, his name *is* Charmant… (I wonder if that's his real name or the invention of a clever agent. I can see someone like Chi-Chi at *De Rigueur* sitting behind closed doors with a cosmo and her More cigarette, coming up with exactly that type of name for the next hottie *du jour.*)

Prince Charming *is* charming—hence, the clever name. Less than charming is synonymous with "to be dumped," n'est-ce pas?

Now, his name notwithstanding, Brandon truly is charming. Or at least, he seems to be. A big princess pitfall is assuming that the seemingly charming truly *are* charming. This happens because she's so charming herself, she just assumes that others who seem charming (particularly hotties with eyes like sapphires, smiles that light up a room, shoulders that…oh, you get the idea!) are charming. Although I firmly believe in an optimistic outlook and a joyful demeanor, here I must advocate what I call "healthy cynicism." (The self-help books I detest would call this "boundaries.") Healthy cynicism is nothing more than self-protection. It isn't to say that you ignore your attractions, but rather that you keep your guard up a bit—that you allow Mr. Hottie to prove to you that he's worth your time and attention.

Don't give your heart away too soon just because your knees go weak every time you see him. Not that the weak-knees thing isn't fantastic. It is. It's just not *everything*. *Everything* is keeping intact your self-respect and your love for yourself, then meeting the man who loves you just as you are. As long as you have your self-respect and self-love, you've got it made. If you lose them—or give them away—you have nothing. And no prince can get them back for you. Neither can a killer wardrobe, a closet full of shoes, diamonds on every finger, nights blurred by too many martinis or too much chocolate…or anything else you try to use to soothe yourself.

A true princess does not kiss frogs.

(Sometimes, by no fault of her own, as has been true for me more than once, a princess will kiss a frog, unbeknownst to her. Once she finds out he's a frog, she remedies the situation immediately. Every frog doesn't hop around saying "gribbit," either. That would make it easy. The worst frogs usually masquerade quite well as princes, tycoons, film stars, or whatever, until the truth comes out. Once you hear that first "gribbit," though, however faint it might be, galvanize yourself into action.)

Now, frogs notwithstanding, what you must remember is that every princess has a Prince Charming. Which is another reason why it's so important to keep your self-respect and self-love intact—no matter how many warty ones you might happen to kiss by no fault of your own. Look at me with Marco/Mark. Some of those frogs have had a lot of practice acting in prince mode, regardless of whether they're professional actors. Life is just life. I may very likely kiss other frogs, and so will you. I have no intention of letting even a pondful of frogs spoil romance for me. And neither should you. I only need one Prince Charming. You only need one, too. The men who aren't Prince Charming just *aren't*. Best to just accept that and move on.

Every princess knows that her Prince Charming will appear when the time is best and right for both of them. The longer it takes, the better it will be when it happens. No matter how disappointed or even heartbroken you might feel, you *must* remember this, as I'm reminding myself of it now. A princess does not settle for any Pseudo-prince Not-So-Charming or Needs-to-Be-Dumped. The man you're with must treat you like the princess you are. That's a *must,* not a *should* or an *it'd-be-nice-if-he-did*. If he doesn't, he's gone. Just give him the boot. I've done it many times prior to Marco/Mark, (with D & G's, of course, but that's besides the point.)

The truly embraced Inner Princess needs no prince to complete her. All she needs★ is herself, and faith in herself.

(★Of course, a few "essentials" make life so much, well, prettier.)

It goes without saying that no matter how sad, disappointed or heartbroken you are, you never let a failed romance change the way you feel about yourself. You are a princess; nothing can change that. If the person you peg as the love of your life (or the love of the week, or however you look at it) turns out to be a frog who doesn't feel the same way about you, that's his loss not yours. You are still you, a radiant, charming, lovable princess, and the man who will recognize this won't need you or anyone else to show him the way. He'll just know, and so will you.

A princess knows how to make the man of her dreams come to *her*.

By this I don't mean that she schemes or plays elaborate games. (I don't advocate either one, because there's too much of a possibility that one or both of you will get hurt.) A princess doesn't have to do that. She attracts the man who's right for her by being herself. Which doesn't mean that men who definitely aren't right for her won't come around, too. A princess can't help being utterly irresistible, after all, and every situation, no matter how wondrous it may be, has its downside.

But a princess will inevitably discern if a man is wrong for her, and if he is, she sends him packing. And she doesn't hesitate to smack him if warranted—*sans* velvet glove, if necessary. The point is, there's no shame in finding yourself involved with or caring about someone who turns out to be other than what he originally seemed. If someone wants you to see him a certain way and goes to great lengths to ensure that you do, he'll usually be able to keep up the charade and keep manipulating you for a while, at least. Don't blame yourself for that. He's the one to blame. And remember: What goes around comes around. Fate (or karma, if you talk to Nirvana) will take care of him.

Tonight, I'm off to Jean-Paul Fameux's sure-to-be-*formidable* premiere, (which is why I'm thinking about romance, I suppose…hoping Brandon Charmant will be there and…sigh…what's meant to be, will be…) Before I go, let me leave you with this:

A princess knows that the only real happily-ever-after is being with a man who will love and respect her as much as she loves and respects herself.

Toujours l'amour, chérie! It will happen for you, for each of my girlfriends, and for me. If it's already happened for you, congratulations, and may it last forever. Every princess enjoys forever love, regardless, because she loves herself no matter what. May that always be true for you.

The premiere is fantastic!! (Very *un*-Hollywood, thank goodness.) Jean-Paul Fameux is my escort, since neither one of us is seeing anyone right now. (I keep looking for Brandon, but don't see him anywhere. Given the size of the crowd, hopefully, I'm just missing him.) Jean-Paul is ecstatic. Not that his popularity has ever waned, but his handling of the Marco/Mark fiasco only served to sky-rocket it. I couldn't be happier for him. (Not to mention how delicious it is to hear him introduce me each time: "This is the ever-exquisite Princess Jacqueline de Soignée, my dear friend and executive producer, who has a cameo in the middle of the film. Look for it." How fabulous is that?!)

The paparazzi are, of course, falling all over themselves trying to get photos. Some legitimate photographers who Jean-Paul and I know are getting quite annoyed. Dressed to the nines in my latest Contessina Sfilato-di Moda— floor-length to-die-for black lamé sheath, if I'm to be photographed, I want it to be for publications you can't buy at a supermarket checkout. Oh, look! It's Chi-Chi Chinobert with a photographer in tow, of course. What timing. With a wave and a dazzling smile, I beckon to her. We air-kiss, then she instructs her shutterbug to start snap-ping. (Look for me on the cover of the next *De Rigueur,* darling!)

As exciting as it all is, even with the ball I'm having, nothing can take my mind off how disappointed I am that Brandon is *nowhere* to be seen. Sighing dejectedly, I look for a quiet corner where I can "take five" (as we say in the biz).

No sooner have I noticed and made for the perfect spot,

then the baritone that turns my knees to jelly comes softly from behind me.

"Jacquie, where have you been hiding yourself?"

Turning to face him, I say, "Why, Brandon, I was going to ask you the same question."

Can anyone's eyes really be *that* blue?

"I've been pretty consumed with rehearsals. You know how into it we method actors get." He smiles at me, dimming the exploding flashbulbs.

I smile back. "You know how I admire method actors."

"You inspire method actors, too. I can only speak for myself, of course." He steps closer.

My knees are so useless now, I practically have to grind my heels into the floor to keep from crumpling in a heap. (Thank God Manolo makes a reliable stiletto!) "Well... Brandon. I'm beyond flattered." (Actually, I'm *liquefied,* but I'm not about to tell him so. Remember that healthy cynicism!)

"And I'm falling pretty hard for you. If I may say so, Your Highness." He lifts my hand, kissing first the back and then the palm, his breath warm on the other side of my silk glove.

"You certainly may say so." A million times every day, preferably.

"Good. Then you'll be able to help me with my next role. It's very important to me."

"What role is that?"

Still holding my hand, he wraps his other arm around my waist. "Prince Charming."

"Jean-Paul didn't tell me his next film was a romance! Who's your leading lady?" For the first time in my life, I feel jealous. How awful is that? Just when things were going along so well, he's going to be in some steamy Fameux romance...without me. And expecting me to help him rehearse. Ha!! Not likely.

"Jacquie, did you hear what I said? Not Prince Charming in a movie. It's not about JPF's next film. I'm playing a double agent with amnesia in it, though. What I meant was my role as *your* Prince Charming. If you'll let me try out for it, that is."

If I'll let him try out? I'll eat him up with a spoon, for God's sake!! How could he think that I wouldn't…? Hmm. I realize he's thinking the same thing about me: I am, after all, a glamorous, gorgeous, brilliant, adorable celebrity. Not to mention a true princess in every sense of the word. Of course he wants to get to know me! Not that I'm feeling complacent, just pleased. Maybe he is Prince Charming and maybe he isn't. I am going to enjoy finding out, though. Most important, I deserve the love I've always dreamed of. Sigh. (And so do you, darling, so remember: Never settle.)

Brandon's arm tightens around me. "You don't have to say anything, Jacquie. Except yes." His blue eyes twinkle at me.

Actually, I can't say anything, because in the same instant, he leans me back and gives me a long, toe-curling kiss. I feel myself melt into him as I return his unbelievably velvety kiss.

"You'll tell me when I've completely swept you off your feet, won't you?" he whispers in my ear.

"Well, you have, but that doesn't mean you can slack off."

Brandon laughs. "Much as I hate to, we ought to get back to the festivities."

Reluctantly, I agree.

"So we'll work on happily-ever-after," he promises, kissing my hand again before folding it into the crook of his arm as he leads me back into the throng.

I keep pace with him as we walk. "That's why real life is better than fairy tales, Brandon. Happily-ever-after is something you have to just live."

"If you're lucky enough to find your princess," he says softly.

I just smile at him.

Truth to tell, you first have to be a princess (or prince, as the case may be) to yourself. If you don't value yourself, how is true love supposed to find you? And if it does, will you believe? I don't think so. I don't tell this to Brandon, of course. I need to find out whether he's a prince or a Prince-in-Training. (And you need to go for the already-trained, too, sweetie. No trainees for you! Too much frog factor.)

Just between you and me, darling, happily-ever-after is a state of mind, or heart, to be precise. Happily-ever-after is nothing more than faith that love exists, is on its way to you and will last forever. True love does, you know. And if you believe in yourself, you believe in love and in life. You can't happily-ever-after until you love yourself. Once you do, look out, Prince Charming! Prepare to be dazzled. Remember, though, his recognizing how wonderful you are in every possible way is what makes him Prince Charming in the first place.

Toujours l'amour, chérie!!

The Last Word

Congratulations, darling! You have successfully completed the Princess-in-Training Program and are now officially a Graduate.

Now, should the princessly mantle slip from your lovely shoulders, just remember to connect with your Inner Princess. Plus, you can always refer back to any (or all) of the chapters, as needed. Your training refreshers will be our secret.

Must run for now. I'm off for my day at Elizabeth Arden, which hopefully will end in time for me to pop in to Tiffany's and Bergdorf's. I'll be thinking of you all the while, and hope you'll long think fondly of our wonderful adventures together. I've so enjoyed having you along.

A bientôt, chérie. Enjoy your life! Be happy. Be hopeful. Be loving. Be loved. Most of all, of course, be yourself and love yourself.

Hugs and kisses!!

Glossary

An indispensable, quick-and-easy reference to princessly terminology:

A bientôt: French, meaning "so long" or "see you later."

Accademia: Florentine art museum most famous for housing Michelangelo's masterpiece *David*.

amour: French, meaning "love." (Compare with "amore" in Italian.)

Après: French, meaning "after."

Arno: River that flows through Florence and Tuscany.

Arrivederci: Italian, meaning "goodbye."

Aubusson: A figured scenic tapestry used for wall hangings and upholstery. Also, rugs made to resemble such tapestries.

au courant: French, meaning "current" (colloquially: "cool" or "hip").

avec: French, meaning "with."

bébé: French, meaning "baby."

Bella Firenze: Italian, meaning "beautiful Florence." Florentines' pet name for their beloved city. (The surrounding region is often called Bella Tuscany.)

bellissima: Italian, meaning "most beautiful." (Superlative of "bella." Usually used as a term of endearment like "beautiful!" or gorgeous!")

Bien sûr: French, meaning "but of course."

Bonjour: French, meaning "good morning" or "good day," also used to mean "hello."

Bonsoir: French, meaning "good evening."

Bon voyage: French, meaning "have a nice trip."

Bonne nuit: French, meaning "good night."

Bravissima (masculine: bravissimo): Italian, meaning "most outstandingly done!" (The superlative form of "brava" ["bravo"].)

Buon giorno: Italian, meaning "good morning" or "good day." Also used to mean "hello."

Buon viaggio: Italian, meaning "have a nice trip."

Buona notte: Italian, meaning "good night."

Buona sera: Italian, meaning "good evening."

Carissima (masculine: carissimo): Italian, meaning "dearest" or "darling." (Superlative form of "cara" ["caro"].)

Cara (masculine: caro): Italian, meaning "dear."

C'est la vie: French, meaning, "that's life."

chamberlain: the head of a royal household.

château (plural: châteaux): French, meaning "castle or fort" or "mansion or estate" (usually in the mountains or countryside).

chérie (masculine: chéri): French, meaning "dear" or "darling."

chocolat: French, meaning "chocolate."

Ciao: Italian, meaning "so long" or "see you later."

collezione: Italian, meaning "collection."

confetti: Italian, meaning "candy." (Originally during parades and triumphal marches, Italians threw wrapped candies. The paper version of confetti didn't develop until relatively recently.)

crème brûlée: A rich French custard with a hard, carmelized-sugar glaze.

demitasse: French, meaning "small cup." Used to refer to small cups of strong coffee, similar to espresso, usually served with dessert.

de rigueur: French, meaning "according to custom" (colloquially: "in").

djellaba: A long, loose garment with full sleeves and a hood.

d'orsay: A style of shoe with a closed vamp and open sides, usually backless but sometimes with a closed heel.

du jour: French, meaning "of the day."

du monde: French, meaning "of the world."

farthingale: A support worn beneath a skirt to expand it at the hipline. (Favored in sixteenth-century European court dress.)

favoloso: Italian, meaning "fabulous."

fete: French, meaning "party."

formidable: French colloquialism, used to mean "terrific!"

framboise: French, meaning "raspberry."

Français: French, meaning "French."

gauche: French, meaning "left side" (colloquially: "crude, boorish, socially inept").

gelato (plural: gelati): Italian, meaning "ice cream."

gioielleria (plural: gioiellerie): Italian, meaning "jewelry shop."

gioiello (plural: gioielli): Italian, meaning "jewel."

glacé: French, meaning "ice cream."

grandmère: French, meaning "grandmother."

grandpère: French, meaning "grandfather."

grenouille: French, meaning "frog."

haute couture: French, meaning "high fashion."

intime: French, meaning "intimate."

J'aime Paris: French, meaning "I love Paris."

jamais: French, meaning "never."

Je ne sais quoi: French, meaning "I know not what" (colloquially: "that certain something" [that defies precise defining]).

joaillerie: French, meaning "jewelry shop."

la dolce vita: Italian, meaning "the good life."

magnifique: French, meaning "magnificent."

mal de tête: French, meaning "headache."

merci: French, meaning "thank you."

merveilleuse (masculine: merveilleux): French, meaning "marvelous."

minaudiere: French. Elegant jeweled evening bag, usually shaped like an object or animal.

monde: French, meaning "world."

moi: French, meaning "me."

n'est-ce pas: French, meaning "isn't it so?"

noblesse oblige: French, meaning "duty of the nobility" (i.e. persons of noble birth should behave nobly).

noisette: French, meaning "hazelnut."

nonpareil: French, meaning "unparalleled."

occhiali: Italian, meaning "sunglasses."

outré: French, meaning "exaggerated" (colloquially: "out there").

pannier: A pair of hoops used to expand women's skirts at the sides; or an overskirt that creates a similar effect by its drapery.

paparazzo (plural: paparazzi): Italian, meaning "aggressive photographer who relentlessly pursues his subjects (descending upon them like a plague of locusts)."

par excellence: French, meaning "the best of its kind."

patisserie: French, meaning "pastry shop" (not to be

confused with "boulangerie," which is French for bread bakery).

pavane: A stately European court dance popular during the sixteenth century.

peau de soie: French, literally meaning "a little silk," but used to denote a particular type of extremely lightweight silk.

pêche: French, meaning "peach."

pièce de résistance: French, meaning "showpiece" or "showcased item or event."

pied-à-terre: French, literally meaning "foot to the ground" (colloquially: "a temporary or secondary domicile" [usually a chic, city apartment]).

Ponte Vecchio: Italian, literally meaning "the old bridge," and the name of the main artery of Florence that runs across the Arno and houses the world-renowned Florentine jewelry artisans.

principessa: Italian, meaning "princess."

Quel dommage!: French, meaning "what a pity!"

Quelle surprise!: French, meaning "what a surprise!" (most effectively used sarcastically).

raison d'être: French, meaning "reason for being."

sans: French, meaning "without."

savoir faire: French, meaning "sophisticated know-how."

sfilato-di moda: Italian, meaning "fashion show."

sine qua non: Latin, meaning "that without which; indispensable thing."

soirée: French, meaning "evening event." (Usually connotes a party of some sort.)

sommelier: French, meaning "wine steward."

sotto voce: Italian, meaning "soft voice," most often used to denote a stage whisper.

sycophant: Servile, self-seeking flatterer.

tartufo: Italian dessert consisting of a ball of ice cream covered in a layer of bittersweet chocolate.

toujours: French, meaning "always."

toute de suite: French, meaning "immediately."

très: French, meaning "very."

Uffizi: Art museum in Florence that boasts most of the finest examples of Italian medieval, Renaissance and Baroque painting and sculpture, including works by Botticelli, Donatello, da Vinci, Michelangelo, Raphael and many, many other masters.

vanille: French, meaning "vanilla."

ABOUT THE AUTHOR

ERICA ORLOFF

is the author of *Spanish Disco* and *Diary of a Blues Goddess*, both published by Red Dress Ink, as well as *The Roofer*, to be published by MIRA Books in May 2004. A transplanted New York writer living in South Florida, she treasures the beach near her home. Though this is a work of fiction, anyone who knows the author will likely attest that she is, in fact, a diva. She enjoys spending time with her extended family of friends and relatives, throwing parties and tending to her menagerie of pets, including a female cockatoo—who is also a diva.

Divas Don't Fake It

Erica Orloff

**RED
DRESS
INK**
™

First edition November 2003

DIVAS DON'T FAKE IT

A Red Dress Ink novel

ISBN 0-373-25039-8

Visit Red Dress Ink at www.reddressink.com

Printed in U.S.A.

Dedicated, with love, to J.D.,
for accepting me as I am—high maintenance and all

ACKNOWLEDGMENTS

As always, a huge thank-you to my agent, Jay Poynor, who recognized from day one that I was a diva, but put up with me anyway.

Another enthusiastic acknowledgment to Margaret Marbury, of Red Dress Ink. I have always felt supported and encouraged with you at the helm. Your insights are so invaluable to me. Thank you also to Laura Morris, in marketing, for your endless creativity. And also to Zareen Jaffery, in editorial, for your support of this concept and editing. Thank yous to Donna Hayes, Publisher and CEO of Harlequin, and Dianne Moggy and Amy Moore-Benson at MIRA for their support of my work. And as always, to the cover design team—you guys are brilliant. The diva is divine!

To the members of Writer's Cramp—Pam, Jon and Gina—we remain a cohesive group, and I value your input. Though our meetings resemble pizza-and-beer sessions (with wine and cheese on our "classier" nights)...I'd never finish a book without you!

To the "Princess," for her creativity and friendship.

To Alexa, for astutely noting, "Mom, you don't take crap from anyone."

To Nicholas and Isabella, for the artwork that adorns my office.

To Chris, Dahl! What more can I say?

To Kathy Levinson, for giving me a place to stay for all my neurotic trips to New York City, including chauffeured drives when I need them, and the intense calming down I require on the way to the airport. I keep waiting for the day when my royalties will allow me a rock star-esque tour bus and I can ditch the flying altogether, but until then, thank you.

And finally, to J.D. Living with a diva cannot be easy, but you manage to make me laugh every day, cook all the meals (divas don't cook) and ignore me when I swear I'm throwing your clothes out on the front lawn.

I was born to be a diva. From a long line of passionate Russians, it was inevitable that I learn how to throw plates and hurl knives at boyfriends—and ex-husbands—who displeased me. These men never complained—not even the time when a Waterford vase was aimed like a SCUD missile at one lover's head. When you're in love with a high-maintenance diva, you have to accept all the passion that comes with it—both in and out of the bedroom.

So what's so great about being a diva…and what place does "divadom" have in the postfeminist millennium?

Let me tell you, people think twice about messing with a diva. And though feminism brought with it certain perks and certain milestones, a true diva doesn't care about any of that. Why not? She is far too concerned about herself.

Selfish? Self-centered? No…a diva is merely totally aware at all times that she needs to be—indeed, was born

to be—the center of attention. It helps if she's an Aries. And she makes no apologies to anyone—not for her temper, not for her attitude. Not for being a bitch. You don't want to mess with her; you don't want to cross her. You do want to be her friend, however, for though she may be a tad eccentric, she will kill—perhaps literally—anyone who messes with her friends.

Can a diva ever find true happiness? Yes! Divas marry and have children. They find peace and happiness. But most of all, they remain ever certain of their status as a diva. Divas don't wait in line. They don't have self-esteem problems. They are not, most definitely not, women who love too much. They don't need anything but their lipstick and eyeliner and a suitcase full of attitude.

Why aspire to be a diva? Well, ladies, divas don't get their hearts broken—they break them. They look out for number one, and enjoy the fawning attention of men who like being with the most exciting woman in the room. They know how to make an entrance, and they know when it's time to make an exit—even if that means making a scene. They do it all with confidence.

So if you've ever been mistreated, not loved enough, dumped by a man, cheated on…not invited to the most dazzling parties, this is for you. But beware: Once you invoke the power of the diva, there's no going back. Once you taste all life has to offer the woman who knows her own power, you wouldn't want to, anyway. So set aside a few plates you want to hurl, and read on.

**Your inner diva has been waiting to
make a scene.**

A Diva Knows
How to Reinvent Herself

"I knew you were going to wear that. It's your gay male-whore uniform." I eye my best friend, Scott, as he sits down in his get-over-a-heartbreak outfit of black muscle T-shirt and tight black jeans.

"First of all…*gay male* and *whore* are redundant." He rolls his eyes. "Second, you're one to talk."

"Well, you look positively sluttish tonight."

"Bitch!"

"But you love me."

"Yes, I do! Air kisses, darling." He motions with his lips in the general direction of my cheek.

I air-kiss back, careful not to smear my own Elizabeth Arden–encased lips (Shade? Sparkling Ruby).

"I'm channeling my inner diva," he says with a toss of his hand. "I'm doing some major scoping of the scenery.

For instance, do you see that guy over there on the dance floor. The one who looks like Moby's ugly twin brother?"

"Uh-huh."

"Well…like, does he not have a mirror *anywhere* in his apartment? What was he thinking?"

"Not everyone has your keen fashion sense, Scott."

"Please. It's in The Gay Handbook. Must have keen sense of fashion and color."

"Well…someone better give him a copy of The Handbook then."

Scott turns to better check out another corner of the room. "And that one." He less than discreetly nods. "It's also in The Handbook that you have to be able to dance. And that move…" He shudders.

"White men can't dance."

"No, white straight men can't dance. That rule doesn't apply to gay boys."

I gasp in mock horror.

"What?"

"Do you think straight men are infiltrating your ranks?"

"Honey, I don't know what to think, but he seriously cannot dance. If I was the bouncer I'd throw him out." Scott covers his eyes with his hands. "It's unsightly. He's giving queers a bad name."

"You'd have him thrown out for having no rhythm?"

"Uh-huh. Hell, I've been thrown out of clubs for less."

Having someone for the three D's—drinking, dancing and dishing—is one of the many blessings of having a best friend who is a queen. Not as in Queen of England, or even Queen of Some-Lesser-European-Nation-So-Obscure-

that-You-Can't-Even-Remember-Its-Place-on-the-Map-from-High-School-Geography, but queen as in…well, queen. And even occasionally drag!

Scott St. James is my oldest and dearest friend and most fearless defender—as well as the hottest dancer in any club on any night. By day, Scott is a laid-off dot-com Web geek now working in a buttoned-up corporation as a temp three days a week and as the file clerk for my PR firm the other two days when he can make it into the office by noon. By night, Scott is whoever he feels he is that particular week. Scott, though a man, is a diva. And all divas and aspiring divas can learn from him.

A Gay Dream waiter in a matching gay male-whore re-dundant muscle shirt and tight black jeans comes over to our table to take our order. His "package" is so big, I swear he has stuffed socks down the front of his pants. Either that or he has a serious moonlighting gig as a porn star. "Ladies?" he asks.

"Two sour-apple martinis, please," Scott purrs.

"Oh no," I beg. "Not another new drink of the week."

"What's the point of reinvention, doll, if you don't change it all?"

I roll my eyes but nod at Gay Dream with Big Package. "Fine. Two sour-apple martinis."

When they arrive, I can't even drink mine without scrunching up my face into a puckered scowl.

"God, this is awful." I squint.

"I just love them!" Scott claps his hands together.

"Last week you loved some Chambord drink that I found mildly tolerable. But this is sickening."

"But that's the fun of it, Xandra."

I look down at my martini glass. "Can't you like…oh, I don't know…a cosmopolitan this week?"

"So last year."

Of course, it's been pointed out to me that I can order my own drink, but it's sort of a tradition with Scott that we switch drinks each week, so I usually go with it. He feels the need to change with his moods. And he has more moods than a PMS-suffering woman denied Midol.

I sip and screw, as in screwing up my face.

"This is the most revolting thing to have ever passed my lips."

"And that's saying a lot."

"Your mind is always in the gutter."

"Of course it is. That's rule number 9,673 in The Handbook."

"I forgot."

He pouts. "I'm insulted you didn't comment on my haircut."

Fawning is a diva national pastime. You must notice everything about a diva, down to the little details.

"What was I thinking? Sorry, honey. And are those a hint of blond tips?"

"Like them?"

"Whorish… They work, though."

"Drink up. I need to get you drunk so you stop picking on me."

I drink down the martini, but I know he secretly loves my barbs. They show I care in some perverse diva way.

I was born a diva. As a child, I was the little girl who couldn't wait to belt out tunes for my parents' dinner guests. I was a miniature Liza, complete with tap-dancing lessons, a dress-up box with feather boas and a *Cabaret*-esque haircut. Other girls wanted little pink sunglasses to wear to the beach. I wanted leopard-spotted frames large enough for Jackie Onassis. Later, I longed to be like Bette Midler, shaking my tits and telling bawdy jokes to anyone who'd listen.

For my sixteenth birthday, my father offered to buy me a car. I held my ground until I got a convertible. Then I needed a Hermès scarf to cover my hair as I tooled around Miami Beach. High school…I was the girl who dumped her lunch tray on her boyfriend when she caught him flirting with any diva's public enemy number one—the Antichrist—a cheerleader.

When I packed my bags for NYU, Dad wanted me to major in something practical. Business or accounting. I did a paper on "The Velvet Rope: Getting Past the Bouncer 101." I majored in club hopping, and racked up an average of 1.1 boyfriends per month for each year I was in school. My GPA was only a little higher.

Through marriages one and two, I believed in grand passion; I've also broken most of the china in the patterns from wedding-registry number one (a rose pattern, if I recall correctly, Wedgwood) and number two (Egyptian-themed). Husband Number Two found all his belongings out on the fire escape and the locks changed. He still begs me to take him back.

Yes…it is destiny that I am a diva.

But Scott was another story. He didn't have the genetic

marker of a diva. And by the time he hit his teens, he was closeted and unhappy. When I met him in college, he was the wittiest guy I knew. Still is. But certainly no Gay Dream. For God's sake, he'd only had two sexual experiences, and one of them was with a woman. Me.

Throughout our friendship, I kept trying to lure him to the light. But the dark side—the dreary doormat world—kept reeling him back to the place where people say, "Oh never mind, it wasn't that important...don't mind me." Then one night, post-college, in our putting-the-rent-on-our-credit-cards years (and paying rent on places with palmetto bugs—Miami cockroaches—so big you could saddle them up and take 'em to the rodeo), we were out at a club on South Beach. He was on the sidelines, watching women in thongs and shirtless men dancing to some club mix, when he looked over at the bar and who should be standing on top of it, grinding with the hottest bartender in the place? A certain diva, of course. And Scott had a "Diva Moment." An epiphany. Fuck what anyone thinks. *He* should have been grinding with the bartender (who, it turned out, was indeed gay). So the next week, when I arrived at his stunningly tiny studio apartment at the time, ready for a night on South Beach, Scott was an imitation of the chick with the beehive in the B-52s. A frighteningly *bad* imitation. But we went with it.

And the week after that, with a new wardrobe (on his overextended credit card—which by then was suffering from credit-card-iac arrest) and new attitude, he was the one bumping and grinding with the hot bar-

tender, in a tight black muscle shirt and jeans—not unlike tonight.

"If it wasn't for you, I'd never have discovered just how fucking hot my ass can look in Versace jeans," he says, pulling me back to the present time.

"True enough. But your inner diva was just waiting to come out of the closet."

"Speaking of which, I better get a new job soon so I can move out of my apartment to one with bigger closets. My wardrobe is sort of taking over. Last night I wrestled with my favorite faux mink thong, thinking I had sat down on a rat."

Divas need a lot of closet space. And if they share their home with a boyfriend, they'll take most of his space, too.

"What do I tell you are the three most important things to look for when apartment shopping." I sigh in mock frustration.

"Closet space." He holds up one finger. "Closet space." He holds up two. "And closet space." The third finger goes up.

"And a close fourth?"

"Someone deliciously fuckable living across the hall."

"Precisely."

"So I have failed miserably in closet space, but there *is* David across the hall."

"And he's straight—which means he's not for you, sweetie. So when are you going to have a cocktail party and invite the two of us?"

"I cannot in good conscience do that to him." He makes a sign of the cross.

"Do what?"

"Do what, she asks. Do what? Hello? Are we even having this conversation? The last time I set you up with someone, the poor man needed therapy to get over the experience. I would be willing to bet he needed *shock therapy* to get over it."

"I'm not that bad."

"You are. But you're worth it." (The diva motto: I'm worth it! L'Oréal, are you listening?)

"Of course I'm worth it."

"But I need to seriously investigate whether he's man enough for you, honey…. So few men are, I'm sorry to say."

"If you don't hurry, I'll just take matters into my own hands."

"Oh God, that means showing up on his doorstep with a bottle of champagne and a push-up bra. And little else. Lesser men have been known to pass out from the shock. Let me see what I can do."

"And while you're thinking, do me a favor and throw out that faux mink thong. It's ludicrous."

"Bob liked it."

"I thought we weren't going to mention his name."

"No…I said *you* couldn't mention his name. It's okay if I bring him up."

"No, it's not. Bring him up again, and I'm castrating you."

"Ouch…you just made my cock shrivel."

"Well, look over at *that* guy on the dance floor. Your cock'll make a comeback."

We sit and continue ogling the men in the bar. The more we drink, the more brazen we become—okay, in my

case, it's an exercise in futility, because it's a bar where none of the men are interested in me, trust me.

Later, I catch myself looking at Scott's profile. He really is beautiful, and I know one day he will meet Mr. Right. For now, he'll have to settle for a little temporary distraction. Scott has sandy-blond hair that does a perfect just-rolled-out-of-bed sexy unmade look with no effort. He has a single earring in his right ear, a small gold hoop and skin that is fake-tanned to movie-star perfect—he won't risk future wrinkles. His eyes are killer, a deep blue, with lashes so long and thick I'm envious, and he uses those lashes to bat away at every Tom, Dick and Harry in the place. I love that Scott now gets it—the whole concept of reinvention. If you don't like who you are one week, change. If you feel stifled and hear a little voice inside saying "go for it," you have no choice but to listen to that little voice—which in Scott's case says go be a male whore dancing on the bar.

Divas reinvent themselves.

Reinvention. Hair, clothes, makeup. Doing something out of character just because you want to. It's about fearlessly entering another relationship even if the last one crashed and burned. Divas dare to go where angels and mere mortals fear to tread.

Change it all. Go out for a night as a seductive siren. Try a new persona on for size. Scott is like a chocaholic faced with a giant box of Godiva. He can bite into each one and taste the fantasy. Caramel? Truffle? Almond? Coconut. Forget Forrest Gump. These chocolates are about

sex and adventure. A world brimming with possibilities. Who does he want to be? Each weekend, each club we hit, Scott is his own heart's delight.

Scott's now dancing on the bar, lost in the music. I stand up and go over to the bar, climb up and grind against him for all it's worth. Then I kiss him full on the mouth, stepping back to wipe off my lipstick.

"What was that for?"

"Because I just think you are so fucking fantastic."

"You want me to set you up with David."

"That, too. But if you don't, I know just what I'm going to do."

"Do I want to hear this?"

"No."

I smile to myself. We get down when the song is over and order two more horrible sour-apple martinis, and I toast to Scott.

"To this week's diva, the queen of reinvention."

We drink, we dish, we laugh. A hunky guy whose name really *is* Richard, aka Dick, asks Scott to dance. Scott shakes his groove thing, bumps, grinds, and gets down and dirty with Dick. Then he asks if I'd mind if he left with his dancing queen.

"Divas are big girls, baby. Go on…I can fend for myself here."

"Are you sure?"

"Listen, I was going to tell you two to get a room soon, anyway. Some major chemistry's going on there."

"You're the best!"

They leave, and I'm a straight woman in a gay bar. It's

not as though I didn't recognize this before, it's just that now I am without my "date." This can only mean one thing: more dancing. I move over to one of the bars—there are four spaced at the four corners of the dance floor. Marcus, the bartender, knows me. I switch to a more palatable tall vodka and tonic, and before too long, I see some of Scott's friends and next thing I am dancing to Madonna—the queen of the divas.

Dance is the ultimate reinvention. While they say white men can't dance, if drunk enough, even a rhythmless doughboy can, for a moment, be John Travolta, and an inhibited mouse can be transformed to a diva. The trick is to remember how you feel when the strobes are flashing all over your glistening body and your breasts are heaving and you *feel* the music pulsating like sex inside you, and take that feeling with you after you leave the club.

And if you don't like how it feels…you can just reinvent yourself next weekend.

After dancing until 3:00 a.m., I grab a cab and head back to my apartment. No roommate. Divas are best living alone. I pull a cold Coke from the fridge and go out on my balcony to listen to the surf roll in.

Feeling contemplative, my thoughts turn to David. Something about Scott's neighbor makes me feel decidedly un-divalike. Okay, I'm not thinking I'm heading for domesticity or anything as insane as that. I'm not about to cook—ha! Takeout is my middle name (all right, it's Summer—blame *that* on my hippie mother). But I wouldn't mind curling up for a quiet evening at home with him. I don't want a man to take care of me—well, he can take

care of me, if you know what I mean—but no one needs to rule my life. But David is different enough to intrigue me. He's studious and quiet. Not, according to Scott—according to my track record with ex-husbands—my type. He looks like a college professor. Maybe because he teaches comparative literature at the University of Miami. (Scott's idea of literature is *Cosmopolitan*.) David makes me want to reach out and muss up his hair. He makes me want to cause him to laugh so hard tears roll down his face. He looks as if he needs a diva in his life. He doesn't know that yet, of course. But he does. And I'm just the woman to show him that.

A Diva Knows
How to Stand Up for Herself

I've just body-slammed a cop. Hard.

I bow to him as he stares up at me, dazed, from the floor, and then I take my place beside Scott.

"You go, girlfriend," he whispers to me.

"He asked for it."

Believe me, I didn't talk Scott into taking tae kwon do classes with me so I could sidekick men with badges. Though I did have a sex dream once in which I flipped George Clooney onto a mat, then straddled him—but I digress. I took up martial arts so I could stay in shape and defend myself if I had to. Anyone will tell you I have the fastest, foulest mouth in Miami, so I stand up for myself verbally. But I wanted to know that if push came to shove, well, I could push and shove with the best of them.

I sought a Korean master of tae kwon do, and I found

the wisest of them all with Master Lee. He has taught me
where my center of power is and how to sidekick an op-
ponent right on his ass. Master Lee also teaches me to be
still for a moment, to remember to breathe. Even a diva
can learn to bow and meditate.

Of course, convincing Scott to go with me took
some doing.

"I don't like to sweat, Xandra."

"We live in Miami. Sweating is like breathing."

"One, that's what air-conditioning is for. Two, that's in-
voluntary sweating. You're asking me to *try* to sweat.
There's something not right about that."

"You sweat when we go clubbing."

"*That's* sweating with a purpose."

"A purpose."

"Yes. We're sweating to get laid."

"Speak for yourself. I like dancing for dancing's sake."

"Come off your sexual high horse. You grind to get
attention."

"I *live* to get attention. Look, all I'm saying is it wouldn't
kill you to take a marital arts class with me."

"It *might* kill me, and that's my point. Gay men don't do
sports with pain involved. We don't play football. You
won't see us in a scrum playing rugby—though isn't there
something sort of perverse about the word *scrum?* And
have you ever seen a gay boxer?"

"Mike Tyson sounds gay."

Divas will do almost anything on a dare.
"Dare you to tell it to his face. No…I take that back. You
would. You'll do almost anything on dare."

"Look, forget your sports phobia. Haven't you ever wanted to be able to walk into a room and *know* you could kick the ass of every person in it if you wanted to."

He stared at me. "No...Xan, that's *your* fantasy."

"I thought it was a universal fantasy."

"No...it's a diva-bitch fantasy."

It also, we found out, was a Napoleon–complex fantasy, with short cops being the most prone.

After much whining (on Scott's part) and pleading (on mine), and eventually some bribing (I treat him to sushi after Wednesday-night class each week), we were officially white belts—peons in the hierarchy of tae kwon do. And now after nearly three years of intentional sweating, board-breaking, roundhouse kicks and enough punches for a Jackie Chan movie, we were ready to take our black-belt test. But one Tony Romeo was determined to humiliate me.

What is it about a five-foot-eleven-inch woman that drives a short man to such fury? Tony had hated me from the moment I walked into class. He seemed determined to leave a bruise on me after every sparring session. He'd offer me a hand if I fell to the mat, snidely saying, "It isn't all fun and games, sister."

"Yeah..." I'd say. "And it won't be when I finally kick your testicles up into your Adam's apple."

Tae kwon do, and the martial arts in general, aren't really about being a badass. The martial arts are about quiet confidence and dignity. But Tony liked to pick on people, and I was his favorite pick-on choice.

So the day I finally flipped Tony, finally put him in his

place, Scott and I celebrate after class with a feast at our favorite Korean restaurant.

"You know he's going to try to get back at you and dump you on your ass, don't you?"

"Of course he is. But I proved my point."

"It took you three years to be able to do that."

Divas never quit.

"Divas don't give up."

"I know. Quitting isn't in your vocabulary, Xan. If I hadn't let you bully me into joining class, I wouldn't have these rippling muscles and a soon-to-be black belt. *Me,* the guy who was picked last for every single sports team in gym class…a *black* belt. Not a pink belt. A black belt!"

"There is no pink belt."

"Purple belt, then."

"Not one of those, either."

"Stop being a pain in the ass."

"Not possible." I pick up a piece of meat and put it on the barbecue in the center of our table, deftly using my chopsticks. "You realize that next we have to talk Libby into joining tae kwon do."

Libby is our new pet project. She is my assistant—I hired her six months ago when my last assistant quit—with my encouragement—to live her dream of breaking into acting, and headed off to New York City, where she promptly landed a role off-Broadway. As to assistants in general…let me get one thing straight: Being a diva does not mean being a royal bitch to your assistant or under-lings. It does not mean being the least bit imperious to

waitstaff or your housekeeper, the maid in your suite at whatever sumptuous hotel you're staying in, or any other person in the service industry. Standing up for yourself isn't about acting like a spoiled actress and demanding you be able to bring an entourage of thirty the next time you have to appear anywhere. It *does* mean that anyone who fucks with you, however, will regret it. Such as the recently dumped-on-his-ass Tony the tae kwon foe.

No, I adore Libby, even if she can't look me in the eye and seems to will herself into the wallpaper whenever a group of people are around. I decided three months ago that she would be my diva makeover project, and enlisted Scott's help. So far, we've managed to talk her into visiting our favorite hairstylist, getting contacts and not being afraid to laugh at our jokes.

"You think she'd come?" Scott asks.

"No. What pretense can we use to get her to class?"

"With you, it's always a pretense."

"What if I tell her that I am thinking of promoting her—which I am, as soon as she can learn to make a presentation without hyperventilating beforehand—and that the first client I want her to design a PR campaign for is Master Lee's studio."

"But he doesn't want PR. He's the most unassuming man on South Beach."

"Besides the point. It's all about the pretense. She can't very well do PR on a tae kwon do studio without actually taking a few classes. Once she's channeled a little *qi,* a little energy, she'll be hooked. I'll dispense with the pretense, promote her anyway, and she'll be on her way to a yellow belt."

"Devious."

"But will it work?"

The next day, Libby resists the entire idea.

"I can't picture myself punching anyone."

"It's not about that, Lib," I assure her.

"Just try a class," Scott suggests. "I didn't want to go at first either, and look at me now. I'm a queer without fear."

"I don't know…" When she's torn, Libby bites her lower lip, making her look like a little girl. As it is, with her light blond hair and pale skin, she looks eighteen instead of twenty-four.

"Lib…just come. Tonight. No time to think about it, you have to pounce on this opportunity," I command.

"I…um…" She looks at me. I hand her a file and turn around to go into my office as if it's a done deal. Decided. Which it is.

Scott follows me into my office, shuts the door and flops down in one of the leather chairs facing my desk.

"You think she'll actually like it? Forty people screaming and kicking at once? Might scare her back to Omaha or wherever she's from."

"Dayton… And she may not like it, but it'll be good for her."

"And you know best."

"Of course. Don't I always? About everything? Take Bob, for instance—"

"Ixnay on the obbay."

"One little point… Now, didn't I—"

"Yes, you told me so. Xan, you are always right. About everything. Drop it."

"God, you're on the rag today." I open my drawer and pull out a bottle of Midol. "Need one of these?"

"Oh, you're priceless today."

"Well…if you refuse to combat your PMS like a woman, then let me take you to lunch. See what a little sake will do for you." I punch up my e-mail and send two fast replies to clients, then grab my purse and head out the door. Libby is still sitting at her desk looking stunned. I know she wants to tell me that she's thought about it and just cannot come to class.

"Lib…grabbing lunch with Scott. Want me to bring you back some sushi?"

"No," she whispers.

"Okay, then…ciao!"

At lunch, it's on to other, more important matters at hand.

"The Fix-up. David. When and how are you going to do it?"

"Look—" Scott eyes me seriously over a teeny-tiny sake cup, making me laugh at the incongruous sight "—you are a she-wolf. You will take the poor, defenseless Professor David White, chew him up, spit him out and leave nothing but bones for the vultures."

"Gruesome imagery."

"Well, the sight of that man once you're through with him *is* bound to be gruesome. You have—single-handedly, mind you—caused one man to up and join the navy when you were done with him, sent two to rehab, another to Sex Addicts Anonymous, and still one more to consider the priesthood."

"That's not true. All right…guilty as charged, but it was

not the priesthood. He went to a retreat at a Buddhist monastery."

"Xandra, you need a man who is an equal, someone who can hold his own when you try to take over his universe. You and your pretenses, your temper tantrums and tirades…not to mention the fact that to you, three times a day isn't enough. You exhaust these men, and then they're out like yesterday's mink thong."

"But David intrigues me with his ever-so-slight English accent, his professorial deep voice…his love of classical music we hear coming across the hallway."

"Don't do this. I am begging you. *Begging you.*"

"Begging is very unbecoming, Scottie. Don't beg. Don't grovel. Give in. You know you will anyway, so why not cut out the middleman, all this stupid nonsense where I try to talk you into it. You *know* you will do this, so…have more sake."

"Xan, I have to *live* across the hall from him. When this blows up—and honey, blow up it will—I'll have to face him in the elevator. I'd have to move."

"You've been wanting to move anyway. For more closet space."

Scott sighs. "All right. Drinks. My place. I'll see when he's available." Under his breath, as he sips his sake, I hear him mutter, "But when you throw his book collection off the balcony and onto the sands of South Beach, for once *I'll* say I told you so."

We finish our lunch, a brilliant array of eel and conch and pieces of salmon, arranged on a little boat display with rosettes of ginger. We drink sake, I slap down my AmEx

and pay for lunch, and then we leave. I head toward my office; Scott to his temp job.

"Libby…call the *Miami Herald* and get Tammy on the phone. I have to tell her about the benefit concert coming up."

"Sure, Xandra. And listen, I don't know if I feel comfortable going to tae kwon do with you. I think I'm too shy. And I think you're… I don't think you want me to take it on as a PR project. I think you just want to convince me to go."

I stare at Libby. Her face is beet red. "I'm so proud of you. That's the first time you've ever stood up to me. Bravo!"

I walk into my office and say over my shoulder as I enter, "But it won't work. You're coming."

And before too long, Libby is a white belt and looking people in the eye when they talk to her.

Divas do know what's best for everyone.

Divas Are Real

What the hell does that mean?
 A diva isn't afraid to:

• Eat dessert

• Laugh so loud tears roll down her face—and fuck it if she gathers a few laugh lines

• Go against fashion and wear last season because she likes it

• Tell a man she's interested in him

Scott plans, instead of drinks, an intimate dinner for David and me and himself. They've been neighbors for three years and occasionally share Friday-night cocktails.

I arrive at Scott's place fashionably late, as in a good forty-five minutes late, because I must make an entrance. I don't care if the only audience I have is my eighty-four-year-old grandmother and her bridge club, I make an entrance.

When Scott comes to the door, we air-kiss as usual and he points to the balcony.

"He's out there, along with a delicious Brie and crackers, and a nice pinot noir that he brought. Expensive bottle. He's got good taste."

"I knew I wasn't wrong about him."

I hand Scott my purse, which he puts in the bedroom, and then we head toward the balcony. I don't ask Scott "How do I look?" because I know how I look. Fucking fantastic. I mean, do you ever hear a man ask, "Do I look fat in this outfit?" Well, actually, Scott asks me if his jeans make his ass look too big sometimes. But you get the idea. I am wearing a black off-the-shoulder dress—no tan lines—and strappy four-inch stilettos.

We step out into the night air, the tropical breezes of Miami ruffling through my long black hair. The stars are a brilliant array across the sky, and the moon reflects on the water.

"David—" Scott sweeps his hand "—this is my dear, dear friend Alexandra."

David shakes my hand firmly, even holding it a fraction of a second too long. "A pleasure to meet you. I've seen you around the building. I didn't know if you lived here or…"

"No. Just visiting."

He looks crestfallen. "You're a snowbird?" he asks, our term for the blue-haireds and tourists who fly down each winter to escape the frigid temperatures up north.

"No. I live down the beach a bit in the South Beach Towers."

"You must have a spectacular view."

"I do. You'll have to come see it sometime."

"Is that an invitation?" His eyes twinkle. God, I *knew* I wasn't wrong about him.

"Yes. But only if you call me Xandra."

"Fast friends, then."

"Yes, fast friends."

We make small talk and Scott excuses himself to go to the kitchen. I let my eyes do the talking, looking David in the eye as I sip my wine. I ask David about his work, and I regale him with stories of my various spoiled clients.

Twenty-minutes fly by and Scott emerges from the kitchen, saying, "Dinner is served." Scott is a fantastic cook, which is how he pays me back for the countless meals I slap on my credit card for him. I've probably bought him a condo price's worth of dinners over the years. He makes a delicious poached salmon with dill-and-mustard sauce, roasted baby red potatoes, and asparagus poached in orange juice. But the best part of all is his dessert, an over-the-top, million-calorie chocolate mousse cake. Maybe two million.

"Hope you saved room for dessert, David." Scott smiles at the very handsome Professor White, who has regaled us with stories of his travels through Europe.

"Barely. I'm stuffed. This was a fantastic dinner. I'm afraid when I reciprocate, I'll never be able to live up to this."

"We're not fussy." Scott smiles again. "Well, Xan is, but you get sort of used to her."

He slices me a *huge* piece, big enough for two to share— but I never share Scott's chocolate mousse cake.

"You're going to tell me you're going to eat that piece?" David stares at me, bemused, those eyes doing a dance.

"Every fucking morsel," I say—and do.

"God, I am captivated by a woman who actually *eats*. The models and beautiful people around here…they don't eat." He sips his wine, his eyes still locked on mine.

"Well, I do. And Scott's cake is orgasmic." I lick a tiny bit of chocolate from my upper lip, ever so seductively. Then I slip off my shoe and start a serious game of foot-sie under the table. What I really like about David is he doesn't look surprised. He only stares at me with a seri-ous I-have-to-fuck-you-soon look.

Scott, ever so wonderful, takes the hint.

"I am bushed, you two, but I'll be happy to pour us all a nightcap."

"Or we could have a nightcap at my place…" David of-fers, adding, "The three of us."

"You two go. I'll clean up the last of these dishes…I'm just wiped out."

"Xandra? A nightcap on my balcony?"

"Do you have Courvoisier?"

"A woman after my own heart."

"Wonderful. I'd love to."

I slip my shoes back on and go to Scott's bedroom to retrieve my purse. Scott sneaks behind me. "Be gentle with him," he whispers.

"Not a chance. He's simply yummy."

"All the good ones are straight."

We laugh, and I kiss him good-night. Then he sees David and me to the door.

"Have fun! Don't do anything I wouldn't do."

"Yes, Dad." I smile and kiss his cheek. David shakes his hand, then gives him a big bear hug. I like a man secure enough in his manhood to hug Scott. Any hint of homophobia and we're talking grounds for divorce, breakup or homicide.

David and I walk across the hall. He unlocks his condo door, and I am transported somewhere else entirely. The place suits him…crammed with beautiful French country antiques, and filled with bookshelves lined with worn volumes of the classics. Instead of sterile Florida white tile, cold and uninviting, he has Oriental rugs.

He sees me out to the balcony, where Biscayne Bay breezes caress my face. I can make out boats on the water, lights on the masts of sailboats, portholes of yachts sending round beams of illumination out into the night. My long dark hair moves wildly around my face, and I turn so the wind instead blows it back off my face.

"I'll go get your brandy," David says huskily. I watch him as he goes to a liquor cabinet concealed in a hutch and pours us two snifters. As he bends to make our drinks, I admire his profile. His hair is thick and black, and it curls slightly at the collar of his white shirt. He's got just a smattering of gray at the temples, and he has laugh lines and the beginnings of crinkles around his eyes. This tells me he knows how to smile. His nose is straight and strong, and his eyes are gray. They startled me in their lightness at dinner.

He brings back my snifter.

"Thank you," I murmur.

"Thank *you* for coming back here. I don't meet many people. I've spent a lifetime with books, and somehow the South Beach scene isn't quite me. But I like a woman who can eat cake without feeling guilty."

I sip my brandy, and then put down my snifter. "And I like that you're very intelligent, know at least one good joke about a rabbi, a priest and the president of the United States, and that you actually *stock* a nice brandy in your home. And I most especially like that you laugh—you really laugh—at a good story. See…you English have a reputation for being kind of stiff…but I don't think you are at all."

I take a step closer to him. He either makes his move now, or I will. But he doesn't disappoint. He puts his snifter down, comes closer, touches my face and kisses me.

Perfection. I bite his lip ever so lightly, then run my tongue along his lower lip. He moans. A good moan, a sexy moan of a man who knows how to moan and please a woman. I *knew* I wasn't wrong about him, I tell myself for the hundredth time tonight. After kissing endlessly, we make our way to the bedroom. We make love…and he doesn't seem to mind when I take control and climb on top of him, my hair sweeping his chest. In fact, it makes him moan louder.

Afterward, as I curl into the crook of his arm, he says, "Would you believe me if I told you nothing quite like this has happened to me before."

"You want me to believe you're a virgin, Professor? I'm afraid I'm not as naive as some of your students."

He laughs and slips away from me so he can roll over on his side and look me in the eye. "No…just meeting

someone as exciting as you are. And so...so absolutely real.
No pretense. No bullshit. You're brilliant. Just brilliant."

I stare back at him. "I'm also high maintenance. You just
don't know what you're in for yet. I demand the best in
people because I give my all to everything."

"I think I can handle that."

We kiss again, and...surprise...he *can* handle things, because before I know it, we're making love again.

I knew I wasn't wrong about him.

Divas Dish
But They Never Gossip

"Spill."

Scott wants details. We're sitting two weeks later at one of South Beach's numerous sidewalk cafés, people watching and drinking the drink of the week—vodka martinis with olives. Thank God, Scott's off the sweet-drink kick. And the sour-drink kick.

"If I was a betting woman—"

"—which you are."

"I'd say this one's a keeper."

"Could this be Husband Number Three?"

"He could be the *real* 'til-death-do-us-part guy."

"And you don't mean until you murder him."

"No…I mean this really has the potential to be, if not *the* love of my life, then one of the great loves of my life."

"But I don't get it."

"What's to get, Scott? He rocks my world. When we're in bed together, the world stops spinning, and then it spins backward on its axis. This is very hot. And you would appreciate this…he is very, *very*…well endowed."

"You have all the luck…. But I still don't understand how you spotted this guy and thought *there's one to rock my universe.* He looks so unassuming. Handsome, but unassuming."

"I don't know. Don't you find intelligence sexy?"

"I'm a whore. Gay Dream over there is sexy." He points at a muscle-bound South Beach god drinking at a table on the teeming sidewalk.

"You say that, but Bob was smart." I see Scott open his mouth. "I know, *ixnay* on Bob, but he was also very insecure. David, on the other hand, is very secure. For instance, dancing is not for him, but he does not mind that at this very minute I am out in a micromini and will soon be dancing at any one of a dozen places we like to go."

"We'll see how long *that* lasts."

"It will last because I can't have it any other way. I'm not going to fuck around on him. I don't do that. But I'm also not about to give up something I love to do just because a man is worried I might be unfaithful. *That* is something a diva won't put up with for two seconds. Insecure men make me break out in hives."

"I've never seen so much as a red splotch on you. You don't get hives. You just send hives and men who try to control you packing."

"Well, it doesn't matter because David is secure in the knowledge that he satisfies me in every way. He goes on sabbatical next semester. I just may go to Canterbury with him to research a book he's writing."

"You and the queen having tea. I'd like to see that."

"I think I'd be more comfortable with Fergie. Didn't she get her toes sucked?"

He shivers. "Feet repulse me."

"Well…if truth be known, the thought doesn't thrill me either. But you know what I *do* like?"

"What?"

"David slipped his hand up my skirt, completely discreetly, at lunch today, at the River Café."

Scott arches an eyebrow. "And?"

"And…take that exponentially to its logical conclusion…. And you know what I especially like?"

"Do tell."

"That this is all rather new for him. He's pushing his own boundaries and loving every minute of it."

We continue to dish about dates, and a small undercurrent of energy runs through us as we talk about the lightning-rod attraction between David and me. And yes, this is dish not gossip.

A diva knows the difference between dish and gossip.

I once was best friends with a woman who moonlighted as a high-priced dominatrix in Manhattan. My friend was often gossiped about because no one really knew just how she was supporting her high-flying lifestyle on her less-

than-stellar salary at the time. This lifestyle included furs, vacations to places as far away as Singapore and Australia, Africa and a hot-air balloon trip over the wine country of France, and the obligatory summer rental on Fire Island— which she didn't share. I mean, she shared by inviting friends out there, but she didn't share the cost. So how did she do it?

People guessed. They gossiped, spitefully, that she must be fucking someone rich, that she was the plaything for a judge she was seen dating at the time. But I didn't even think the judge could afford her lifestyle. I never chimed in on the speculation, though. That would have been gossip—half-truths and jealous lies. When she told me, over many margaritas, that she was working at night spanking the rich and famous, I didn't gasp. I didn't blink an eye. And I didn't judge.

Over the next couple of years, my divaesque friend told me about the unusual proclivities of some of the more famous men in Manhattan. I knew who liked to be talked dirty to, which news anchor had a thing for being turned over her knee and which politician liked leather. I even knew which very gregarious morning-show host had a thing for licking her boots.

Also, over the course of my friendship with this woman who knew all the secrets the rest of New York City was dying to know, I learned the difference between *dish* and *gossip*.

There is a difference, of course.

Dish is something you serve up over drinks to regale a table of acquaintances. Because of my friendship with this

high-priced diva in stilettos, if the man you saw at sunrise on a certain talk show was really a closet cross-dresser, I was only too happy to dish. Dish is the whispers that follow the famous. And I never feel guilty for dishing. After all, they ask to be in the limelight, and they bought and paid for their behavior with my friend, and therefore they are fair game.

But my friend—she was off-limits. No matter how many mutual acquaintances cornered me demanding to know how she afforded the mink she wore so stylishly, or asked if she was sleeping with you-know-who, I never divulged her secret. That would be gossip.

Gossip hurts. It's that moment you find out that someone you trusted with your most heartrending secret spilled it to someone else. A true diva will talk sex and spankings, will make her friends laugh with that silly nickname she calls her new boyfriend's cock (for the record, I call David's Big Man), but she won't, not even for a laugh, betray the trust her friends have placed in her. She won't take a secret between friends and use it to make herself seem worldlier, funnier, more in the know.

When your close friend shares she's fucking her boss, who's married, and swears you to secrecy, that is a sacred conversation between divas. It isn't dish to serve up like a number-two special of scrambled eggs with a side of hash browns and bacon at the Waffle House.

I trust Scott implicitly. We know where all the skeletons are in each other's closets. I know that Bob was poorly endowed and insecure about it. I know that Scott is a bottom—as in on the bottom. And he knows

I always like it on top. But I never tell anyone the real gossip.

I don't tell anyone that Scott's father disowned him the minute he came out of the closet, and not even his father's near-fatal heart attack last year has brought them together again. I know Scott is HIV negative and won't play Russian roulette and do it without a condom because he is terrified of death. I know he wants, more than anything, to own a restaurant, but doesn't have the money to open up a place—as sure as I know one day I will back him.

And I know, as sure as I know that I'm a diva, that he will never tell a soul that I like to experiment with a little bondage, that I am a moaner in bed. He knows that growing up with a succession of nannies and stepmothers made for a very lonely childhood after my mother died when I was ten. Cancer. He knows my heart shattered like a thrown plate when my lover, Dylan, died in a single-car collision three years ago, and that I took to my bed for three weeks. He knows I am terrified of becoming a mother, and that I really hate menstrual cramps, so the thought of labor repulses me. But he also knows that deep down, I can't wait to have a daughter to whom I can reveal all the secrets of divadom—and how to always be right and always get your man…and your way.

We continue dishing, Scott and me. I tell him all the ways David is sensual, and how he and I sit in his gigantic bathtub, covered in bubbles, and reading aloud to each other from Henry Miller. I even tell Scott that I actually made David scrambled eggs for breakfast the night he stayed at my place. Trust me, this was an immense con-

cession to love on my part. I think, in the four years I've owned my penthouse apartment, I've only turned the stove on once, and that was at closing to make sure it actually worked.

I even tell Scott that this is the deepest I've ever fallen for anyone. Because I know, like the honorary diva he is, Scott won't ever tell a soul.

Silicone Sluts and Implant Invasions: Divas Aren't Afraid of the Word *Fuck*

"Libby, get me that bastard Jack Shaw on the telephone."

Jack Shaw, for the record, is the lowest, most loathsome, most lugubrious lawyer on the planet. With his receding hairline and two-thousand-dollar suits, he is also hell-bent on bringing a lawsuit against one of my high-profile clients, for a paternity and palimony claim we all know is bullshit, but Shaw's statements to the press are a PR nightmare.

"Right away, Xandra." Libby looks frightened, but not nearly as frightened as before she started taking tae kwon do. And, amazingly, she is wearing a shorter skirt, showing off her tighter calves, courtesy of the five hundred roundhouse kicks we do three times a week.

"Jack Shaw here." His voice echoes in my office, courtesy of a speakerphone.

"Jack, you motherfucking bastard, how are you?"

"Xandra Kingston," he chortles. "Let me guess. You've seen the morning paper."

"Seen it? I've put it on the floor so my puppy can use it for training paper."

"You with a puppy? I don't see you as the cute-and-cuddly dog-loving type. What'd ya get? A pit bull?"

"If I did, I would be training it to eat your balls for breakfast." Out of the corner of my eye, I could see Libby at her desk, mouth agape, hanging on my every word.

Surprisingly, Jack had no comeback. "What's the matter?" I taunt him. "Did your tiny prick shrivel up at the thought?"

He sighs. "Whatta you want, Xandra?"

"I want you to stop making inflammatory statements to that reporter you're banging so you can plant all this rumor, innuendo and total crap on the front page. Besides, I hear that reporter has herpes. I'd watch it if I were you."

Dead silence. But this is Jack Shaw after all. He recovers. "What we're saying about Martin Dannerhurst is not rumor and innuendo. Martin Dannerhurst did, in fact, promise to take care of my client for the rest of her life. And he did, in fact, father little Martin Jr."

"He did, did he? I think your client might want to re-examine her line of bullshit here before you two speak to the press again."

"We're doing fine in the media."

"I'm warning you. Why am I warning you? Why am I being so nice to such a little shit shoveler?"

"Don't try to intimidate me—or my client. You'll lose this battle."

"When I paint her out to be the whore she is, I won't lose," I retort.

Libby's cheeks, I could see, were flushed pink.

"You kiss your mother with that mouth, Xandra?" Jack growls into the phone.

I wince. "No, but I suck my boyfriend's cock with it. And now I'll let you in on a little secret. Not only did Martin Dannerhurst *not* sleep with your lap-dancing slut of a client…not only did he *not* promise to support her…he didn't father little Martin."

"The DNA tests will prove otherwise."

"No…they won't. Because Martin's little Marty, if you catch my drift, shoots blanks."

There is dead silence on the other end.

"Still there, Jack?"

Still silence.

"Well, Jack, unless you want me to advise my client to file a libel suit, keep yourself and that tramp out of the papers. I don't want to see so much as a blind item about him. If I do, I'm frying your balls for breakfast."

I hang up the phone, relishing that I had *yet again* beaten Jack Shaw at his own game.

Libby brings in the Dannerhurst file.

"You were amazing, Xandra."

"I was, wasn't I?"

"Yes…" She stands there, and I can tell the way she is biting her bottom lip that she wants to ask me something.

"What is it, Lib?"

"I just don't know how you can think up all those things to say. How you can just decimate the other guy like that."

"Years of practice. Listen and observe, and one day, you, too, will be telling men like Shaw to fuck off."

She flushes. "I could never do that."

"Yes, you can."

"I was taught that ladies never curse."

"Yeah, well, I'm not a lady. I'm a woman. And I can be as ladylike and classy as the next one, when I want. But I'm telling you that sometimes, to get your point across, particularly to men like Jack Shaw who think they rule the world, you have to grab the guy by the balls and speak his language. It's the language men like him understand."

Libby visually cringes. "I couldn't."

"Try it. Say 'fuck.'"

"I can't."

"It's very liberating. Why don't you whisper it?"

Laughing (something she's doing a lot more of lately), Libby whispers, "Fuck."

"There...doesn't that feel good?"

"Kind of."

"Practice it at home. Soon you'll be holding your own around here."

"Thanks, Xandra."

"Anytime."

Yes, the Libby Experiment is coming along nicely. Eventually, I'll teach her to toss her drink on rude men, do a tequila shot with gusto, and how to tell a man off in five languages. In the meantime, she is learning to loosen up.

Scott calls me at four o'clock. "Did you get ahold of Jack Shaw?"

"Yes. Don't think they'll be planting any more lies in the paper."

"Did he sleep with her?"

"Martin? With the bimbo from the strip club?"

"Yeah."

"Sure he did. But I find it pathetic when women take that as some sign that because the guy is wealthy, that entitles them to a blank check."

"I would have loved to be a fly on the wall."

"Trust me, you've heard a variation of that tirade a hundred times before."

"Liberal use of the f-word?"

"The f-word. Scott, how old are you?"

"Thirty."

"Well, it's time to stop using euphemisms."

"Sorry. Bad habit."

"It's all right. Anyway…Jack Shaw is probably going to remember that conversation for a long, long time."

"Have you ever done anything like that?"

"What?"

"Used someone for a blank check. A guy."

"Not likely, Gay Wonder."

"Really? Never?"

"No. Being a diva isn't about using people. You should know that. What about the old guy who wanted you to be his boy toy. You didn't go for it."

"I thought about it."

"Thinking is okay."

"But I shuddered every time I thought of a wrinkled penis."

I shudder myself. "Listen, I have to have dinner with my father and Wife Number Six. Will you come with me?"

"Xan…that's a torture even *I,* your bestest friend, can only do if wildly intoxicated."

"So, I'll take you for a two-martini warm-up before we go. Please…I never ask you to do anything for me."

"Excuse me?" he squawks into the phone. "Excuse me?! Let me count the ways."

"You're being impossible."

"Impossible? Let me remind you that I painted your apartment the weekend you decided you had to have bloodred walls in your bedroom. Then I painted it back to a sea-foam green—not an easy task, mind you—the very next weekend. Four—count 'em—four coats of primer, Xan! And what about the time I ran out for tampons and Midol in the pouring rain? When Hurricane Irene blew threw here."

"Hurricane missions don't count."

"All right then. My sewing skills. How many hemlines have I taken up for you? And then there're the hundreds of times I've gone out for lunch with you."

"And how is that doing something for me? I always pay."

"I know. I'm just trying to get out of this dinner. Xandra, your step—"

"Don't!" I scream.

"Don't what?"

"Don't put the word *mother* on the end of that Silicone Slut's name."

He speaks soothingly, knowing I am drifting closer to homicide at the prospect of dinner with Daddy.

"All right then…I can tell the thought of seeing your father and *Slutsky* is driving you to the edge. Where and when?"

"Meet me at the Delano bar. Two strong martinis should elevate the evening into the barely tolerable category. Then we'll meet them at the restaurant. See you at six o'clock."

He sighs. "Only for you, Xan. Only for you."

"I won't even *mention* the way I mopped up after you when you got so drunk after Bob left."

"You just mentioned it."

"I know. Ta-ta!"

I hang up and look out the window of my office at the azure ocean outside. My father and Silicone Slut. Maybe we'll have *three* martinis.

"Alexandra, darling." My father, still a dashing figure with nary a gray strand in his black hair, and just reading glasses to show his age, rises from his chair at the best table at The Blue Door. He kisses each cheek, and hugs me, and gives a hearty back slap to Scott, whom he's always loved.

That's the puzzling thing about my father. For someone so wonderful and warm, he has a blind side when it comes to women. They're his addiction. And Silicone Slut is the worst of them all. She's also all of six years older than I am. Thank God their prenup is airtight.

She barely looks up from her glass of champagne as we sit down.

"Janice, a fresh dose of collagen in those lips? New Botox? There's something different about you, I just can't put my finger on it."

"Here we go," Scott mutters. He takes his seat opposite me and promptly kicks me in the shin.

She smiles tightly. "Must be this *dazzling* new diamond ring your father bought me. It's rather overpowering, isn't it?" She flashes her hand and wiggles her ring finger.

"No." I smile back. "I don't think that's it. But never mind. The diamond is nice. Of course, not as lovely as my tennis bracelet." I wave my wrist. My bracelet was a gift when I started my own firm and got my first big account in Miami. Dad was separated from Wife Number Five and treated me to it. I don't wear it often—I'd be mugged for it, it's so brilliant—but dinner with Slutsky calls for all my arsenal of antipathy.

Her eyes pop and she flushes, but before we can whip our claws out further, Dad signals for our waiter.

"A martini. Lots of olives." I smile at the waiter, who tells me his name is Jorge. "And keep 'em coming."

"Ditto." Scott smiles. He gives me a "behave" look over the top of his menu, and he checks out Jorge's ass as the guy makes his way to the bar.

"So tell me, my genius daughter, what is new in your life?" Dad asks.

"New account. The Magdalene house of fashion. Very hot. Very controversial. Very rich."

He beams. "You make me proud. Isn't that wonderful, Janice?"

Slutsky looks at her acrylic nails, so long they're like daggers. She tosses her long platinum mane, à la Donatella Versace. "Interesting, of course." She pretends to stifle a yawn. "But what about your personal life? It seems like you just can't hold on to a man."

Scott is mid sip of water, and sputters down his chin.

I smile with all the animosity I can muster. "Well, Janice, I can hold on to anyone I want. *They* can't hold on to *me*. I won't settle. And besides, there is someone new and wonderful in my life."

"What? Alexandra, you've been keeping your poor old dad in the dark." Dad grins and the smile makes it to those green eyes of his. "Tell me about him."

"First, you're neither poor, nor old, Dad. But his name is David, and he's a comparative literature professor at the University of Miami. Brilliant. Authored three books. World traveler. Speaks four languages." I turn to Slutsky. "That means he speaks languages other than *English*," I enunciate as if she is an imbecile. Which she is. "I don't want to confuse you, Janice."

"We'll see how long this one lasts."

Jorge arrives with my martini, and I suck down most of it in a gulp. The guy is no idiot. He takes in Janice's outfit, watches me guzzle my drink, has gaydar that tells him Scott isn't really my date, and does some sort of mental calculation adding up to he better get another round, pronto.

"So anyone see the Dolphins game on Sunday?" Scott says in singsong fashion, though he wouldn't know a football from a testicle. Well...maybe that, but...

I ignore him. The martinis have hit me.

"Excellent game," Dad says nervously. "We had box seats, isn't that right, dear?"

I ignore him.

"Janice...Janice, Janice, Janice...what are you? Wife Number SIX? As in one, two, three, four, five, six? With

an airtight prenup? *You* should be the last person on this entire earth talking to me about how long a fucking relationship lasts."

"Here we go." Scott throws up his hands. Then he drinks down the rest of his martini and hails the waiter, who is already arriving with two more. When the waiter leans down to put Scott's on the table, Scott whispers, "Better make it another two."

"I don't understand her, Charles." Janice now looks demurely at my father. "You *claim* she's very educated, but every time we get together it's f-this and f-that."

"Well, at least when I fuck this and fuck that, Janice, I fuck *only* this and *only* that and keep my legs closed for everyone else."

Scott gasps. He starts on his next martini, watching this like a tennis match.

My father raises his hands. "Look, you two…you don't have to like each other, but could you, for me, learn to be civil? Janice, honey, Alexandra is a tough cookie in a tough profession, and if she liberally sprinkles a few curse words here or there, that's part of the game. And as for you, Xannie—" he calls me by my pet name "—Janice really isn't all that bad if you would just get to know her."

As soon as he says it, Scott's eyes grow round as the plates in The Blue Door. *Isn't all that bad?* The fallout should be good.

"Excuse me?" Janice looks as if Dad's stabbed her in the implant.

"I didn't mean that how it came out," Dad says, but he

can't help himself and starts to laugh. Soon Scott and I are laughing under our breath so hard, tears are rolling down our faces.

"I've had it!" Janice stands and slams down her napkin. "I'm tired of competing with your precious daughter. She's nothing but a bitch, and a stupid one at that."

My father stares at his wife. He has ice water where his eyes should be. "She's no pushover, Janice, but she's anything but stupid. And if you were just the least bit smart, you'd realize you'll lose whatever contest it is you're insisting on trying to win."

"You prick!" she shouts, attracting the stares of neighboring tables. "I'll tell you one thing…my lawyer will be going over that prenup with a magnifying glass."

Scott can't resist. "Isn't this a replay of Wife Number Five's departure?"

"I believe so, Scotty my boy," Dad says.

"And she got the clothes on her back," I add. "You'll be lucky if you walk with that diamond. And Janice?"

"What?!"

"That diamond looks very flawed."

She shrieks and leaves the restaurant. I look at Dad. He starts to laugh. Next thing I know, Scott, Dad and I are laughing so hard we're wiping our napkins at our eyes. We order foie gras and Dom Perignon and have a wonderful time.

Later, I kiss Dad good-night, just a bit tipsy. All right. Drunk.

"Good night, Dad. Sorry about everything with Slutsky."

"That's all right, angel. It all boils down to the fact that no one, ever—" he takes my chin in his hand and tilts my

head so I am looking him in the eyes "—will hold a candle to your mother. Or you."

I well up and give him a hug. Then Scott and I grab a cab and head back to our respective apartments, dropping him off first.

"Your father loves you, Xandra," he says, getting ready to climb out of the cab.

"I know."

"Well…we'll have to see what Number Seven is like."

"Please. No more wives. Though I didn't mind Number Three."

"Hmm. Me, too. But she was jealous of you, just like the rest of them."

"Why?"

"Don't you know, you silly diva, you. Xandra, you're larger than life. Who can compete?"

"I love you."

"Love you, too….and I'm not coming into the office tomorrow."

"No problem. I'll pay you for the day, though. For God's sake, you earned it tonight."

"I must be the only file clerk on South Beach earning forty dollars an hour."

"Maybe."

"Just know I know how much you take care of me."

"I do."

He exits the cab, and I ride in a sort of melancholy funk back to South Beach Towers.

After entering my apartment, I look at my watch. Thank

God, David is a night owl, too, though in his case less from clubbing and more from reading.

"Hello?" He answers on the first ring. "Xan?" He has caller ID.

"Hello…" I sniffle.

"Are you okay, honey?"

"Yes. No."

"What? Tell me."

"It's nothing," I insist.

"Xandra…I just want to know I can be there for you. That you'll let me in."

"You're in. You have no idea how in."

He laughs. Then he grows serious and takes a deep breath. "Please? Please tell me what's wrong."

I sigh. "My father's sixth marriage just blew up. In no small part because of me."

"I know you well enough by now not to argue. High maintenance you are, my dear. But if it was Wife Number Six…doesn't that say something, too?"

"Maybe… I've been married twice, you know."

"I know."

"And two broken engagements."

He inhales audibly.

"In fact, David, there's a two-carat diamond somewhere off the shores of South Beach that got tossed in off of a yacht."

He laughs. "Whoever he was, he probably deserved it."

"Maybe. Then there's also the guy who joined the navy."

"Scott did tell me about Ensign Johnson."

"Yes…and then there's the guy who took off for

Tibet. He's living in a monestary rather than risk running into me."

"Xandra?"

"Hmm?"

"None of that matters to me. Can I tell you something?"

"Sure." I wander with my cordless phone over to my balcony. The moon is full. Maybe that's why I feel this way. I open the sliding glass doors.

"Is that the ocean I hear?"

"Mmm, hmm."

"Looking at the moon?"

"Yes. It's really beautiful. Orange."

"Well, I'm looking at it, too. We're together even though we're apart."

"That's sweet, David."

He grows quiet. Then he whispers, "I thought I was set in my ways. I thought I was content being the way I am. I thought I could settle."

"For what?"

"For whatever it was that passed as a relationship before. But it was never what this is. What's between us. Xandra…I'm trying to tell you I love you."

I think back over marriages one and two. Broken engagements. One-night stands. Love affairs. But it is this man. I know it.

"I love you, too, Professor White."

"Would you think I'm crazy if I came over there right now and made love to you?"

I feel my stomach dip. "No. You better get here soon."

We each hang up, and I go to my bedroom and un-

dress. I light a candle. On my dresser is a picture of my mother. She was my father's sun and moon. I never really knew her. I only knew that she was elegant. One of the few memories I have is of her dressing for a black-tie function and putting on her pearls. She smelled of jasmine. And a hint of lilies. Her hair was wrapped in a chignon. And I remember how my father looked at her.

Just the way David looks at me.

"Fuck," I say aloud. Sometimes that's the only word that will do. I've got it bad. I've fallen in love.

Fuck.

Divas aren't afraid to say it. And sometimes no other word will do.

Divas Never Fake It

Men don't fake it. So why should we?

This little mystery has been confounding me since my friend Naomi confessed to me, at age twenty-two, that she had never had the "Big O"—this despite the fact that she was dating just about the sexiest man I had ever seen.

"What?!" I had screamed from across the table, and had immediately downed my martini. "'Cause if Damian ain't doing it for you, honey, I'll be glad to take him off your hands."

Naomi laughed. "I mean…I get…excited, but…"

"But what? You cannot be telling me this."

She shrugged.

"What about your high-school boyfriend?" I asked, thinking of the prom picture she once showed me with the tall, dark and handsome quarterback on her arm.

Shook her head.

"What about Ted? What about Julian? What about Andrew?"

She was a serial faker.

As we ticked off boyfriends from the loss of her virginity on, she admitted they just didn't do it for her.

So before we go any further, let's get this one out in the open.

Divas never fake it.

No exceptions.

Not ever.

No matter how hard he's trying.

Women who fake it, I have come to conclude, acquire puppy dogs, not men. They feel sorry that the poor man is running through his entire repertoire and he's not moving the earth. He's not even inducing a little tremor.

So this is one of my cardinal rules.

Two months after the demise of my father's sixth marriage, I meet Scott at a sidewalk café. I stare into my Singapore sling.

"Xandra...you look like you've lost your best friend. And since I'm here, Sugar Pops, that's not possible. So what's up?"

"Why are we drinking this?"

"I don't know. I was lacking inspiration this week."

"I'm going to gag."

"Enough of that. What is the matter? You're in need of a little more blush and some under-eye coverstick. Circles, honey. You've got circles under your eyes. This has got to

be serious. Don't tell me you've discovered you're headed for Stepmother Number Seven."

"No. Though he says he wants me to meet his latest girlfriend. A double date so he can meet David. The thought is almost as gag-inducing as this drink. No…it's worse…. Brace yourself."

He grips the table.

"Last night I didn't come."

"Come where?"

I look up from my drink and stare at him.

"Oh my God! Not that! Not you, Xandra!"

"Oh yes! Oh yes, indeed."

He flags our waiter. "Two stiff vodka and tonics. Hold the tonic."

He pats my hand. "There, there. Tell Scotty all about it."

"There's nothing to tell. It would have been so simple to just fake it. But here we are…what…it's been a couple of months. And I don't want David and myself to get lazy. So I just didn't fake it. I won't fake it. I told him he had to work harder, to work at keeping it exciting, and I would do the same."

"Sounds reasonable."

"To you, perhaps. But he didn't take it well."

"What do you mean?"

"He…he accused me of not loving him. Then he wondered aloud if I was interested in *someone else!*"

Scotty shook his head. "Tsk, tsk, Professor White. This is not the way to treat our Xandra."

Our drinks arrive, and we do a quick shot. Scott suddenly grows wide-eyed. "I just thought of some-

thing. He all but accused you of being interested in someone else."

"Yes." I nod.

"Which I know you're not. You're hopelessly in love with him. So that means he not only *didn't* satisfy you...he pissed you off.... Oh God...I hate to ask what happened next. Waiter? Two more." He signals.

"Well...you said it would happen eventually."

He cringes. "Please...tell me you didn't. Not his books."

I nod.

"In the surf?" he asks.

I nod.

"Not his first-edition Edgar Allan Poe."

"No. I spared his favorites, but I accused him of being more interested in his books than pleasing me."

"Ouch."

I nod again.

"Honey, can I say something here?"

"Not before I get a vodka."

We people watch, scoping out the thong and in-line skating crowd until another round comes. The waiter, with the name Chad embroidered on his polo shirt, sets down our drinks. "This is a boyfriend fight," Scott whispers to him. The two of them exchange looks. I sense some chemistry.

Still, I am too distraught to work at a fix-up. I fight back tears. Divas cry, too.

"Baby..." Scott touches my hand. "I thought you were crazy to go after Professor David White. He's a *professor* for God's sake. You're a diva. You like sunbathing topless. And bottomless. He sits on the beach under an umbrella. You

like loud clubs and trendy restaurants. He likes eating in.
You like Versace and Gucci. He likes khakis and depart-
ment-store polo shirts. You wear—" he looks under the
table "—four-inch stilettos. He wears sensible loafers. But
somehow, someway, I can see adoration, love and sexual
tension so strong it's palpable."

"Exactly. So why does he doubt me?"

"Look, Baby Bitch, you have to realize that you can be
intimidating."

"What the fuck are you talking about?"

"I rest my case. I mean, after all these years, I find it adorable, endearing…but you scare the shit out of the average
person. Look at poor Jack Shaw."

(Two days after my confrontation with Jack Shaw, he had
packed his bags for a Hazeldon clinic in the Midwest to
beat a cocaine addiction.)

"But I love David. I don't look at other men. And I don't
want to intimidate him."

"Of course not, but you do. It's almost like you were
born to terrify people."

"So how come I don't scare you?"

"Too many years together. The good. The bad. I've out-
lasted your husbands. But we've had our tiffs. Remember
the time you accused me of telling Naomi that you like
to tie men up?"

"Yes." (I had a screaming match with Scott in the middle of a hotel lobby where we'd met to go out.) "Turns
out Naomi was just making an educated guess."

I sip my drink and spot a twentysomething guy with a
tan and a white muscle shirt, tight jeans and Ray-Bans, his

smile dazzling. I recognize him as a Calvin Klein under-wear model. Ah, the joys of South Beach.

"All right. I swear on all the vodka in the world that even if that guy over there came over and wanted to fuck me on the table right here, right now, I wouldn't."

"I would."

"Can we stay focused?"

"*You* pointed him out!"

"Fine, but Scott…I don't know what it is. David is my soul mate. Even when I got married before, I never said that."

"Then have you considered that perhaps…and don't bite my head off…but perhaps throwing his books into the ocean and…let me guess, hurling a plate—"

"It was a wineglass."

"A wineglass then…that perhaps this isn't the best way to settle conflict."

"Maybe you're right."

We drink and dish, but at the end of the night I don't feel much better, plus I am well on my way to a case of bed spins. Around midnight, David calls me a half-dozen times. I see his number flashing on caller ID, but I don't pick up. I'm not ready.

**A diva doesn't demand the best from others…
she demands it from herself.**

"You threw his books into the ocean."

"Yes."

Dr. Alfred Duncan is taking notes. A lot of them.

In desperation over my decision not to fake the Big O, I call up Miami's top therapist and bully my way in to an

appointment. Dr. Duncan is filling a steno pad with, from my vantage point, scribble.

"And have you always been this way? Always…resolved your differences with people in this way?"

"Yup. Look, Doc, I don't feel any remorse, if that's what you're pushing me for."

He purses his lips. "I see."

"I'm not a sociopath, if that's what you're thinking. It's a two-way street. I don't just demand the best from others…I demand it from myself. Dr. Duncan, life is not a dress rehearsal. I'm grabbing it by the balls and living it to the fullest. And the people around me can either come along for the ride or get out of my way."

"I see."

"Stop saying 'I see.'"

"I see…uh…I see that you believe you are correct in how you handle things. You're comfortable with that. So why are you here? If not because you have some remorse."

"I want to know if it's okay not to fake it. Do I have some sort of obligation to not hurt his feelings? It's just once in a while. This is the first occurrence. With him. I mean, Doc…he will drive me wild. But this one time…"

"I'm more concerned with your throwing his books in the ocean."

"*I'm* more concerned with him being lazy in bed. What's next? Gaining twenty pounds? Quickies with no foreplay? Now, that's okay once in a while, but you don't want to make a steady habit of it."

I notice beads of sweat on the good doctor's forehead. "What is your lovemaking normally like?"

"Well…normally we might indulge in a little bondage. I might tie him up and spend three hours just torturing him sexually, not letting him come until he's literally insane with animal lust. Or we might role-play. I pretend I'm a college student and he's the headmaster. Or even if it's just, you know, us climbing into bed and making love, it's usually so intense it's like a drug."

"So you're a sex addict, perhaps?"

"I think you're missing the point."

"Perhaps he was just tired then. This pace you suggest… it could be exhausting, the pressure to always make each encounter so, as you say, intense."

It hits me. "You know, Doc…I think I know what I need to do."

"What's that?"

"Get back on the horse. Or the cock, so to speak. I love him. He loves me. What am I doing talking to a shrink? I need to go fuck my boyfriend. If you'll excuse me—"

"But you have another forty-five minutes in the session!"

"Don't need 'em. Sorry, Dr. Duncan…I've never been to a shrink. I'm sure you're helpful to many people, but what I really need is to be with David right now. Thanks."

"You're welcome," he said, puzzled.

"It's like this, Doctor. Once you start lying, even if it's faking it in the bedroom once or twice, you lose something. You lose something special. I don't want to ever lie to David."

I shake Dr. Duncan's hand and rush out to my car and head over to David's apartment building. I enter the building, say hi to the doorman and rush to the elevator.

I press twelve and ride to his and Scott's floor. I knock on the door. No answer. I ring the little bell positioned beneath the peephole. I hear nothing, but he has carpeting, so that's not surprising. I look at my watch. Four-thirty. I realize he still has class. I knock on Scott's door. He's at his temp job. I let myself in with my key and pour myself a drink.

Two hours later, I hear David fiddling with the lock across the hall. I open the door and David turns around briefcase in one hand, a stack of books in the other. His eyes well up, and he sets his things down and comes over to kiss me.

"I'm sorry, Xandra. I never should have insinuated you were interested in someone else."

"Shh." I put my hand to his soft lips. "Well…I'm not sorry I threw your books in the ocean. But I am sorry I hurt you. I never want to hurt you."

He turns his head, fumbles for his keys and opens the door. "Come inside. Let's talk."

He picks up his things, and I lock up Scott's place. No sooner are we inside David's apartment than he drops his books with a soft thud on the carpet and throws his brief-case half across the room. He is kissing me suddenly, running his lips down my neck, pulling at my hair, taking my face in his hands. He moans.

"David," I gasp. "Sometimes we're going to be out of sync, but I don't want to lie. It's not that I don't enjoy—"

He covers my mouth with his hand, gently. "Shh. I understand. We've set the bar so high for ourselves. But I

don't want us to start deceiving each other in the bedroom. I'd rather work at keeping this passion alive."

I begin unbuttoning the oxford-cloth shirt he's wearing. "Fuck me, David. Just shut up and fuck me."

He lifts my dress over my head, and we somehow, while kissing and touching each other, make our way to the bedroom.

"Promise me something?"

"That I won't throw your books in the ocean?" I ask breathily.

He shakes his head then takes off my bra and nibbles down my neck. (Note: Divas only wear sexy underwear. Thongs. Lace. Garter belts.)

"That I won't break your crystal wineglasses again?"

He shakes his head and pulls off my panties. He licks his way down to my thighs.

"What then?" I gasp.

"That you won't ever fake it. That you'll keep challenging us."

"Deal," I whisper. But it soon becomes clear to me that tonight, faking it won't be a problem.

A Diva Doesn't Have to Be the Most Beautiful Woman in the Room— Just the Most Fearless

First, let's get one thing straight: The diva is not the most beautiful woman in the room. She is the most-looked-at woman in the room. She is the woman with presence. Most important, she is the woman with attitude.

Take a look at the self-help section of the bookstore. You've got *Women Who Love Too Much* and women trying to capture and tame Peter Pan–syndrome men. You've got, frankly, women trying to fix their relationships—and themselves—and what are men doing? Nothing. They're leaving their underwear on the floor, forgetting to change the toilet-paper roll, and watching football and drinking beer on Sundays. They're not freaking out about the cellulite on their thighs, and they're sure as hell not meeting at Starbucks with their buddies to dissect everything the women in their lives are saying to them, trying to gauge

whether it means "commitment" or not. I don't blame them. They have a good thing going.

If I do nothing else, then I hope to inspire a legion of women to become divas, to develop that diva attitude. Honey, a diva doesn't care if she doesn't get a diamond for Valentine's Day. She *will*. And if she doesn't…baby, he'll be eating a candy heart—one of the ones with lettering on their pastel-colored sweetness—that says "Get out!"

Of course, I won't deny it helps to be the best-looking woman in the room. But most of that is about what you believe. This is a lesson I try to teach my various friends and loved ones. Which brings me to…

Valentine's Day.

Ahh, the day of love and candy and flowers. The day immortalized by Cupid. The day for lovers and fools for love.

The day when a diva's mind turns to nothing else but The Fix-up.

DIVA DOSSIER
Victim #1

Name: Scott St. James

Age: 30. Though victim lies about his age. Could be 33. But who's counting?

Last relationship: One year ago, the crash and burn of St. James and Robert M. King.

Reason for lack of a boyfriend: Always goes for the boy toy, never someone with substance. Case in point, Robert King aka Mr. Muscles; aka Bob; aka Hairless Whore; aka the man who cheated on Scott in Scott's own bed. With an eighteen-year-old hustler.

Plan: The Fix-up

Date: February 12

Parties involved: Alexandra Kingston aka Moi and Professor David White aka The Boyfriend Sucked Into Fixing Up Scott With Professor Julian Crane from the Drama Department.

Location: Xandra's apartment

Occasion: Cocktails

Outcome: Read on

"Stop sulking. Stop sulking this minute or I am making you pay me back that loan for that ridiculous car you had to buy."

"It's not ridiculous."

"A six-foot-two-inch man does *not* need an MG. You look like a circus clown climbing out of it. I don't even know how you drive it. Your knee must hit your chin as you're pressing the gas."

"Shut up."

"No, you shut up and start putting these appetizers on a tray so it looks like I made them."

"You're not fooling anyone, Xan. Everyone knows you didn't make these."

"No," I snap. "*You* and *David* know I didn't make these. Professor Crane has no idea."

"I have a very bad feeling about this, Xan."

"You're being a big baby. You haven't had a relationship since the Hairless Whore, Bob, and it's time."

"What about that waiter I picked up?"

"I said—read my lips—re-la-tion-ship. It's time."

He starts pulling little canapés out of the box from the restaurant. "But David isn't exactly the best judge of what my type is. Like most straight men, he thinks, *homo…meet homo.* It's as if by virtue of two guys being queer, they're meant to be together."

"That's not true. David gave this a great deal of thought."

"What if this professor guy is ugly? Or dresses in tweed? You know tweed makes me break out in hives."

"You're just allergic to the ugliness of it.... Besides, David assures me that Julian Crane is the hottest professor on campus. He fends off *both* sexes on a routine basis."

"I don't know." He pouts again, sticking his lip out and looking pathetic.

"It's too late now, chickadee."

As if on cue, my doorbell rings.

"Oh God...I'm going to throw up."

I slap Scott across the face. Lightly. But enough to snap him out of it.

"Thanks," he says. "I needed that."

I open my door, and for once am speechless. For there, standing on my doorstep, is my love, my lust, Professor David White. And there, standing next to him, is an Adonis. I've seen a lot of men in my life. A *lot* of men. But this one...he looks half-Cuban, his skin a soft mocha, his eyes jet black and rimmed with long lashes, his teeth as white as a toothpaste-commercial model's, his hair dark brown and thick. His chin is chiseled with one of those adorable little dimples in the center of it. And that body. Sculpted and taut. His dress understated and elegant. He shakes my hand and smiles. "You must be Xandra. I've heard so much about you."

I shut my mouth, which I am sure was gaping, and smile. Then I manage to say, "I hope David didn't tell you the dreaded books-off-the-balcony story, but I'll take that as a compliment."

"It is one. In fact, you're all he talks about."

"Where are my manners? Come in." I step aside to let Professors Crane and White in. David sweeps close to me and wraps an arm around my waist. His breath is in my ear, driving me wild. Then he whispers, "Did I do good?"

"Darling," I whisper back, "your reward for this will leave you weak."

I usher them into the living room. Scott is nowhere to be found. "Scott must be in the kitchen. You two wait here. David, would you mind pouring Professor Crane a cocktail?"

"Please call me Julian." He grins. I need sunglasses his smile is so bright.

I race to the kitchen. "Scott! Scott…oh my God, Scott, you are going to be indebted to me forever. Beyond forever. You so owe me."

"I'm sure. If he's so great, what's he need a fix-up for two days before Valentine's Day?"

"I don't know. What's *your* excuse?" I grab Scott by the arm.

"You're pinching me. In the spot under my arm where it really hurts."

"Good. Now come on. And bring that tray of appetizers I slaved over."

He rolls his eyes, but brings the tray. I should have known better. When we enter the living room, he takes one look at Julian and drops the tray right then and there.

"Oh sweet Jesus!" Scott says, his face flushing.

Julian immediately gets up and dashes to Scott's aid. They pick up the canapés, laughing.

"I'm Julian."

"Scott St. James, professional klutz."

They giggle, Scott a little *too* uncontrollably. Once they get the now topsy-turvy canapés back on the tray, I am clueless as to what to do for food. "Scott, dear, could I see you in the kitchen?"

"Sure."

We take the mangled little finger sandwiches and what-nots back into my kitchen.

"I can't do this, Alexandra Summer Kingston."

"This must be serious. You're calling me by my full name."

"He's too gorgeous."

"What?"

"Did you not see what I just did?"

"Yes. In fact, I now have to run out for more food because," I say, opening a cabinet, "other than a can of salted peanuts, I don't have anything to serve."

Scott opens the fridge. "You have olives."

"For the martinis, Gay Wonder. And what am I supposed to do, put out a bowl of green olives?"

He shrugs.

"And back," I say, "to the more important issue at hand. What does 'too gorgeous' mean? Ordinarily, on a blind date, you're worried about the opposite problem."

"I would just be a bundle of nerves. Yes, I work out courtesy of tae kwon do. Yes, we're testing for our black belt in a month. But that man in there is the most beautiful specimen of homo—homo sapiens I have ever seen."

I look at Scott and am suddenly filled with feeling a cross between maternal instinct and pity. "Love—" I reach out and touch his cheek "—you are more than those rippling abs you've worked so hard to get. You are a beautiful person. You are funny and clever, and very smart. And you don't *have* to be some goddess/diva/gay god. All you have to be is you, and trust me, the handsome professor can't help but fall for you. Just in time for Valentine's Day."

"You think so?"

I nod. "You're an honorary diva. You'll have him eating out of your palm in no time. Of course, what he'll be eating are peanuts and green olives, but..."

Scott takes a deep breath. We open the olives, put them in a bowl. Pop the peanuts in a bowl, and go out to visit with out guests.

By the end of the night, courtesy of no real food served with our drinks, all four of us are smashed, but as I nuzzle David on the couch, I can't help but glance out on the balcony where Scott is showing Julian the view of a thousand stars.

"I did good, didn't I?" David asks.

"If I didn't know any better, I'd say there was a diva underneath that serious college professor exterior."

I kiss David. Then I whisper, "After they leave, I'm going to blow your mind…and a few other things."

DIVA DOSSIER
Victim #2

Name: Olivia "Libby" Maxwell

Age: 24. Looks 19.

Last relationship: One serious boyfriend in college. Since then a string of duds.

Plan: The Fix-up

Date: February 13

Parties involved: Alexandra Kingston aka Moi and Scott St. James, still reeling with delight from his date with Mr. Wonderful aka The Gorgeous Professor Crane.

Location: Tokyo Sushi

Occasion: Dinner

Intended Fix-up: Tae kwon do instructor, Master "Sam" Kwon

Outcome: Read on

Divas can be good listeners.

"I can't do it, Xandra," Libby whines as I urge her to get her purse so we can make our way to Tokyo Sushi.

"Do what?"

"Dinner with Master Kwon."

"Yes, you can. Besides, Scott and I are going, too, so it doesn't look like a date. Just four friends gathering for sake and sushi."

Libby has been in love with Master Kwon since she first set eyes on him in class. In fact, I think that's why she is now a yellow belt and even goes to Saturday class—which Scott and I never attend because it would interfere with sleeping in after Friday-night clubbing.

Master Kwon is an instructor at the studio. He is in his late twenties, tall, lanky and lightning fast. A third-degree black belt, he has a deft and gentle touch with new students. He also has an amazingly good sense of humor, and when he smiles, his eyes look like they're laughing, too. It also turns out that he is very single and very lonely. So when we asked him to join us for sushi, he said yes before we'd even totally spit out our invitation.

"Come on, Libby." I tug at her sleeve. "Scott and Sam will be waiting."

When we invited Master Kwon, we all sort of realized we couldn't spend the whole evening calling him "Master Kwon." His real name, in his own language, is quite long and I garbled it terribly. But he says we can call him Sam, so we do.

Libby is near tears. "He is so…perfect."

"No one's perfect—except me. Now, let's go!"

I drag her to the elevator, and then down to ground level where we walk to Tokyo Sushi. February in Miami, today, means a breeze and sixty degrees. I shiver. That's kind of cold for me. What can I say? Your blood thins when you live in South Beach awhile.

"What am I going to talk to him about?"

"Class. His home country of Korea. What kind of food he likes. Movies. Whatever it is you usually talk to dates about. He likes you, Libby. I can tell."

"I get all sweaty in class and then my hair frizzes."

"Being a diva isn't about looking perfect. Come on, haven't I taught you better than that? Don't you notice the way he always comes to you—in a dojo full of students—and helps you with your punches. How he smiles when you do it right. How he laughs just a little *too* hard at your attempts at humor?"

We arrive at the restaurant.

"I want you to hold your head up," I tell her. "March in there and look him in the eye. Be a diva. Be sexy and play-ful. And know that no one else in that room is as vibrant as you are. Except me, of course."

She looks at me for courage and does. She's dazzling. Heads turn. It isn't the outfit (personally, I would have worn a shorter skirt and a higher heel). It's the way, when she sees Sam, that her eyes shine.

He stands and bows to her. She bows to him. Scott air-kisses me. I air-kiss him.

We all sit down. Libby has learned well. She knows that asking others about themselves is the sure way to get a con-

versation rolling. Divas may have to be the center of attention, but they don't have to hog the spotlight. They can be good listeners.

"Tell me, Master Kwon—"

"Please, Olivia, call me Sam…"

I look at him closely. My God, he's blushing. Pink! I kick Scott under the table and subtly roll my eyes in the direction of Sam. Scott sees it. He smiles at me. We've scored a home run. Or a well-placed roundhouse kick. Whatever your analogy.

"Okay…Sam. And please, call me Libby. All my friends do." God…that's one of my lines. I swell with pride.

"Tell me more about how you became interested in the martial arts."

He spreads his palms and smiles. "I don't know." He shrugs. "In my country, seems like it is the thing to do. Like here boys play baseball. There, you begin study with a master…. Tell me, do you like tae kwon do?"

She stares deep into his eyes. "I love it." I know what she wants to say is "I love you." But I sense that conversation won't be far off.

We order enough sushi for the city of Tokyo and eat and laugh and drink hot sake until our heads spin. When the bill comes, Sam insists on treating. We all stand to leave, and he takes Libby by the hand. When we get out to the sidewalk, I pinch Scott under the arm as I link mine through the crook of it.

"We have to go," I say. "Why don't you walk Libby home, Sam. If you don't mind."

"I don't mind." He bows to Scott and me. We bow back.

I kiss Libby and whisper in her ear, "This is your night. You are a star."

She radiates. Maybe it's the sake. But I don't think so. The two of them walk off, hand in hand. It's then I notice their body language. It's not just that they're holding hands, it's how they walk in step with each other. How they move as one.

"Our baby is growing up," I say to Scott.

"Yes, Ma, our Libby is a grown-up girl."

"With highlights, contacts, a better wardrobe—she wore DK tonight—laughter in her life and now a totally hot lover. I'll sleep well tonight."

And I do.

DIVA DOSSIER
Final Valentine's Victim

Name: Dad

Age: 62. Looks 45.

Last relationship: Silicone Slut

Plan: The Fix-up

Date: February 14

Parties involved: Alexandra Kingston aka Moi

Location: Bluefin Café

Occasion: Lunch

Intended Fix-up: Madeline Swenson, the widow downstairs

Outcome: Read on

A diva never takes no for an answer.

After six failed marriages (my mother doesn't count; that was a love match), I believe in my little diva heart that Dad has learned his lesson.

No…it's time for him to stop chasing these bimbos. He was right not too long ago when his marriage to Janice imploded like a bad implant. No one can live up to my mother. But on the other hand, he has never really tried to find true love again. Instead, he picks women he knows are using him, so he never is truly in love, and he never has to worry about her dying or leaving him and breaking his heart all over again. He doesn't get hurt. He just finds another Starsky and Slutsky and moves on.

I decide it's time to remedy this. And Madeline Swenson is just the ticket. Her husband, Will, died four years ago. She grieved, and then she set about rebuilding her life. She's a beautiful fiftysomething, with vibrant auburn hair and dancing brown eyes. And she lives, she really lives. She backpacks in Europe. She volunteers at the hospital and cuddles AIDS and drug-addicted babies. She reads everything she can get her hands on, and she laughs with no thought of Botox. Yet for her laugh lines, she actually looks younger than the taut-faced wicked stepmonsters I've had before. It's all in the way she dances through life, living each moment for all it's worth. She lives in my building and we have had dinner together a few times… sometimes meet at my condo's palm-tree surrounded pool. It's time they meet, so I arrange a lunch. She has no idea

it's a fix-up. I just tell her that no one should be alone for Valentine's Day. ("But I'm not alone, dear, I'm going to the hospital to volunteer." I don't take no for an answer, however. When do I?)

Madeline and I walk to the restaurant together.

"By the way, Madeline, since my father wasn't doing anything for lunch, I asked him to join us. He's an avid reader, too."

"Oh really?" She smiles. I'm not fooling her. My guess is she just may be a "mature" diva herself. She didn't get older; she got better.

"Really." I play along.

At the restaurant, Dad is blindsided. I knew he wouldn't come otherwise. He tries to avoid looking surprised, but he can't help it. Madeline is so not his type. She's not blond, not dumb, and she doesn't have fake tits. But I have faith.

Being a diva is about being exciting, and she is.
Before too long, over salmon (for me) and fresh mahimahi (for each of them), Madeline is regaling my father and me with tales of haunted castles in Scotland and rowdy Irish pubs, along with poignant stories of babies shaking and writhing until she swaddles them. Before my eyes, she grows more and more beautiful. The mark of a real diva. The mark of a woman worth loving and knowing.

When she excuses herself to go to the ladies' room, my father rises like a gentleman, then sits down. As soon as she is out of earshot, he says, "I should wring your elegant little neck."

"But you won't. Admit it. If I had told you I had a fifty-ish widow for you to meet, you would have told me to go jump off my balcony. But she's great."

"She's more than great. She's fantastic. Vibrant. Smart. Funny. Beautiful."

"When will people realize I always know what's best for them? I'm three for three this Valentine's Day."

"Do you think she'd think I was crazy if I asked her to dinner tonight?"

"Dad…you sound nervous. Like a little schoolboy with sweaty palms, about to deliver his first Valentine's Day card."

"That's how I feel."

She rejoins us a moment later. Dad asks her to dinner. He blurts it out, instead of behaving in his usual suave fashion. She agrees.

"Or better yet," she says, "I could make you dinner. All the restaurants will be packed tonight."

"No one has cooked me a meal since…well, probably since my first wife died."

"How does rock Cornish game hen sound?"

"You can whip that up on such short notice?"

Madeline, who insists we call her Maddie, smiles demurely. "It's not short notice, my dear. I was going to make myself an elaborate Valentine's Day dinner anyway. Just because you're alone doesn't mean you can't want the very best for yourself."

Dad reaches across the table and touches her hand.

I just sit back, self-satisfied. She is a woman after my own heart.

★ ★ ★

As for the handsome Professor David White, he buys me a telescope for Valentine's Day. The card says "So I can give you the stars."

"David, this is so wonderful. Though I want to make mad passionate love to you right this instant, in fact, I have to kiss you—" I do indeed stop to kiss him as he and I sit amid red wrapping paper. "Can we set this up? I so want to see Orion."

He looks delighted. "Of course. You wait here and open another bottle of champagne."

I do. Then I pour two glasses and call out to the balcony, "Did you know Julian and Scott are down on Coconut Grove at this very instant, spending the night at the Mayfair Hotel? Probably sitting in the piano bar right now."

"Come on out, it's set up," he calls back. Taking the outstretched glass of champagne I offer him, he asks me, "Do you mind that we stayed in? That we're not out at one of SoBe's hot spots?"

"No. I like knowing that Scott and I can still go out dancing or to a place where we can people watch and that you're okay with that. But I also like staying home with you. I can't explain it, but somehow it's just as exciting as that first night together."

"Why don't you see if you can spot Orion. I think I have the telescope aiming right for it."

I bend down and put my left eye to the telescope. "David, darling, you must have had too much champagne. I can't see a goddamn thing."

"Let me look."

He bends down and adjusts things. "Try now."

"I still can't, love. Nothing. It's like this telescope is defective."

"Maybe there's something on the lens. Sea spray got it all cloudy."

I walk to the front of the telescope to clean it. And there, taped to the lens, is a diamond ring.

"Oh, David." My voice catches in my throat.

"You infuriate me, amuse me, challenge me and make me ache for you every day. I have to marry you, Xandra. Say yes."

I unstick the diamond ring. It's emerald-cut in a platinum band.

"Is it big enough? Beautiful enough?"

"Of course, David."

"Then say yes. Put it on your finger."

"David…are you sure you understand what you're getting into? I've tried marriage. Divas don't do well caged."

"I'd never try to cage you. It's when you're hatching these schemes of yours, setting up your father and Scott, and poor Libby, and painting your apartment three times in a month, and throwing my books off the balcony, and… serving olives for dinner, that I think I can't possibly be without the rush, the drug, the excitement that is you, my darling Xan. My diva."

Can it be a man finally gets me? Scott gets me. Always has, but he is an honorary diva, after all. And this man, with his quiet good looks, his book collection, the meticulous way he folds his laundry, the way, despite all that is studious about him, he grabs me and makes love to me standing up, my back

against the shower wall, water everywhere, laughing and loving and not caring about any of it, he seems to get it.

That I am a diva. And when I walk in a room, you know it.

And yet, with him, I am home.

I slip the ring on my finger.

And that night, anyone with a telescope on a boat out at sea got quite an eyeful on my balcony.

A Diva Knows
How to Make an Exit

Scott is beside himself. "Third time's a charm, Xan! I'm so happy for you." He clutches me to him and then steps back to admire my ring.

"That's a big honkin' diamond!"

"My thoughts exactly."

"We have a million things to do."

"What do you mean?"

He rolls his eyes as if I am stupid, which I am not. "First wedding at the Plaza in New York. A huge affair attended by all the beautiful people. Your father and Wife Number...what was it?"

"I think Two." We sit down on the floor at the hottest new sushi place in town, on embroidered red silk pillows with elaborate dragons on them.

"Wife Number Two takes over and plans the whole thing. All that is required of Alexandra is that she show up. Late, of course. In her twenty-thousand-no-that's-a-real-figure-not-my-salary-dollar Caroline Herrera gown. We dine on pheasant and foie gras. Cocktail hour…I recall ice sculptures of the statue *David,* and shrimp as big as my fist, for God's sake. Caviar."

"Yes. I think those are some of the highlights."

"Oh no…I'm not done. There were mountains of caviar. Mountains! And iced vodka. A martini bar. Enough Kristal champagne to create a lake. Bridesmaids in silk dresses in an oyster-shell pink. Also designed by Herrera."

"Yes."

"And note that one Scott St. James, your *best* friend, did not get to throw you a bridal shower. That job was stolen from me by your aforementioned stepmother."

"Yes, it was. She was a bit overbearing, though she meant well. And your point, darling?"

We are perusing the menus.

"I'm not finished. Marriage number one doesn't just end in divorce. It ends in a nuclear holocaust, combusted in less than two years."

"He was incredibly jealous and controlling. He may have been great in bed, but it was impossible to overlook his other flaws."

"Yes. So we move on to Husband Number Two. One very nice Mark Carson, whom, I may add, I am still in touch with because he is still quite madly in love with you."

I roll my eyes. "Is there a point to this speech?"

The waitress arrives, bows to us and takes our order.

When she leaves, Scott says, "Yes, there is, because for marriage number two, Xandra insists on outsmarting Stepmother Number Three or Four, can't remember."

"The Face," I say, prompting his memory. This is our nickname for one particular stepmother who had had so many lifts she looked like something out of a wax museum.

"Yes, Xandra outwits The Face by flying to Las Vegas for a quickie nuptial. No shower. No engagement party. No bachelorette party with male strippers—and God, don't we all need one of those? No wedding party. No nothing. I didn't even get to throw so much as a fucking grain of rice."

As the waitress arrives with our sake, I can see where this is headed.

"Just say what's on your mind, Scott."

"I want to be your wedding planner. I want to plan it, throw the bridal shower, do all of the things I've been *robbed* of doing."

Scott looks at me with the most sincere of expressions. I never doubt that his love for me is completely pure and untainted by jealousy.

"But Scott…by your third wedding, darling, it's not as if you're lacking in peignoir sets. In fact, at this stage of my life, it's nudity in bed. A bridal shower would be…downright redundant."

"David deserves a shower."

"David?"

"Yes. Garter belts. Sexy negligees. Doesn't he deserve those on the honeymoon? And don't *I*, your loyalest,

bestest, cutest, gayest friend, deserve to get to be able to do all this? I want to plan a classy wedding. I want to shop for the dress with you. I want to be part of it."

The thought of putting a white wedding dress on my body makes me break out in hives. As I think of this, our sushi arrives. Scott raises his sake glass and toasts me and my big honkin' diamond. Then he adds, "Besides, I was the catalyst for your meeting David. You owe this relationship to *moi*."

I see the look of love on his face, how he's thrilled with my happiness. I hear myself say, "All right. You can plan the wedding."

"You won't regret this! I love you, Xandra."

"I love you, too," I say, but deep in my gut I wonder if this is really such a good idea. I have visions of Chippendale dancers and bridesmaids in purple hoop skirts.

Despite Scott's keen fashion sense, when it comes to events, he thinks there's no such thing as too O.T.T., as in Over The Top.

David is content to leave the details to Scott. "All I ask is that my family fly in from London. I'd like my brother, Henry, to be my best man. It isn't every day a man gets married. Beyond that, as long as you show up and say 'I do,' it can be a circus theme for all I care."

"You may live to regret that statement. Overkill is Scott's middle name, but we'll see what happens."

"Where do you want to go on our honeymoon?"

"You've never been married before."

He shakes his head, although, of course, I know this already.

"So you're planning on a honeymoon, bachelor party, the whole nine yards?"

"You don't want a honeymoon?"

"It's not that. I guess I would just call it a vacation together. But honeymoon it is. How does Paris sound?"

"Perfect. Or Venice. Someplace romantic."

"Venice then."

I walk toward my fiancé and touch his face. Behind his mild-mannered but very sexy exterior is a wild man. He rocks my world—and isn't threatened by sex toys and a little begging in the bedroom. But it's something else that thrills me about him. Something quiet and deep and still. It's past the diva stuff and even deeper than that.

"Let's go for a sunset walk on the beach," I say.

He nods. "Let me go change into shorts."

"I love your legs. Have I told you that?"

He looks at me slyly. "Yes, you have. More than once. I'm beginning to feel like a bit of a sex object."

"Get used to it." I wink at him.

He goes into the bedroom to change, and I suddenly realize we haven't decided who is going to move in with whom. He lives in a beautiful apartment, with antiques and most of his books—minus the ones I threw off the balcony. I live in a huge penthouse apartment with a view only a lot of money can buy down here in South Beach.

My furniture leans toward Art Deco, and I have gauzy linen curtains that flutter in the cross-breeze.

He comes back out in his shorts. God, that man has great legs.

"David…have you given a thought to combining our two universes? You with…French country and antiques. Me with…"

"I call your place Early South Beach Sexy."

I laugh. "Yes…well, the two places couldn't be more different."

"Immaterial to me, love. I need my books. Those I can't part with. But the furniture is frankly something to sit down on. I may have excellent taste, as you say, but I'm still a man."

As I've grown older, I realize being a diva does not mean *always* having your own way. Not to the detriment of those you love. "Well…I don't even use my kitchen, and yours is bigger."

"You have the better view."

I stop and stare at him. "So you'd sell and move into my place?"

"Your place is bigger anyway. All I ask for are my books. And my desk over there." He points to a beautiful Chippendale secretary.

"Fine. But you'd sell? This place? You'd invest in this marriage and sell this apartment you love?"

"If you're asking whether after living and loving all my years I'm still willing to throw a little caution to the wind and invest one hundred percent in you and me, then yes."

I take his hand and we venture to the door, down the hallway, down the elevator, to the beach.

"You're awfully quiet, Xan."

"I was just thinking…"

"About what?"

"That you surprise me, Professor White. And the element of surprise is always a good thing."

I smile to myself as we walk down near the surf. His hand feels so strong to me, but it's the electricity that passes between him and me when we walk that surprises me, too. Maybe you *can* teach an old diva new tricks.

A diva knows the value of a well-hurled plate.

The London contingent has arrived. No, it's not the wedding yet, but an engagement party that Scott has planned and my father is paying for. Dad had shocked me by actually welling up when I told him about David and me.

"Why are you crying, Dad?"

"Because I can tell this one is like your mother's and mine. I can tell. And you still believe in love."

"Aren't all your ex-wives proof you still believe in love?"

"No. Call it proof of my loneliness. Though now, with Maddie, I am never lonely. Can you believe it? Searching all this time for something…an elusive something…and my daughter is the one who finds it for me."

After a warm hug, he told me whatever I wanted was mine. So I told him Scott was the Official Wedding Planner, a title he would surely drive us to drink with, and that the two of them should put their heads together.

My father trusts Scott. Adores him. In a world in which friends can sometimes come and go, I've watched girlfriends abandon me when a new boyfriend comes on the

scene (something a true diva would never do!), and I've
seen potential women friends steer clear of me, as if my
forward nature, my diva-ness, is dangerous and I would
steal their boyfriends (something no real diva would do either—listen, there are enough men to go around…all is
not fair in love and war). But Scott, he has been there
through it all. Marriages, breakups, thrown plates, scenes
and entrances, parties, laughter, sadness, death, stepmonsters, he has been my real and true friend, and my father
values Scott for that reason.

Which is how I now find myself meeting a bunch of
Brits at my engagement party. Libby is here with Sam, my
father with Maddie, and Scott with Julian. I invited a few
people I know well from my various client functions, but
am deliberately keeping my side rather small—how many
times can you register for gifts from Tiffany's? Well, the
answer is there's never too many times, but still. I want to
be tasteful about it all, so my side was a paltry twenty people. But the London contingent…well, it seems like the
entire House of Lords has shown up to meet the diva who
finally captured the heart of the elusive bachelor, Professor David White.

Scott has chosen a room in a little sushi place, the Lotus
Club, with rice-paper walls, hanging lanterns and floor
seating. Out come giant boats of raw fish, which don't
seem to be a favorite with the fish-and-chips crowd. They
pick at the boats with their chopsticks. Some of them
laugh, but they all seem most interested in me. And not
in a good way. David's parents seem a tad shocked by my
appearance. Frankly, I look damn hot. I am wearing a sim-

ple black kimono-style dress with sleeves that flutter as I move my arms, and a plunging neckline that shows off the beautiful antique pendant David bought me last week at an antiques show we went to. What is it about me? I wonder.

Is it my four-inch stilettos?

My *real* breasts perched in my push-up bra?

My elaborate jade bracelet and showy earrings?

My bloodred lipstick (hardly the demure little virgin)?

I decide it is none of these things. It is the fact that I am self-secure, that I am confident, that I have a clear sexuality and chemistry with David. That I am not English. That I am bold and fearless and a Yank.

And maybe that I am thirty-four and have been married twice already. Yeah…that could be it.

His mother asks if I intend to keep working after we marry.

"Why wouldn't I?" I ask her back. I smile. But she doesn't smile in return.

"I don't know. David has a very good job. His books. I thought you might support that, my dear."

"I do support him. And *he* supports *me*."

"I see."

I see. Code for "I don't see," as in "I don't see what he sees in *you*."

Scott senses a little tension between me and the Queen Mum, so he offers a toast.

"To the wonderful couple… Xan spotted him in my building and just knew he was the one for her."

This elicits a raised eyebrow or two.

Scott continues. "And I thought Xan was wrong. That a professor and a city girl—a diva—couldn't find true love. But I was wrong. Though Xan will be the first to tell you that she is *always* right and everyone else is always wrong, anyway."

This elicits laughter from my friends, but not the Londoners. David seems oblivious to it all. Gazing at me, stroking my arm, occasionally putting his hand on my thigh as we sit side by side on cushions. I can't decide whether this is endearing or annoying. Why hasn't he noticed the tension? Is he that obtuse? I find my blood pressure rising.

After dinner, and a dessert of bananas tempura and little chocolate-covered fruits, and hot green tea, we all rise to go home. The Brits are staying at the Ritz-Carleton and we are all supposed to meet for brunch tomorrow. As we stand bidding our goodbyes, I whisper to David that I am going to the ladies' room.

I find the ladies' room, powder my nose and take a deep breath. It isn't easy pulling families from two different parts of the world together, though thank God for Maddie, who somehow managed to keep the conversation flowing and ask interesting questions of each guest. If my father doesn't propose to her soon, I will do it for him. I realize he's been around the track a few times before, but *this* one is a keeper.

I exit the ladies' room and head back toward the lobby of the restaurant. Rice-paper walls are thin. So thin I can hear everything being discussed, though I am not yet visible.

"All we're saying is you're rushing into this, David. You barely know this girl. She isn't your type at all…"

"How do you know what my type is? And I'm a little too old to be having anyone worrying about my choice of a wife."

"So you don't find it odd—" I hear his mother's voice "—that she's been married twice before? That she dresses like a strumpet—"

"A strumpet, Mother. Really…let's all grow up here—"

David starts to defend me, but he is soon drowned out by a cacophony of voices, all urging him to be careful. I stop hearing him defend me. All I hear are his sighs.

Now I am pissed.

He should be defending me with every breath, every bit of life in that soon-to-be-lifeless professorial body of his. He is a champion debater, and he can speak on a thousand subjects intelligently—in four languages!—so you would think he could reasonably be expected to speak on the subject of his fiancée with absolute clarity.

I feel a surge in my blood pressure. A rising spike. Instead of going to greet my fiancé, the bastard, I head toward the front door.

"Where are you going?" Scott asks. He has been rather pleased with himself. And in truth, the food and decor, and flowers on the table—single orchids in bud vases—were all perfect.

"I'm leaving."

"But—"

Maddie looks at the crowd surrounding David in the next room, and she deduces the scenario in an instant.

"Honey…" She stretches out her arms to offer me a little comfort.

But let me tell you, a hug is the *last* thing I need right now. I need a plate to hurl. I need a book to toss in the ocean. I'll even settle for a few love letters to set ablaze.

"It's okay, Maddie." I hold up my hands. "I just need to go right now."

Now David spots me.

"Xan! Where are you going?"

Libby, Sam, Julian, Scott, my dad and Maddie all hold their collective breath. Scott softly says, "Easy there, Xan…remember, you *love* him."

"I'm leaving."

"Why?"

"David…if you can't even defend me to your family, how do you expect us to weather the storms of marriage?"

"But—"

"Please…spare me," I say and turn my back.

I exit the door and slam it as hard as I can. Bad move— or good one—it depends on your opinions on making a scene. Because, unintentionally, you understand, the force of my martial-arts-trained slam results in the beautiful Asian-inspired Art Deco glass door of the Lotus Club to smash into a million pieces.

I don't look back.

It would ruin a perfect exit.

A diva always makes a perfect exit.

A Diva Is Spontaneous

I know staying in Miami is futile.

David will call me a hundred times a day.

He will send me dozens of roses.

He will buy me gifts.

He will send me cards and love letters filled with the rather good poetry he writes.

In short, if I am to banish the thought of David White from my brain, I must get out of town. This requires a partner in crime. Make that two.

Back at my condominium, I call Scott on my cell phone.

"Thank God you called. David's a mess. His family is leaving on the next British Airways flight out of Miami. He screamed at the lot of them. And you have to come back to him."

"Scott…rice-paper walls are thin. You get the picture. His family was *ripping* me to shreds. I heard it all. At first he argued with them, but then he did the unforgivable and said nothing. *Nada.* Zip. His mouth slammed shut like a fucking clam."

"Xandra…I am telling you, this time, for once, you are *wrong.* You jumped the gun. You can't expect a man, at his own engagement party, to start family warfare."

I am silent.

"Xan?"

I am still silent.

"Xan, honey?"

Still silent.

"So you do think total warfare was in order."

"Of course I do."

He sighs. "And what are you doing right now? Please don't tell me you are in his apartment dousing his clothes in paint, dumping his books off the balcony or smashing his brandy snifters."

"No. I am in my own apartment. Packing."

"Packing?" I hear the panic in Scott's voice.

"And you're packing, too."

"No, I'm not."

"Yes, you are," I coo. "I need a cooling-off period. We're heading to Vegas. Let's go. I'll pick you up in an hour."

"But—"

"I'm not coming up. I could run into him on the elevator. So be downstairs. One hour from now. Synchronize your watch."

"That'll be 11:30 p.m."

"We'll catch a red-eye. I'm calling Libby."

"Can we at least wait until sunup?"

He knows it's pointless to try to talk me out of going to Vegas. But I can be reasonable.

"First morning flight out then. I'll pick you up in a limo at 6:00 a.m. Be ready or be dead."

"Charming."

Next I call Libby.

"Libby? You there?" I speak into her machine.

She picks up the phone instantly. "Xandra! Are you okay? There was a huge mess at the restaurant. Your father had to pay for the door. David was distraught. I've never seen a man so upset. And you should have heard him telling his family they were a bunch of snobs. Except his brother, Henry. He liked you. Henry did."

"Pack your bags."

"What?"

"I am taking you to Las Vegas. Consider it a reward for all your hard work."

"But—"

"But nothing. I'll pick you up at six-thirty tomorrow morning. And we'll be back in two days. I just need to get away."

"I hate to leave Sam."

"You're not leaving him. You're just going on a mini-vacation. Besides, absence makes the heart grow fonder. Haven't you ever heard that?"

"Uh-huh," she says unconvincingly.

"Pack. And bring your shortest miniskirts, honey. Vegas is the city of sin."

"I was afraid of that," Libby says as she bids me good-night.

We land in Vegas. I have already consoled myself with four Bloody Marys on the plane. Scott is also a few vod-kas short of total inebriation. Only Libby is sensible, hav-ing only drunk a Coke on the plane.

Of course, as I'd packed, and all night long, David had called. Finally, I ripped the phone out of the wall. Then he called my cell. The deadly 5:00 a.m. wake-up call arrived, and I directed the limo driver to pick up my two sidekicks.

Now the three of us are heading down the Strip in another stretch limo, taking in the busy streets, even at midday.

We are deposited at the Bellagio by our very patient driver, and we pile out and up to our rooms—one room for Scott and me, and another for Libby, who re-marks this is the first time she's had a hotel room all to herself.

"You have one hour to rest, then we go gambling, shop-ping, eating, drinking, and generally forgetting my recent engagement disaster. Come on, Scott." I unlock our room. The bell captain brings our bags up shortly.

"Thank you." I tip him a twenty. I realize my life re-volves around twenty-dollar bills. A five is too cheap. A ten…better but not memorable. A twenty at least means you won't be forgotten. Not that I am *ever* easy to forget.

At this thought, I feel a little pang. For David. What is wrong with me?

Nothing the minibar won't cure.

Five hours later, I am down two thousand dollars in blackjack, which I blame on my now very inebriated state and a lack of good judgment clouded by romantic disaster.

Scott is on my right. He is winning. How this is technically possible when the man knows less about blackjack than he does about baseball, I have no idea. But for the man who has to ask me how many balls before you are walked in baseball each time we go to a Florida Marlins game, he is up five hundred.

Libby sits on my left. She is moping about Sam, but is loosening up as the evening progresses and more and more high rollers and enough strange Vegas creatures to make your neck snap from people watching descend on the casino.

"Xannie." Scott tugs on my sleeve. "I'm hungry."

"And?"

"And? Are you taking us to dinner?"

"Not until my luck changes."

"Honey pie, your luck isn't going to change until you admit you love David, you've been a fool, and it's time to go back home."

"No chance."

"This little spontaneous getaway of yours is nothing but a well-disguised attempt to avoid the handsome Professor White. You need to go home."

I show him my diamond engagement ring, which I am

still wearing, though I have no idea where my views on marriage number three now stand. "Shut up, or I will deck you with my big honkin' diamond."

"You don't scare me. Besides, I'm getting hypoglycemic. You get me food or I'll faint right here on the table."

"Go ahead and faint. I'll stay here with Libby."

"I'm actually hungry, too," Libby whispers.

"You two are such amateurs. Come on, we're in Vegas. The city of lights, neon, slot machines and hookers. They don't sleep here, and neither will we."

Scott and Libby exchange a look. I sense a mutiny. The dealer announces, "Bets, please."

I push a tall stack of chips forward. Chips. Goodbye, Mr. Chips. He was an Englishman. This reminds me of David. *Is there no escaping him?*

I signal for another drink.

Libby stands up. "Xandra, you need to go up to bed or come to dinner. Losing all your money will not help you forget David."

"I've already forgotten him," I say even as I ask the dealer to hit me on 14. Why? This is an idiot move. I get a face card. Bust. I lose.

"We're going to dinner," Scott says solemnly.

Mutiny. I knew I smelled it.

"Fine. Charge it to the room. I'm staying put."

"Suit yourself. Come on, Lib." They link arms and abandon me at the table.

I sit and lose some more. A tall Texan in a ten-gallon hat and a deep tan sits down next to me.

"Hello, little lady."

"Hello," I purr. Mr. Tall, Dark and Texan is handsome and masculine, in a rodeo kind of way.

"Winning tonight?"

"No. But maybe you'll change my luck."

"Well, you've already changed mine." He flashes me his pearly whites. He's smooth as oil.

What if David was sitting in a bar right now, being enticed by a Texas A&M cheerleader with a blond bouffant? How would I feel? There he is again—David. In my thoughts and my mind. I shake my head, as if to exorcise him from my brain.

I flirt with the Texan. I begin to win. My confidence grows.

The Texan wins. Only, he's betting a thousand a hand. The table limit.

"You're bringing me good luck," he drawls.

His face is slightly weathered, like the old Marlboro Man. I imagine him in cowboy boots and Levi's instead of the suit he's wearing.

"Well, mine's changed, too."

We talk. We gamble. We win. He tells me his name is Tom. His friends just call him Big T.

And then I have an epiphany.

Me and a good ol' boy?

What the fuck am I thinking?

Me and *anyone* other than David would be a huge mistake. And if it's not David, then it might as well be nobody—which doesn't frighten me. I've been alone before. Divas are never afraid of that, because without being com-

fortable being alone, we would settle. But I don't have to be alone.

I rise from the table and stick out my hand. "Big T, it was a pleasure meeting you, but I'm afraid I'm heading home for greener pastures."

Big T adjusts his belt buckle and looks at my BHD (big honkin' diamond) and just smiles amiably. A good good ol' boy—but still not for me.

I cash in my chips and realize I've broken even. Just barely.

I make my way past the blackjack tables to the *ching-ching-ching* of the slot machines. On a whim, I put a dollar into one of the slots.

Money pours down. It rains money into the tray, and I am suddenly five hundred dollars richer.

Is it my luck? Or have I finally returned to my senses, and now all is right with the universe?

All that is left is making up with my two pals who came all this way, I know, not because they want to see the Bellagio's excesses, or to ride in a gondola under a simulated Venetian sky, or to ride a roller coaster, or even to see Siegfried and Roy.

They came for me.

They came because they love me.

I check in at the Bellagio's you-ain't-seen-excess-until-you've-gorged-on-our-buffet spread. It's a disgusting array of excess. Beautiful food, but mountains of it!

In a corner, I spot Lib and Scott. In front of him is a mound of shrimp so high it almost comes to midchest level.

I walk over to their table.

"Xan!" Libby is effusive and jumps up to hug me.

I hug her back.

"Sit down, Xannie." Scott pushes out a chair.

I sit and signal the waiter. "Just a Coke, please." I've got to think clearly.

"Are you broke?" Scott asks.

"No. I broke even at the table and then hit the slots."

"And?" Scott looks hopeful.

"And I've come to my senses."

They both sigh. In fact, they both look like hundred-pound weights have just been lifted from their shoulders.

"And you're going to go home?"

"In the morning. We're all going home."

"And you'll call him."

"I don't even know what to say to him."

"You'll think of something."

"Maybe I'm not meant to be married. You know it really is a ridiculous convention."

"I want to be married," Libby says, starry-eyed.

"We'll work on Sam when we get home."

"Shrimp?" Scott holds one up.

"No. But let's head over to the nightclub. We'll party tonight while I figure out what I want to do."

We go see some dynamite act with women in *Cabaret*-esque outfits doing high-stepping Vegas topless dances.

Relieved that we're not going to be on the lam from my wedding anymore, Libby and Scott really enjoy themselves. Libby is absolutely amazed at the dancers. No, I don't suppose they have anything quite like that in Dayton.

Later, long after midnight, we return to our rooms. Libby is giggly now and says she's going to call Sam. Scott and I go into our room and flop down on our respective beds.

"I'm sorry," I say.

"What was that?"

"You heard me."

"I know. But I want to hear it again."

"I'm sorry. About the door, the scene…well, not really…those people were stuffy and pompous. 'I thought you'd support him,' his mother said. What the hell does that mean? How could he come from that and be so perfect himself? Anyway…I was wrong about leaving town. I'm sure he's worried sick. And I was wrong to bully you and Libby into coming and for bringing you to the verge of a hypoglycemic attack on the blackjack table."

"God…let me bask in this moment. You know…this is almost as good as an orgasm. This might possibly be the most wonderful moment in the life of one Scott St. James."

"Shut up!" I hurl a pillow at him.

"Stop…do you feel that?"

"What?"

"The earth is spinning backward on its axis. The diva has said she's sorry. And…spinning still backward, that she was the w-word. *Wrong.* Oh rejoice!"

"I'm going to have to kill you."

"Ahh…the natural order has been restored. She's back to threatening bodily harm."

"Go to sleep."

We do. Or try to. But I can't sleep.

Can a diva find true love?

Can it last?

And can she walk out on her own engagement party and live to tell about it?

A Diva Isn't Afraid to Love—
with Grand Passion

As we land at Miami International Airport, I feel my stomach do a little flip-flop.

"Take a deep breath, Xan," Scott orders me, knowing me so well.

"Who are you, Spider-Man? Your Spidey senses tingle when I get tense?"

"What can I say? This is honed from years of living with you."

We disembark the plane, a process I find aggravating. I hate dealing with the idiots who hog the aisle, fussing with their luggage in the overhead bins while the rest of us just want to get off. I sigh loudly. And this is why I always sit in first-class.

Libby, Scott and I retrieve our overnight bags from the carousel. Rather, they do. Mine has been lost.

"Oh God," Scott moans. "We've had peace from her tirades for less than twelve hours and already something comes along to fuck it up."

But I am calm. I file a report and even smile at the man who tells me they'll do "their best" to find my LV bag.

"Please do," I mutter. But I don't scream at him. Maybe Scott is right. Maybe the world really *is* spinning backward on its axis.

Our limo driver is standing in a herd of limo drivers. I just see his arm perched high above the crowd, "KINGSTON" in capital letters in black marker on white paper.

"There's our driver." I point.

We head that way. The driver's back is to me as I arrive. Then he turns around and beneath his cap is David. My David.

Despite all those little diva voices in my head that tell me to play it cool, I rush forward and kiss him. I smell a traitor though and turn around to stare at Scott. He had to be in on this charade.

"Sorry, honey. You think you were going to tell me you were coming home and have me not call him?"

He grabs Libby by the arm. "Come on, we'll take a cab."

"Can we stop by the studio so I can see Sam?"

"Sure thing. And then I get to stop by Julian's drama class."

Young love.

Off they go, and I am alone with David.

"Your luggage, madam?"

"Lost."

He raises one eyebrow. "You're surprisingly calm for someone who has just lost her luggage, madam."

"Yes, I am. I'm a diva, but this is my attempt at keeping my blood pressure under control."

"I see…. Well, come along, the limo is this way."

We walk through the terminal and then outside into the balmy Miami air.

"First time in Miami?"

"Yes."

"Well, then let me point out some of the sights on the way to your accommodations, madam."

"Certainly."

We arrive at a real limo. I open the front door.

"No…no. I never allow passengers to sit up front." He shuts the door and opens the rear door. "Here you go." He sweeps his arm out with a little bow. I suppress a little smile.

"Thank you…what did you say your name was?"

"David."

"Thank you, David."

The rear of the limousine is filled with orchids, lilies and roses. A bottle of Dom Perignon chills in a bucket.

"Shall I uncork your champagne?"

"Thank you."

An obligatory *pop* echoes in the parking garage.

He climbs into the front seat as I settle in the back with my glass of champagne.

"What brings you to Miami? Business or pleasure?"

"Both. Mostly pleasure." I grin.

"May I be so bold as to say you look smashing for someone who's just had a grueling airplane ride?"

"That's a bit forward for a limousine driver, but I'll allow you that."

"I'll try to control myself, madam."

"Good." I mutter under my breath, loud enough for him to hear, "Can't find good help these days."

I see his eyes twinkling in the rearview mirror. We pull out into the traffic, and he drives carefully to the parking lot checkout where he pays the parking fee and then gets on the highway.

"May I also say, madam, that whoever filled your limousine with all these flowers must really adore you."

"Perhaps. But then again, maybe this is really just a grand gesture designed to make me forget a little tiff we had, rather than a sign of true apology."

"I don't think so. I would say that the man who found those lilies probably went to at least a dozen florists to locate the exact varieties in those bouquets."

"Really? What sort of man would go to all that trouble, do you think?"

"I think the type of man who would give you—pardon me, but I just learned this expression from one of my American friends by the name of Scott—a big, *honkin'* diamond."

"Oh, this little bauble." I dangle my left ring finger.

"It's lovely. Are you engaged?"

"Well…that's a tricky question, um…what did you say your name is? Dave…? You see, I don't do well in captivity. I'm a bit like a caged tigress."

"Like to play the field, eh?"

"No…it's not that at all. I just find the whole pressure-filled meeting of the families, the big day, the whole

thing…well, it isn't as important as the two people in-volved, you know? But I don't know if this man understands that. You see, I've been married before. I'm a bit of a diva. I know what I want. But this man…he may be swayed by family pressures, by what other people say about me."

"Anyone who says anything but the most wonderful things about you is crazy. Utterly mad."

"Really?" I lower the window a little and let the sea breeze kiss my face and ruffle my hair.

"Really," he says. We exchange an intense look in the rearview mirror.

"You're awfully brazen."

"Then let me be still more brazen. Forget this man, this man so in love with you he would go to twelve florists and rent a limousine and hire a driver. I want to take you right here, right now."

"Pull over near the beach then. And climb in back here with me. The windows are tinted."

He does. He slides across the leather seats next to me.

"I love you, Xan."

"I love you, too."

"I need you. I miss you. I'm sorry about my family—"

"Silliness. We're all that matters."

We begin making love. Slowly, so that a rocking limou-sine isn't a telltale sign of two people getting busy in the back.

The slowness of it is ecstasy. I can barely hold myself back as his hands slide under my skirt.

"I'm sorry about the big engagement party scene. I guess I wanted a fight to the death, but really…what I want most is you."

He slides inside me, and we move as one. As we always have.

"Xan…we don't have to get married. Just wear the diamond and tell everyone you're mine. Be mine. It doesn't have to be this high-pressure thing."

I can't answer. It's too close. We both come at the same time.

We wait until we can each talk again.

"I'll make you a deal." I smile.

"Anything."

"Let's get married, but let it be just us and our friends. On the beach. Let it just be about us. Not the day. Not the families."

"Anything."

I expect Scott to be disappointed. Bitterly. But he's not.

"But you won't get to plan this big ostentatious event."

"I know. But I have to tell you, after you broke the door…I was getting hives just *thinking* about bringing both sides of the family together under one roof again. And I'm not sure there's a restaurant in town that would have let us book it anyway!"

"Will you be my maid of honor?"

"Wouldn't miss it!"

So in the end it is just us.

Scott and Julian.

Dad and Maddie.

Libby and Sam.

Henry, David's brother, who liked me anyway.

And a justice of the peace.

And the stars. They cascade across the sky as the wind whips my hair.

I am wearing white, but not because of tradition. Because I look fucking hot in white. It shows off my complexion and my dark hair. It's a slip dress.

David wears a linen suit.

We're both barefoot. Even a diva can give up heels for a little sand.

And we say I do.

Scott is crying. Dad is crying. I am crying. David is crying.

And I realize, fundamentally, that whatever a diva is—and she is many things—she is fearless about one thing.

She is unafraid to love. With great passion and total abandon. She is unafraid to march forward with her heart even in the face of heartbreak.

She can say I'm sorry and live to tell about it.

She can let people into her heart, and they can stay there forever.

David is my shining star. He is my lover. He is my friend. And he is fearless, too.

And in a pinch?

He can double as a limo driver.

On sale in December from Red Dress Ink...

Up and Out

Ariella Papa

Life on the up and up was great for Rebecca Cole,
creator of the new cartoon sensation Esme—fancy
nights out and a trendy new wardrobe. But thanks
to a corporate takeover, Rebecca soon finds herself
on the up and out. Can this food snob find a way
to afford her rent and her penchant for fine dining?

RED DRESS INK

™